PENGUIN CRIME FICTION

TIP ON A DEAD CRAB

William Murray was born in New York City and educated at Phillips Exeter Academy and Harvard. A staff writer for *The New Yorker* and author of that magazine's "Letters from Italy," he has written nine novels, including *Malibu*, recently made into a film produced for a television mini-series, and *The Sweet Ride*; five nonfiction books, including *Horse Fever* and *The Dream Girls*; as well as two volumes of translations of the plays of Luigi Pirandello. His most recent nonfiction book, *Italy: The Fatal Gift*, was chosen by the American Library Association as one of the most notable adult books published in 1982. A contributor to many major periodicals, Mr. Murray lives with his wife, Alice, and divides his time between Los Angeles and Rome.

TIP ON A DEAD CRAB

by
William Murray

PENGUIN BOOKS

PENGUIN BOOKS

Viking Penguin Inc., 40 West 23rd Street,
New York, New York 10010, U.S.A.
Penguin Books Ltd, Harmondsworth,
Middlesex, England
Penguin Books Australia Ltd, Ringwood,
Victoria, Australia
Penguin Books Canada Limited, 2801 John Street,
Markham, Ontario, Canada L3R 1B4
Penguin Books (N.Z.) Ltd, 182–190 Wairau Road,
Auckland 10, New Zealand

First published in the United States of America by
Viking Penguin Inc. 1984
Published in Penguin Books 1985
Reprinted 1985

LIBRARY OF CONGRESS CATALOGING IN PUBLICATION DATA
Murray, William, 1926–
Tip on a dead crab.
(Penguin crime fiction)
I. Title.
[PS3563.U8T5   1985]   813'.54   84-26394
ISBN 0 14 00.7662 X

Printed in the United States of America by
George Banta Co., Inc., Harrisonburg, Virginia
Set in Baskerville

For Alice

God forbid that I should go to any heaven in which there are no horses.
—ROBERT BONTINE CUNNINGHAME-GRAHAM

TIP ON A DEAD CRAB

ONE

Form

"HEY, GET UP," the distant voice insisted, "you got to get out of here. Hey, it's late. Get up."

"What time is it?" I couldn't see; I was busy hauling myself up from the bottom of a well.

"It's after eight. My old man's coming in from L.A. this morning. I told you. He'll kill us."

I rolled over and leaned back, my head resting against the bare wall above the king-sized mattress. Hot July sunlight flooded the room through the open slats of the Venetian blinds, but I still couldn't see anything. For a moment I imagined myself dead, a corpse laid out on a slab inside some big-city morgue; I was simply another victim of hard times. "Who's coming in?" I mumbled. "Who?"

"I told you," the voice said. "Kretch'll kill us. You've got to leave."

I saw her now. She was standing naked in the doorway and holding her underwear in both hands out in front of her, as an offering of some sort, I imagined. I didn't recognize her. In fact, I was sure I had never seen her before in my life. "Who are you?" I asked. "What is this?"

"Very hilarious, a panic. You got five minutes to beat it or I'll call the cops. I'll say you broke in here. I mean it, Lou. You got to get out of here and fast."

A little of it came back to me, a thin slice of dim yellow light in the darkness. I remembered that freckled, bucktoothed face looming toward me through the smoke of the polluted air above the bar at Bully's, a vision out of some flirtation with the forces of despair. "You're Bunny, right?"

"Right, right. Now beat it."

She disappeared temporarily and I heard the sound of water splashing into a sink. I sat up now and swung my legs over the side of the bed. My feet rested on the floor like wounded rabbits, pale white and pink against the orange shag that stretched like a rotting kelp bed from wall to wall of this dreadful room. I still had no idea where I was, but I had a sudden remembered glimpse of long, thin, white legs embedded in a torso like celery stalks in a cheese ball, a flash of memory awesome in its dismal implications. What lies had I told? What tricks performed? Even blind drunk, I could shuffle a deck of cards as easily as Rubinstein could ripple a keyboard. I could make magic, that always. Any move a blind, if I so chose. So what had I done last night?

I forced myself to stand up, leaned a hand against the wall for support and groped over the floor for my missing clothes. I began painfully to assemble myself. What *had* I imbibed? What not-so-rare poison had I inflicted on myself that I could emerge feeling like this?

"Oh," she said, reappearing, still naked, in the doorway. "Good. Hurry up, Lou."

"Bunny Lehrman," I mumbled. "Cocktail waitress of the woeful countenance and abundant bosom. Like the song, it all comes back to me now."

"You promised you'd be gone by eight."

"I meant to be, yes, I did."

"You don't know Kretch, do you?"

"Who?"

"Kretch, my old man. He'll kill us both."

"That could be unfortunate," I admitted. "Where are my socks?"

"You weren't wearing any. Come on now . . ."

"What was I drinking?"

"Brandy, straight. Lou, please . . ."

"It must have been Christian Brothers."

She thrust herself into a green terrycloth robe that clung to her like moss on a damp stone and helped me finish dressing, then guided me like a nurse leading a patient in shock toward the front door. "Did I say I loved you?" I asked, as we reached the foot of the stairs. "Did I say that?"

"Don't be an asshole. We just got it on," she said. "We had a good time."

"Oh, that's nice, Bunny. I'm glad."

She opened the front door and propelled me into the street. "I'll see you," she said, shutting the door firmly behind me.

I walked very slowly down to the end of the street, then shuffled back and knocked on her door. She opened it and stared at me, her eyes wide with dismay "Lou . . . I told you—"

"Listen, where's my car?"

"Damn you, it's down there," she said, fluttering a long-fingered hand toward the avenue, "around the corner "

"Listen," I said, as she started again to close the door on me, "what did we do, really? Was I good?"

"Do? Good? You were so-so. Like limp—"

"No, no, not that," I said. "I know I drank too much. I mean, what tricks did I try? What moves? Three-Card Monte? The Multiplying Rabbit? The Erdnase Shift? I mean, what was I *doing?*"

"You got great hands, Lou," she said. "And you can talk up a storm, but you're also totally crazy." She shut the door again on me and this time for good.

Just as I reached the corner, a big silver-gray Cadillac nosed down the street. The man at the wheel had the unshaven face of a primordial anthropoid. The dreaded Kretch? Who else? I began to understand the lady's anxiety. Before I could get into my own car and escape, however, I had to sit down for a few minutes on the curb, at least until the nausea passed. With it came more unwelcome memories, of terrible old jokes and tricks and fast, phony talk, and it shook me badly. At such times I feel as if I'm not in control of any part of my life and it sickens me. I jabbed a finger down my throat and forced myself to heave into the gutter. Emptied, the last of the night soured against my palate, I stood up to go home. A lean blond youth on a skateboard swooped past me. "Hey, man, you okay?" he called back. "You all right?"

I didn't answer. I lowered myself carefully into the front seat of my ancient Datsun as if I were made of frosted crystal and carefully drove home. As I left, I glanced up into the rearview mirror and saw Kretch again. The monster was standing in the doorway glaring out into the street. Had this Hunding sniffed the premises and detected the lingering scent of an intruder in his lair? I didn't wait to find out. I remembered now what Bunny Lehrman had told me about him. He liked to break people up piece by piece, like a man snapping kindling, after which he sometimes set them on fire. Had Bunny actually said that? I thought so, which made it imperative to keep going.

When I walked in our front door, Jay was already seated at the dining table and at work. He glanced up once as I passed him on my way to the kitchenette. "You look wonderful," he said. "Fresh, rested."

"Thanks. Any coffee?"

"On the stove. So?"

"So what?"

"Who was it? The cocktail waitress? The bucktoothed, bosomy one you wowed with your charm, your patter and swift fingers?"

"I don't want to talk about it right this minute."

"Shifty, when the fever seizes you, it makes me want to cry."

"Yeah? Me, too."

I spent the rest of that morning soothing my nerves by watching Jay crack the *Racing Form*, which is not unlike witnessing a great painter readying his palette for an assault on bare canvas. I wasn't about to do any work of my own that day and I found the spectacle as soothing to my nerves as an ecclesiastical ritual.

Jay never varies his routine. First, he spreads the tabloid out flat, making certain it's divided exactly in half. It's now ready to be perused, but before doing so Jay refolds it very carefully, making certain the borders match exactly and are what he calls "pin straight." Once that basic task has been accomplished, he's ready, like Rembrandt, to go to work. His brushes are his black, red and green felt-tips, lined up parallel to each other on his kitchen table, where the *Form* is spread invitingly open.

With his black pen, Jay now begins by crossing out in the past-performance charts the names and records of horses that have been scratched from the day's entries, information gleaned from listening to an early-morning racing program over one of the local stations. He also makes a note, based on this broadcast, on the condition of the racing surface (whether it's fast, muddy, slow, sloppy, good, or what), after which he writes in other pertinent data—the name of each jockey over each horse, changes in equipment, and the season record of each animal's trainer, with emphasis on recent achievements or lack of same.

Once this information has been carefully noted, Jay is ready to create his daily masterpiece and reaches for his flashier colors. It is now about eight-thirty and the really creative work will take him another two or two and a half hours of concentrated effort, by which time he'll be ready for the telephone call from Alex and the other brain drains he services. Jay never begrudges a second of this time he spends on the *Form*. "Think of it," he once said, "the incredible effrontery of the person walking into the track and buying a *Form* fifteen minutes before post time and imagining he'll know anything well enough to risk money on it! You'd have a better chance learning how to walk on water that way than figuring out how to make money at the races."

What Jay does with his colored pens is dictated entirely by his analysis and interpretation not only of what he sees in the

Form's printed information on each horse, but mainly from what he has previously noted down about each animal in his loose-leaf notebooks, in which he has pasted past-performance charts at the Southern California tracks for the past four years. These black books accompany Jay wherever he goes and are as precious to him as the Philosopher's Stone (He once thought of insuring them with Lloyd's of London for a million dollars, but was dissuaded from doing so by a crippling losing streak that temporarily clouded his reason.) During his serious creative hours, the books repose on a chair beside the table where he works, so that Jay can consult them horse by horse, race by race. Based on what he gleans from his books, with his nose five or six inches above the paper, as if to sniff out the most elusive of the subtleties immortalized in his charts, Jay now begins to paint.

In red, he enters all the negative information he can muster on a horse; in green, all the positive intelligence. The red will usually dominate, but from time to time an entry will come looming verdantly through the cobwebbed mist of black and red like Sir Lancelot cantering triumphantly out of an ensnaring bog. It is at such moments that Jay's heart will begin to glow with hope and pride, and the entire day will begin to assume rainbow hues. One or two such apparitions are all Jay expects from his day's effort and will be enough, he feels, to justify his time; three or more and he will begin to doubt his senses. He will back off, perhaps even start over, looking for bits and scraps of negative knowledge hitherto concealed. To Jay, too much green would cheapen his creations, like superimposing a clown's face on the Mona Lisa. "The worst day I ever had," he once told me, "I went into Hollywood Park with five good numbers and got killed. There are no five good numbers on any nine-race card. That's gospel."

By ten-thirty or eleven o'clock, Jay is done. The *Form* reposes on the table in front of him, a masterpiece of jottings, scrawls, checks, crosses, stars, numbers, dots, tiny circles, other symbols of all kinds, as well as loops and lines, crossing and recrossing each other across the printed matter of the empty canvas. Incomprehensible to the layman (to anyone, in fact, but Jay himself), the picture is nevertheless as solid and reassuring to him as the nifty, little notations of an Einstein on a blackboard. This is the way Jay thinks the *Form* should look; otherwise it could not be trusted. "Most people's *Form*s are the way their minds are," he says. "They look like garbage." To the uninitiated, a Jackson Pollock could look the same; it takes a connoisseur to spot a masterpiece in the making.

Jay now permits himself a light beer, the only drink he'll concede himself until the end of his working day, and sits back to wait for his phone calls. He's as ready as he can be, and as relaxed right now as a superbly conditioned athlete still two hours away from the true test of competition.

I like to watch Jay at work; it soothes me and I can bask in his confidence. My own approach to the track is more casual, more open, and it pleases me to be in the presence of a master of form, a keeper of the sacred flame who will not deviate by so much as a dollar from the cabalistic message emanating from the page before him. On this particular day in July, with my hangover in full flower, I had no strong opinion of my own concerning the card, so it was easy for me to fall back on Jay and revel in his artful expertise. I was still on hand, of course, when the first of the calls came in, this one from Alex. I don't have a very high opinion of Alex, but one thing I can say for him, he understands the rules of the game; he always pays off on time and he doesn't have a point of view of his own, which saves Jay a lot of anguish on the phone.

Alex called, as he always did, exactly three hours before post time and Jay quickly gave him the rundown of the day. "We've got one major bet and maybe two minor ones," Jay said to him. "The main action horse is Falkland Flyer in the fifth. It's the right distance for him, a sprint on the dirt." I glanced over Jay's shoulder and noted that the horse showed lots of green on the *Form* and only one red notation, which had to do with the high weight of a hundred and twenty pounds the animal was being asked to shoulder. "I'm going to bet him straight and take him in exactas back and forth to Parsimonious. I'll press this bet if I win the double." Jay gave Alex the names of two long shots in the first to Flow Gently, the solid-looking favorite in the second. "If we hit the double, we'll have some extra money to push a little bit on Flyer."

Alex listened, thanked Jay and hung up. No sooner had he done so than the phone rang again and Jay had to deal with his syndicate, which was a little harder to do. Jay's syndicate consisted of a bunch of investors who revered his expertise and wanted to make money without having to pay income taxes on their profits. Theoretically, winning gamblers are expected to declare their earnings and pay taxes like everybody else, but in practice none of us does. The federal government requires winning horse fanciers to sign a tax form and withholds twenty percent at the parimutuel windows on all payoffs at three hundred to one or more on a single wager. Furthermore, the winning bettor is expected to declare such earnings when he files his yearly income-tax report and perhaps have to pay still more taxes on his hard-earned coup. This practice, on top of the normal vigorish from every dollar wagered, is considered triple jeopardy, a form of legalized theft, by Jay and all of us who live by this game. On the very rare occasions when such payoffs do occur, almost always in exotic-wagering contests, we all pay some Social Security pensioner or terminal loser like Tap-out fifty or a hundred bucks to collect the money for us. This technique removes us from the basilisk stare of the Internal Revenue Service and contributes significantly to the survival of the species.

It also makes it possible for Jay to bet at the track for his syndicate without having to account for the large sums of money he periodically shoves into the tote. Jay insists that he wouldn't mind paying normal taxes like every other citizen if the feds weren't prejudiced against him and his kind. "I'd have to register as a professional gambler and pay still another tax of something like fifty bucks a year for the privilege," he contends. "I'd have to save every single losing ticket against my winnings and I'd be audited every year." He'd also lose his syndicate bettors, who want to have nothing to do with the IRS and for whom daily action on horses is recreation, or at best a minor source of income. "What the government would really like to do is hang bells around our necks and declare us unclean, like lepers," Jay once said. He doesn't intend to give the government that satisfaction.

Jay's betting syndicate consisted at the time of a young married couple in Oceanside and four of their friends in the San Diego area. The couple owned a successful seafood restaurant in the North County area and their friends were all reasonably well-heeled, if not actually rich. Jay had met the couple during a hot streak at Del Mar the year before and counseled them one afternoon on their betting. He picked three winners for them, none at less than seven to two. Impressed, the couple hung around Jay for the next two weeks and made more money, then they told several of their friends about him. At Jay's suggestion, five interests in all came up with a total of twelve thousand dollars for Jay to invest for them. His commission was pegged at thirty percent of net winnings. The investors could withdraw their money at any time, but they had to keep a minimum of two thousand dollars each in action or drop out entirely.

Every racing day some member of the syndicate would telephone Jay for his day's action and he would return the call in the evening to give an exact accounting. He wasn't locked into his selections, but he did have to account for what he did and why. Within those limits he had absolute freedom of action. The biggest hazard, of course, was the inevitable second-guessing that went on from one or two members of the syndicate whenever the horses didn't run quite the way Jay expected them to, but so far that summer only one man, who had unluckily joined during a brief losing streak, had dropped out, while Jay himself had fired one of the original syndicate members, a female dental technician who never thanked him when she won and always complained when she lost. "She thought betting horses was a sure thing, like putting a gold crown on a molar," Jay said to me. "I decided I didn't need the aggravation."

When the syndicate call came in that day, it didn't take Jay long to explain the action, since it consisted of only one major bet, but the caller, the male end of the seafood restaurateurs, seemed unconvinced. He had come up with Parsimonious, the favorite in the race. With the patience of a kindergarten teacher explaining the theory of relativity to a precocious five-year-old, Jay quickly demolished the caller's reasoning. "I'm going to use Parsimonious in exactas to Falkland Flyer," he said, "but he's going to be less than even money, which makes him a bad bet, especially since he's in the one hole and could get pinned on the rail and shuffled back on the turn if he doesn't get out of the box cleanly. The Flyer's in the four hole and he's as honest as they come, he always runs his brains out. He could easily win and he'll be a decent price, at least three to one. So we're going to put a thousand on the Flyer's nose and four hundred in exactas to Parsimonious. We'll cover by taking Parsimonious back to him for six hundred, as a saver. We'll press the bet if we win the double." Jay went on to tell the restaurateur that he planned to play two one-hundred-dollar daily doubles from the two long shots in the first to Flow Gently in the second, and he got no further argument from the man.

After hanging up, though, Jay seemed momentarily depressed. "How can you explain to these people what it's taken me most of my life to find out?" he asked. "Every day I got to explain my action, as if it could make any difference to them. What do they know? Nothing." He said this sadly, with the cautious compassion Galileo must have felt when compelled to defend the Copernican system to the Inquisition. "See, I also liked a horse in the third called Disc Jockey and I'm going to play him for myself," he added. "But there are too many negatives on him, so I could never explain my reasoning to my group." So far at the meet, Jay's flock was showing a net profit of about twenty-four hundred dollars, but the past few days had been only so-so and the pressure on Jay to justify his action mounted always in direct ratio to his lack of success at the windows. "About once a month, I feel like telling these people to pack it in," he confessed, "but then we'll have some real good days and I decide not to."

He also admitted that taking a percentage of other people's winnings while not having to get involved in their losses gave him a cushion that enabled him to bet for himself with more panache than when he was risking only his own capital. Of course, if Jay faltered for too long in the sort of losing streak that can afflict even the shrewdest of gamblers, most of his syndicate would undoubtedly desert him. This was why he bet charily and rarely involved his group in the sort of risks he himself would occasionally take. "I got to tell you, though," he said to me that morning, "it gives me a great feeling to walk up to these schmucks at the betting windows and push heavy money at them." The ego factor in gambling is not to be underestimated.

It was about eleven-thirty when Jay hung up on the syndicate caller. The sun had burned off the early-morning cloud cover and a bright blue sky glowed over the soft green hills of Del Mar. From our terrace I could catch a distant glimpse of the beach, already full of kids and bronzed older bodies, and I was going to get out there with or without Jay. "No, no, I'm coming," he shouted at me from the bathroom. "Just let me shave and I'll be right there." If Jay is going sour, he'll deny himself frivolity entirely and spend the rest of the morning going over his figures and rehearsing his action, so as to overlook nothing, but most of the time he'll permit himself a break, especially during the seven delicious weeks of the summer season at Del Mar, when at least two hours of every day can be spent on the sand in a romp with sun and surf and festive youth.

We drove, as usual, to our favorite part of the beach, just north of the public parking lot, which was already full at that hour. Jay could always find space on the street for our Datsun, after which we'd tramp out onto the sand and set our blankets and towels down not too far from the water and always near, if possible, the best-looking summer bodies. The beach view is an important component of every day in Del Mar, a resort town that in the hot months teems with golden California hard-bodies of the kind Jay favors. I'm not as big on muscles as Jay is, but then I have to remember that he is, after all, an aging jock to whom soft flesh seems a betrayal of standards. Anyway, that summer we always knew exactly where to encamp, because we had tapped into the morning routine of a really spectacular-looking woman Jay had begun to call the Princess, mainly because she looked like one.

She was tall, about five-ten or more, with broad, square shoulders, a torso like a Greek statue and long, perfectly proportioned legs. She usually wore white shorts and a blue sweatshirt and she'd come running past our position at about the same time every day, a little before noon. Her hair was copper-colored, long and curly, and it flew out behind her like a mane when she ran. Sam Vespucci had spotted her first one day and told us about her and we had positioned ourselves for her ever since, though no one had yet made a move in her direction. I think she had intimidated us a little; she was so glorious to look at when she ran that we were afraid she'd disappoint us in conversation and turn out be just another California bubblehead. "She's a princess," Jay had said that first day. "If she were a horse, she'd be a stakes animal for sure."

"I clocked her in one-o-two and change," Sam had said, "but then she was just breezing."

"Sam," Jay had told him, "your contribution to the season is already complete. This is one filly I'm not putting a saddle on, not yet."

On this warm July day, the Princess came by on time, barefoot as usual, her long legs eating up the sand down by the water's edge. She ran past us about a hundred yards, then turned and came jogging back. Sam, who had been having a coffee and toast on the terrace of the restaurant overlooking the beach, now came tramping toward us, his *Form* sticking out of his rear pocket. Jay saw him coming and grimaced. "Look at him," he said with evident distaste, "he's as out of place as a cart horse in Alfred Vanderbilt's stable."

Sam certainly didn't look the beach part. He was wearing baggy Bermuda shorts with loafers and ankle socks and his short-sleeved shirt bulged out over his belt line. His face, already red from too much reflected sunlight, was half hidden by the brim of a battered porkpie hat, perched like a lid on his balding dome. He reached us about the same time as the Princess ended her run on the sand about fifteen yards from us and proceeded to prepare herself for her morning dip.

"All right," Sam said, "if you can come up with a winner today, you're immortal."

Jay cut him off with an upraised palm. Sam sat down on a corner of the blanket and we stared at the Princess, who turned her back to us and now slipped out of her shorts to reveal a trim, tight runner's bottom thinly disguised by an infinitesimal strip of green bikini. As we stared openmouthed in wonder, she pulled the sweatshirt over her head, folded it and dropped it on the sand at her feet. She turned briefly to look at us, then loped like a lazy gazelle toward the water, her dark, lightly freckled torso gleaming in the sun and her hair falling loosely over her shoulders. Even Sam grunted appreciatively. "Oh, thank you, God," Jay whispered.

"I'd bet on her," Sam said, "but nothing else that's running today."

"You have no faith, Sam," I said. "A wise man once observed that there's a winner in every race."

"They buried him early," Sam said. "So what's good, huh?"

Jay was staring dreamily at the water where, now well out beyond the breakers, we could see the Princess swimming like a porpoise, her long brown arms flashing spray into the clear air. "That is a wonder," Jay said. "That is a wonder of the universe. You don't see more than two or three of those in a whole summer out here."

"Yeah," Sam agreed, "but about the card—"

Jay turned to stare disapprovingly at him. "Sam," he said, "there are times when even horses don't count."

"I don't know when that could be," Sam said. "Women come and go, but horses are forever."

So are you, Sam, I thought, so are you. I tried to imagine Sam as a small, innocent child and I couldn't. He had been born with the face of a suffering pawnbroker. His parents must have gotten tired of looking at it, because he had been turned out to fend for himself at fourteen. He had gone to work for a barber in Hoboken, New Jersey, sweeping up and running numbers in the neighborhood, but then his boss had taken him one day to the old Aqueduct track and Sam had found his real life's work. The barber had picked five winners in a row and Sam had contributed a sixth, at nineteen to one, and he had never looked back since. For a while he had been a bookie, like his father, but it had violated Sam's Sicilian code of honor to side with the forces of exploitation, so he had struck out on his own. He owned nothing, but he had survived. "Don't you kid yourself about Sam," Jay had once told me. "He keeps his money in a shoebox under his bed and he knows what to do with it. You ever see Sam buy anybody a drink or even a cigar? No, and you never will. The shoebox is never empty, no matter how low Sam gets. That's because he lives like a miser and he is one."

"I like Sam," I told Jay. "He exudes an aura of incorruptibility."

"I wouldn't know about that," Jay answered. "Sam knows about survival."

Jay told Sam that morning about his day's action and the older man heard him out, nodding thoughtfully. "You maybe got something," he conceded, "but it's no bargain, Jay. I mean, the favorite don't lose, I don't think."

"Well, that's my play," Jay said. One thing about Jay, once he's made his mind up about a horse, there's no shaking him.

I glanced out to sea and my attention was riveted. The

Princess was treading water facing the shore and waving at us. I told Jay, who jumped to his feet. "Hey, maybe she's in trouble," he said.

"Call the lifeguard," Sam advised. "They're specialists. She could drag you under, she's a big girl."

"No time," Jay barked. "Let's go."

We hit the water together, but Jay was a better swimmer than I was and by the time I reached her through the waves Jay was already bobbing alongside her, his face alight with glee. "She's lost her pants," he confided, as I came up to them, spitting salt water out of my mouth.

"I am so sorry," the Princess said, smiling sheepishly, her face pink from embarrassment. "I bought this suit in France last year and it is a little fragile, yes? I would need you to be so kind with the towels."

"Sure thing," Jay said. "We'll meet you coming in. We promise not to look."

"Oh, that," the Princess said, "pouf! What is there to see?"

By the time I fought my way back to shore, Jay had already grabbed a beach towel and was wading back into the water to meet the Princess, who had waited for him and now caught a long, rolling breaker in toward him. We caught a glimpse of a perfectly shaped white bottom bobbing through the foam. Jay met her as she emerged and wrapped her up, then escorted her up to our nest on the sand where Sam, looking like an obscene Buddha, sat disapprovingly. Jay introduced us.

"How nice," the Princess said. "You are so sweet, really."

"And what's your name, Princess?" Jay asked.

"Princess?" the woman echoed. "Oh, yes. No, I am not a princess. I am sort of a countess, but what does that matter? My name is Marina."

"Marina? You're Italian?"

"No, French. But I am an American citizen. I was married," she explained.

"Were?"

"Yes. My ex-husband is in New York. He is a movie producer."

"What's your last name?"

"De Nevers," she said. "My husband was Dino Caretoni. You have heard of him?"

"Of course," Jay said. "A true *schlockmeister*."

"I beg your pardon?"

"He makes huge trashy movies," Jay explained, "the kind I like best. Too bad he doesn't make any horror movies. I'm nuts about horror movies."

"Those are for children," Marina informed him.

"All movies are for children," Sam observed.

"I have always thought so," Marina agreed. "Now, it was most kind of you, but I must go." She slipped back into her white shorts under Jay's protective towel, then handed it back to him. "Thank you again, but I shall be late."

"Where are you staying, Princess?"

"At my beach house," she said, "down that way." She waved vaguely toward the north. "Dino owns a little house that he has loaned me. We have parted in good taste, with only minor fighting over money. I have money of my own. Now you must forgive me, but I am going to see my horse run."

This announcement was equivalent to the launching of a small rocket. "A horse?" Jay said.

"You own horses?" Sam asked.

"Yes," she said. "I have always loved racing. My father owned horses in France when I was growing up. Now that I have the freedom and the money to indulge myself, I intend to have a good stable."

"What horse are you running?"

"Piquant, in the fourth race. He is untried, still not ready."

Jay reached out for his *Form* and quickly snapped it open to the fourth race, where Piquant, Marina's horse, an unraced two-year-old colt, lay dormant behind a fence of crisscrossing red lines. "A Buckingham first-time starter," Jay observed. "He's out for the air, right?"

"I am sorry?"

"He's giving him the race."

"Giving him the race?"

Marina spoke very clear, grammatically sound English, but evidently she was weak on track terminology. "I mean, most of your trainer's horses don't run in sprints," Jay explained. "He uses these sprints as workouts. Your horse got any speed?"

"Yes, I think so," she said, "but Bert agrees that he will run better at a mile or more."

"Of course he will," Sam said. "Till then he won't let him run."

"I think he is not without talent," Marina said.

"You're not going to bet on him?" Jay asked.

"Oh, only a few dollars, because he is my horse."

"I think you should save your money."

"Oh? Are you also a racing owner?" she asked.

"No, not exactly," Jay said, "but I have a vested interest. I do this for a living."

"Do what?"

"I bet on horses."

"Oh, I see, but isn't that very risky?"

"Oh, yes," Sam agreed, "very risky. How many horses do you have, Marina?"

"I am not certain," she said. "Ten or eleven here and there. Some are for breeding only."

"Marina, can I see you again?" Jay asked. "Dinner?"

"Well, perhaps." Marina smiled. "After all, you did save me from being arrested." Before he could answer or even ask for her phone number, she suddenly loped away up the beach. "I will see you at the races. Come down to the paddock," she called back.

Jay watched her run. "I'm in love," he said.

Sam shook his head in sorrowful disapproval. "This is going to be a tough summer," he said.

Sam regarded women on the scene of action with the same disapproving eye the only doctor of a small walled town might cast on the first victim of the plague to drop dead at his feet.

TWO

Winners and Losers

ONE OF THE HIGH POINTS of Jay's working day was his arrival at the track. There was, first of all, the minor thrill of gaining admission to the premises without having to pay. By the start of every meet, Jay would usually have acquired, through his many acquaintances and friends, all the necessary documents—parking stickers, some sort of horseman's license, admission coupons to the box areas—to assure his entrance into the sanctums of privilege without having to part with a dollar. Even on the occasions when he found himself temporarily minus a key document, he would find a way to get in gratis, usually by bluffing. He was a well-known figure to most of the parking attendants, gatemen and ushers, who were never quite sure of his actual status and were reluctant to waste their energies in vain attempts to part him from even a token gratuity. Crashing the races was a point of honor with Jay, who referred to the track as "my office." "Would you pay every day to go to your office?" he'd ask rhetorically, while insisting that he was the sort of patron who ought to be given a lifetime free pass. "Instead of that, the clowns who run these places not only expect me to pay just to have the privilege of risking my money," he once contended, "they also put on special promotions to lure the squares. They even name races after them." He pointed to the program, which listed the names of special groups in attendance that day. I remember that they included the

Kiwanis Club of Moon Bay, the Fedco Retired Executives, the Moose of Pacific Palisades, and the South Pasadena Ladies' Auxiliary. "Who are they kidding?" Jay asked. "I'm going to run more money through the tote in one race than these dummies will all year."

Jay's turf at the track was the second-floor grandstand box area near the finish line. This is where most of the owners and trainers sit and it was holy ground to the pros, most of whom frequented the area and maintained a rough sort of pecking order within it. Jay usually settled with his notebooks into any one of a dozen private boxes near the finish line, where he could watch the races in comfort and, like a Renaissance prince, hold court for visiting dignitaries and petitioners. Should the rightful owner of the box he had chosen to grace with his presence put in an appearance, Jay would shift to less crowded premises; even on the most heavily populated big-race days, he would always manage to find himself a good spot, if only because his favors, in the form of superior expertise, had endeared him to a good number of box-owners and ushers, who would often seek out his advice. Unlike Waldo the Zip Kid, Billy the Bell, Cold Al, the Mole and some of the other pros, who wouldn't part with a free nosebleed, Jay was not at all stingy about dispensing information. In fact, like Smokey Okie, Lucky Bucks, our friend Sour Sam and one or two others, he enjoyed sharing the fruits of his wisdom with less favored mortals. An afternoon spent at the races with Jay Fox consisted partly of a procession of suppliants trooping by to scoop up enough crumbs to stave off famine. "There's plenty of action to go around," Jay would say. "Anyway, most of these people don't know what to do with the information you give them, because they can't handle their money. Anybody can pick an occasional winner. Managing your money well is the hardest thing to do in gambling. These guys will bet every race and start pressing when they get behind. They'll have the occasional big day, but they're all losers."

In addition to such regular beneficiaries as Tap-Out,

Lend-Me-Ten, Action Jackson, Bet-a-Million, Whodoyalike and the Desperado, all track junkies whom no one could help, we'd occasionally receive visits from our equals, especially Sam, who liked to hang around under the TV monitors and watch the races from there, and Fido. Sam was not as thorough a handicapper as Jay, but he had access to useful workout information from a couple of the better clockers on the grounds and he had a finely tuned cynical mind, with a talent for separating nuggets of useful knowledge from the tons of misinformation that foul the premises during the course of any racing day. Fido, a chunky, curly-haired enthusiast in his thirties, was not a handicapper at all but knew it and would plunge heavily on horses he liked, usually heavy favorites. He replenished his frequently depleted finances by publishing a subscription tout sheet that was advertised daily in the *Form* as a talisman to wealth and had misled thousands. His real talent was for promotion, at which he was an expert, and gossip, which helped kill the half hours between races. Both men spent at least part of every afternoon sitting with Jay, who enjoyed Sam's company and tolerated Fido's. Of the latter he once said, "He's like one of those big mangy dogs who means well but who's always screwing up. Just when you think you kind of like him, he craps on your Persian rug."

This particular day, a Thursday, did not begin well for us. Jay and I settled into a front-row box near the sixteenth pole just in time to see the first race go off. One of Jay's long shots won that race, but his horse in the second ran out of the money. Then Disc Jockey, Jay's semi-hunch play in the third, went off at four to one, a good price, but received an atrocious ride from a normally competent jockey and finished fourth, which cost Jay fifty dollars out of his own bankroll and ten out of mine. Everything now depended on the fifth race and I could tell that Jay was under pressure. Nevertheless, we got up and went down to the paddock for the fourth in order to catch up with the Princess, whose animal was debuting in the race.

I wasn't sure the Princess would speak to us, mainly because we looked pretty disreputable. Although we usually dress at least passably for Santa Anita and Hollywood Park, at Del Mar we tend to get informal. I was wearing scuffed blue jeans sawed off just below the knees and a short-sleeved Hawaiian shirt, while jay was attired in sandals, dirty tennis shorts and a green sports shirt open practically to his waist, revealing great masses of curly black hair. Marina, on the other hand, had dressed for the occasion and looked positively regal in an elegant beige pants suit. I thought she might cut us dead, but the moment she saw us she smiled and beckoned us over to join her. She even introduced us to her friends, a tony couple from La Jolla who regarded us with the horrified contempt with which Madame de Pompadour must have regarded the Parisian street rabble. Wilbert Buckingham, who subsequently appeared with Marina's unraced colt in tow, chose to ignore us. He was a tall, aristocratic-looking horseman with a thick head of iron-gray hair cropped very close to his skull, a long, slightly hooked nose and the cold, blue eyes of a card shark. To him we were obviously horse degenerates, poachers who had somehow wangled their way into a private hunting preserve but whom he'd eventually arrange to have banished. Meanwhile, he concentrated on the animal in his charge and gave the veteran Bill Scarpe, one of his favorite riders, just the sort of instructions we had expected to hear. "He may be a little short," the trainer said. "I wouldn't rush him, because he'll need a little time to hit his stride."

"Are you still going to bet him?" Jay asked Marina, as the horses filed out toward the track and we headed back toward the grandstand.

"But of course."

"Your trainer just told the jockey to stiff the horse. Didn't you hear him?"

"Really? I didn't hear that," Marina answered in astonishment.

"Princess," Jay said, "you may know horses, but you got a lot to learn about racing. How much are you going to bet?"

"Fifty dollars."

"OK, I'll buy you the ticket."

"Oh, no, I'll do it."

"Go watch your horse warm up. I'll take care of it."

"Well, all right." She handed him the money. "If he wins, you must come to the winner's circle."

"He won't win. How about dinner?"

"I don't know. Perhaps. Please call me." She gave us her number and hurried away to rejoin her friends in the Turf Club.

Jay watched her go admiringly. "I can't take her friends, but *she* is a vision of loveliness."

"You going to bet the horse for her?"

"Don't be crazy. I just saved her fifty bucks."

When the starting gate opened for the fourth race, Piquant broke sluggishly in the middle of the pack, then fell back to last, began to make up some ground late and finished sixth in the ten-horse field, beaten by seven or eight lengths. Jay made notes on the race. "The first time at a distance, pow!" he observed.

"You going to give the lady back her fifty bucks?"

"Right after the fifth, if I can find her. They won't let us in the Turf Club dressed like this."

"I was wondering if you knew that. You've never been in the Turf Club."

"If not, I'll call her tonight."

With the fifth race looming, Jay managed to put Marina out of his thoughts. He was under pressure, because Parsimonious was being very heavily bet and, according to Sam's best estimate, could not lose except by falling down; Falkland Flyer was the public's second choice, at seven to two. Nevertheless, Jay stuck to his game plan. He still bet a thousand to win for his group on the Flyer, but he adapted his action in exacta wagering by risking only two hundred from his horse to Parsimonious and bet eight hundred on the latter to finish on top of the Flyer. Either way now, the syndicate stood to win, but considerably more, of course, if Jay turned out to be right about his top selection. For himself he bet a hundred to win and another hundred in exactas, a tenth of what he was risking for his syndicate.

As the horses were being loaded into the starting gate, Jay focused a huge pair of Japanese binoculars on the stall containing Falkland Flyer and began to talk softly to the animal. "All right, Junior," he said, "keep your head up now, don't go to sleep in there, just take it easy, you can do it, Junior, just break clean now, no problems, just get out of there and show them who's boss. . . ." A small line of perspiration became visible just over Jay's brows and the binoculars, clutched tightly in both hands, trembled slightly, even as his voice remained a cool, nerveless monotone, barely audible to anyone but Jay himself.

When the horses exploded out of the gate in a tangle of legs and brightly colored jockeys' silks, Jay jumped visibly, but kept his glasses glued on the race. He mumbled instructions directed at the horse's rider, Dickie Wharton: "Okay, Dickie, baby, keep him out of trouble now, don't get him boxed, get him clear by the turn, go with him, Dickie, don't wait on him, you can beat this mother and cut him off on the inside, don't get fanned, damn it, keep him going, that's it, that's it, stay with him now, yes, now set him down, bring him home, Dickie, get into him now, keep him going, that's it, that's it . . ." His voice began to trail off into silence as it became evident in the stretch that Falkland Flyer was not going to beat the favorite; he did, however, finish second.

As the horses crossed the finish line, Jay lowered his binoculars and slumped back in his seat, an expression of extreme disappointment on his face. After a few seconds, however, he rallied, produced a pocket calculator and quickly began to add up pluses and minuses. The official Falkland Flyer-Parsimonious exacta payoff was twenty-one dollars, which meant that the syndicate had won thirteen hundred and sixty dollars on the race. After the two-hundred-dollar loss in the double and Jay's percentage had been subtracted, the group was showing net earnings for the day of eight hundred and twelve dollars. Jay had picked up three hundred and forty-eight dollars as his commission and his personal action had yielded him another eighty-six dollars, for a total of four hundred and thirty-four dollars, a better than average winning day. "With a little better luck, we'd have really cleaned up," was his only observation. "Dickie never should have let the one horse get the lead."

"How was he going to stop him?" Sam asked. "With a cannon?" Jay chose to ignore the comment. He scribbled in his notebooks and sat back to enjoy the rest of the afternoon.

The time passed pleasantly enough, punctuated by the frequent interruptions of Whodoyalike, a plump, gray-haired little man in a baggy business suit, who stopped by several times between races to solicit Jay's opinion. "Who do ya like?" he asked, thrusting his anxious face into our box. "Who do ya like?" Each time, after Jay informed him that he wasn't betting the race, Whodoyalike rushed away, only to reappear minutes later to make sure the handicapper hadn't changed his mind. "Why don't you put him out of his misery?" I asked Jay, after one of these visits. "Give him a horse that can't win, Jay. Maybe it'll shut him off."

Jay only smiled. His professional pride would never have let him do that. Besides, nothing could have shut off Whodoyalike, whose whole life was founded on the assumption that someone somewhere knew something that would unlock all the secrets of the universe. "He can't be married," Sam observed. "He'd be asking his wife the same question every night."

Just before the feature race, Fido showed up, the buttoned side pockets of his lavender leisure suit bulging with hundred-dollar bills salvaged from having wagered heavily on Parsimonious. He was not only triumphant, but awash in gossip. He informed us that the Actor had a new scam. The Actor was famous for never repaying loans and for stiffing anyone incautious enough to become involved with him financially. "He's selling off pieces of his Pick Six action to squares for a hundred or two hundred a clip," Fido confided, "after which he disappears into the Turf Club, where the boobs can't follow him. At the end of the day, he reappears and says, 'Gee, I'm sorry, we blew it.'"

"He'll end up on his back one day, like the Pig Man," I said. The Pig Man, so named because he had once raised porkers in Oklahoma, not only failed to repay a bookie he had borrowed money from at the track one day, but committed the unforgivable sin of turning the bookie in to the police. A few days later, the Pig Man had received a head massage outside his house from a couple of husky citizens wielding two-by-fours and ended up in the hospital with a cracked skull. "He's back now," I told Fido. "He and the bookie are even doing business again, I hear. You break the rules here, you pay the price. But after that, it's like it was before."

After a horse called Crater ran third in the eighth at odds of eight to five, Fido, who had blown most of his winnings on the animal, stopped by our box again to sound off angrily about "the lousy ride" the horse's jockey had put in. We heard him out in silence and then departed, right after the ninth, through the usual blizzard of paper—discarded losing tickets, shredded programs, crumpled newspapers, torn *Form*s, paper cups, cardboard trays, all the trash left behind by the fans on their way out to the parking lots. Most of the crowd shuffled out in silence, soured by the day's events. Jay, however, marched out briskly, his notebooks tucked under his arm and humming softly to himself. "You seem cheerful enough," I said.

"Why wouldn't I?" he answered. "I had a good day and so did my group. They don't know I pressed the exacta the other way, so they're going to be real happy when they find out." As we inched our way out of the parking lot, he suddenly laughed aloud. "Isn't this the greatest? We have the whole summer down here still ahead of us and now I've got the Princess to look forward to."

"If she wants to see you after today," I observed. "We didn't cut a dashing figure in the paddock. I have a feeling she lives in a different world, Jay."

"Nah," he said, "horses is all one world, believe me."

Jay turned out to be right about the Princess. As soon as we got back to our condo, he called her and told her that he had fifty dollars of hers. Astounded, she replied that the money would buy them both a very nice dinner for two at the restaurant of his choice. Jay picked the Windjammer, a seafood emporium a mile or so up the coast and arranged to meet Marina at the bar there. Then he spent the next hour grooming himself. By the time he was ready to leave, just after seven o'clock, he looked sleek and elegant in white ducks and a long-sleeved striped shirt, his thinning curly black hair carefully combed and his cheeks aglow with cologne. "This is a pretty classy lady," he explained. "Tonight I have to make a good impression."

"You smell like the perfume counter at Schwab's," I told him.

"No kidding?" he answered, looking more than slightly alarmed. "You think I overdid it?"

"A little, but it's okay."

"It's not okay," he said and dashed back into the bathroom to splash a little water on his face. As he left, he turned and winked. "If I come in late, you'll know it was a success," he said.

"I won't hold my breath," I told him.

To my amazement he didn't come in at all, not until nearly ten the next morning. I was reading the sports pages at the breakfast table when he appeared in the doorway. He looked as if he'd had a major religious experience. "Are you all right?" I asked. "You look wiped out."

He laughed. "Shifty, you have no idea," he said, "simply no idea. It's a miracle."

"Tell me about it."

"No way," he said, heading for his bedroom. "Just take my word for it."

"I'll have to."

He suddenly popped his head back around the corner. "And she's got a horse."

"I know that," I said. "We saw it run."

"No, a real horse, a stakes animal, name of Balthazar."

"Never heard of it."

"He's a South American import, from Argentina," Jay explained. "He's supposed to be something special. He's a Group One winner down there. He was the three-year-old champion of Argentina."

"When's he going to run?"

"Soon. We're going to go out and see him one morning. Want to come along?"

"Sure. Where is he?"

"Oakview Downs. It's a training and boarding facility about an hour from here." He popped back into his room and I could hear him singing now. He was obviously in love, which implied possible complications, as far as I was concerned anyway. Women and betting generally don't go together at all. In fact, later, when I told Sam about Jay's night out with the Princess, he just shook his head and sighed. "I can feel it coming," he said. "Love and horses, it's a sure losing streak." But then they didn't call him Sour Sam because of his rosy outlook.

THREE

The Office

SAM TRIED TO EXPLAIN it all to Marina one morning by telling her a joke. Jay had been losing for several days and was devoting an extra hour to the *Form*, which left us all sitting around on the beach waiting for him. Marina had run past, taken her dip and joined us. She was an unsettling presence, with her long legs and nearly naked body stretched out on our blanket and glistening under the hot sun. I could tell that she was restless, a little unhappy, perhaps, about Jay's absence. Finally, she sat up and shook her hair out, as if to banish whatever had been going through her mind. "I don't understand this," she said.

"What don't you understand?" I asked.

"This business he does every morning with the newspaper," she said. "It is absurd."

"Not to him."

"That is because he does not see himself as I see him."

Sam grunted, which was about as close as he ever came to a laugh. "You want to know something about Jay?" he said. "I'll tell you a story. There's this guy who dies and goes to heaven and Saint Peter asks him at the gate what it is that he does for a living and the guy tells Saint Peter, 'I'm a horse-player.' Well, there's quotas, even in heaven, and there's no more room for another horseplayer. Saint Peter tells the guy he'll have to go to hell."

"This is a silly story," Marina said.

"Wait, wait," Sam insisted, patiently holding up a hand to

stifle her protest. "Now the guy says to Saint Peter, 'Listen, if I can talk some poor jerk into leaving, can I take his place?' 'Leave heaven?' Saint Peter says. 'Nobody ever has, but you're welcome to try.' So the guy gets a twenty-four-hour pass and goes in and finds this very nice complex where the horseplayers are. It's got gardens and pools and tennis courts and beautiful broads and TV monitors with reruns of all the great races from history, everything, and naturally our guy knows everybody there and everybody knows him. They come flocking around to find out how it's been going down on earth, who are the good three-year-olds, stuff like that. So he fills them in on the latest news, including colorful accounts of all the horses so-and-so has stiffed and all the wrong rides so-and-so has given and then, just when he's got everybody misty-eyed, he says, 'Oh, by the way, on my way up here I seen a notice that down in hell they got a meet going with twelve races a day seven days a week and dollar exactas, quinellas and trifectas on every race as well as two daily doubles and a Pick Six.' Well, everybody gets very quiet and then they all start to drift away on some excuse or other and pretty soon there's this tremendous flapping of wings and the sky is full of horseplayers getting out of there. By nightfall the joint is empty and our guy has got his pick of apartments and broads."

"I don't think I want to hear any more of this," Marina said.

"Wait," Sam told her, "I'm not through. You'll miss the whole point. After four or five days, see, nobody comes back and the guy gets to thinking, 'Hey, there must be something in it,' and so he leaves, too."

"I don't understand," Marina said.

"No? The guy in the story," Sam explained, "that's Jay."

"It's a silly story."

"Yeah," Sam agreed, "I've heard better. But it's to show you that if you want to keep Jay permanently interested, see, you'd better put a saddle on your back and start munching hay."

"That is coarse," she said. "You are not a nice person."

"Yes, I am," Sam protested. "I'm just trying to explain to you what this means, Princess." He stood up and brushed sand off his baggy gray trousers. "I'm going to get some coffee. Anybody want anything?" We shook our heads and Sam departed, plunging heavily off into the soft sand toward the dining terrace of the restaurant nearby. "I'll be back. I want to hear Jay's thoughts about the day. I couldn't find one pig to risk a dime on."

The Princess and I watched him go, an ungainly, heavy-set figure lurching majestically over the beach like an over-loaded Spanish galleon bucking a head wind. "I do not understand his costume," Marina said. "Why does he not remove his shoes at least?"

"Sam doesn't trust the great outdoors," I explained. "He doesn't know about sunshine and water and trees. Sam doesn't know country. Sam knows sidewalks and racetracks."

"It is very strange," she said. "Has he always been this way?"

"He comes by it naturally," I said. "His father was a bookie. Only Sam hated it and didn't want to be part of the system, so he became a horseplayer instead."

"Please?"

I explained to her that being a bookie, like Sam's father, meant playing with the house and against the right to earn a living as a free spirit without making yourself miserable by profiting from a rigged game. Sam had rejected that way of life very early, especially after he noticed that no one came to his father's funeral, not even his brother. Sam had allied himself from then on with the forces of light. "I still do not understand," Marina said, "but he does make money betting?"

"Oh, yes," I said. "Sam's a survivor. You know what you need to survive at the track?"

"No."

"An iron ass."

"I beg your pardon?"

"You have to be prepared to sit still for several days, if you have to, and not make a bet. Sam can do that better than anybody."

"It sounds so boring."

"It is," I agreed. "I can't do it. I have to make at least one or two bets a day."

"Do you bet what Jay tells you?"

"Some of the time. Jay's the best handicapper I know."

"And is that all you do, too?"

"No, not quite. I have a profession of my own, but it's not very lucrative."

"I'm sorry?"

"It doesn't make much money," I explained. "I'm a magician."

Marina beamed with delight, as if I had just handed her an unexpected gift. "Really? How marvelous! And can you make things disappear and come out of hats and so on?"

"Small things, Princess. I'm a close-up artist."

"Oh, you must perform for me. I'll give a party."

"I'd be happy to."

"But where do you do this magic?"

"Here and there. Sometimes at the Magic Castle in L.A. Sometimes in Reno or Vegas, wherever. I also play cruise ships, but in the winter only."

"What fun! Are you very good?"

"I think I am."

"But then what are you doing here?"

"Between jobs I go to the races," I told her. "And every summer I come to Del Mar, no matter what, because I really like it down here. Don't you?"

"Yes, it's beautiful," she admitted, "but I could not do this, only this, all the time. I would go mad. I need music and theater. Don't you?"

"In moderation," I said, "but not really."

"It is a mystery. What is it you all want, *au fond?*"

"Oh, what?"

"In the end," she translated. "What is it you all want?"

"Winners."

Sam rejoined us with his coffee in hand and a few minutes later Jay showed up. The Princess began to glow when she saw him plowing across the sand toward us, a blanket and wooden backrest under his arm, as if he had turned on a light inside her. Before setting his stuff down, he leaned over and kissed her on the mouth. It was more than an affectionate peck and it wasn't hard to see what was happening between them. They had a physical relationship going that almost caused the air around them to vibrate, as if electrically charged by some secret force. It made me envious, though it only caused Sam to sigh and look away in disgust.

Jay set his equipment down, took his shirt off and stretched in the sun. "How's the water?"

"Nice," I said. "How's the card look?"

"Two good things today," Jay answered confidently. "We ought to do all right."

"Yeah? What are they?" Sam growled suspiciously. "The way we been going the last two days, I couldn't spot a Secretariat in a field of ten-thousand-dollar platers."

"Let's have a swim," Marina suggested. "You have all afternoon for the races."

"True enough," Jay agreed, smilingly helping her to her feet. "Sam, look at it this way—even on your worst day in Del Mar you can tell yourself it's just another shitty day in paradise."

Hand in hand, Jay and his golden goddess sprinted for the water and hurled themselves recklessly into the foam of a breaking wave. They looked like gamboling children and the sight astonished me. I had never seen Jay Fox in love before.

Jay had just turned thirty-seven that summer, but he looked five or six years younger. Although for the past fifteen years he had been making his living at the track, he didn't look at all like the popular conception of a horse degenerate. He was about five-eleven, stocky, with thinning curly black hair, blue eyes, a dark-complexioned face, and the bouncy stride of a man in excellent physical condition, which he was. Jay had majored in political science at UCLA, until he had flunked out in his third year. He had also played on the tennis team and had been nationally ranked. For several years he had taught tennis, played in a few local tournaments and done a little hustling of the Hollywood crowd that hung about the La Cienega public courts in Beverly Hills. Although he'd given up tennis entirely for the much more sedentary life of a full-time professional handicapper, he'd kept in shape by running two or three miles a day, five days a week. He drank moderately in the evenings and smoked only an occasional cigar, mainly because he believed that staying in excellent physical condition helped to keep his mind clear for his gambling.

Jay had been a racetrack aficionado since the age of sixteen, when his older brother took him to Hollywood Park. At first, he'd only gone to the track on weekends and holidays, but very soon the horses had begun to dominate his life. Apart from the immediate appreciation he had for the athletes the horses themselves were and the thrill he derived from the challenge of trying to beat a really tough game, Jay had soon discovered that nothing else in his life gave him the same amount of pleasure as being at the track and picking winners. This had distressed his essentially conservative middle-class WASP parents, who had expected him to enter one of the professions or at least get into retail sales, like his older brother Morton. Jay, however, had early on acquired a distaste for any form of work, which, he claimed, was stultifying to the human spirit, a negation of the *élan vital*. "If you'd rather be doing something else," he once said, "then it's work."

When tennis had become work, Jay had dropped it. The only real pleasure in his life that seemed to offer any hope of remuneration had been the track, so he had decided systematically to conquer it. If he hadn't exactly managed to do that, he had been able at least to survive, occasionally quite lucratively. There had, of course, been hard times as well, but Jay had never not been able to stay in action, which is the bottom line for all gamblers. "There's always fresh," he liked to say.

Jay estimated that it had taken him the better part of a decade to solve the complexities of survival at the track. Many of the lessons he'd learned had been painful to the point of agony. In addition to mastering the basic knowledge, which consisted of the hundreds of factors that had to be taken into consideration before an intelligent wager could be made, there were several unavoidable basic handicaps to overcome, especially the house takeout, which in California was fifteen percent on every straight wager and higher on the combination bets, such as exactas, daily doubles and Pick Sixes. There was the occasional cheating that went on and, worst of all from Jay's point of view, just plain dumb luck. Adjustments and compensations could be made against the odds, cheating could be anticipated in certain kinds of races, but dumb luck was a killer. "On some days," Jay explained to Marina, "nothing goes right. Bad favorites win most of the races, which gets all the dummies and little old ladies screaming." When this happened, there was nothing to be done but survive, with as much dignity and containment as the circumstances permitted. "In the long run, I'm going to bury the dummies," Jay said. "They're the ones I'm basically in competition with, after the house vigorish has been peeled off. My basic attitude toward almost everybody at the track is respectful contempt. Respectful because on some days I'm going to get my brains beaten out."

Unlike most big gamblers, who are usually described as being utterly devoid of visible emotion, Jay felt that he shouldn't deprive himself of one of the chief recompenses of gambling, that very special moment of exhilaration that accompanied a big score. He had been known to cheer some of his winners loudly, but never for too long and never under certain circumstances. "There are some rules," he said. "It's okay to make noise for a long shot, but on an obvious favorite you root silently. Rule Two is, you don't keep screaming and yelling when you know you've got it won. That's bad form. Rule Three, don't relive the past. The track is replete with liars who all want to tell you horse stories. If the jockeys hadn't screwed up, if the horse hadn't gotten fanned on the turns or shut off in the stretch or bumped out of the gate—forget it, it's ancient history. You go on to the next race."

The biggest hazard to avoid at the track, Jay maintained, was hot tips. Pros like Jay don't need tips, even though they always value another pro's judgment. Information from a reliable source, such as a respected clocker of morning workouts or another good handicapper, could be helpful in confirming or denying one's own figures on an animal, but tips, especially of the kind available on every racing day, were to be shunned. Jay then told Marina the story of an encounter he'd witnessed the year before between a pro named Waldo (better known to the regulars as the Zip Kid, because of his preference for front-running speed horses) and Tap-Out, our favorite loser. "It happened just before the nightcap," Jay said. "Waldo was standing under a TV monitor and checking out the possible exacta payoffs when Tap-Out, who was obviously broke, spotted him and came up behind him. 'I got the winner of the ninth,' he announced. Waldo gave him this real cold stare, but he couldn't shake him. Finally, with his fingers in his ears, he walked away from him. Tap-Out followed him, until Waldo finally turned on him and looked into his eyes right down to his arches. 'I don't want to know,' he said, in this voice like an ice pick. There was this big pause and then Tap-Out said, 'Give me ten bucks and I won't tell you.'"

"You must like what you do," Marina told him. "I can see that it is a real love affair for you."

Jay laughed. "What's not to love?" he answered. "I spend every day in the open, enjoying a glorious spectacle, with the thrill of the gamble itself to lend spice to the scene."

"It is not work."

"No, you're right about that. But it's no different from what any speculator or investor does, basically. The one difference is that I get my thrill several times a day instead of weekly or monthly and that I get to look at something beautiful while I'm getting it."

Jay told Marina all this one morning while they were sitting around the condo waiting for the phone to ring and I could see her taking it all in, her eyes roving about our rented summer quarters, which to her must have looked dismal. We had rented a place across from the track, but it had been left much the worse for wear by the three students who had occupied it the rest of the year and neither Jay nor I had bothered to make any improvements. We were going to be around only for the seven weeks of the Del Mar meet, so what was the point? The furnishings were motel-room walnut, with a dusty shag carpet on the floor and travel posters pasted to the walls with Scotch tape. A bulky black TV set squatted against one wall and the lamps were ornate floor models topped by plain globes. We didn't care. In fact, we hadn't even considered the aesthetics of the place; it had been enough for us to know that the location was convenient, the beds comfortable and the rental price not outrageous. Still, a general air of dilapidation cloaked the premises like hanging moss on a B-picture plantation set, not ameliorated in the least by our somewhat casual approach to housekeeping. The sink and counters in the kitchen seemed to be permanently awash in dirty dishes, silverware and half-empty glasses, while Jay's old *Racing Form*s and programs lay scattered about over the chairs, the sofa and in various corners of every room. On her second visit to our digs, Marina had discovered the five-gallon Sparkletts water jug Jay always kept under his dirty laundry in the closet. It was full of the small change he dropped into it from his pockets at the end of every racing day. "Hamburger money," he'd explained to her. "Sometimes, no matter what you do, you get caught in a long losing streak. You gotta be ready for it, babe."

"Has there ever been anyone in your life?" Marina asked.

Jay looked surprised. "Why?"

"I cannot imagine any woman tolerating this for very long."

He smiled. "No, I suppose not. It isn't that I don't like girls," he said.

"That I have understood about you."

"It's just that I never wanted to saddle myself with excess weight."

"Comment?"

"It's like the weight they put on horses, see, Princess?" he explained. "With animals, it's the lead strips they slip into the saddle cloths. With gamblers, it's the overhead, mostly in the form of women and what goes with them—kids, possessions, commitments. That's killing weight, Princess."

Marina looked puzzled at first, then sat back in her chair with a sigh and sipped from the California Chablis Jay had poured for her minutes earlier. "I think that we are going to have a very peculiar relationship, Jay," she said, almost plaintively.

"You're different," he said.

"How?"

He grinned wolfishly at her. "You're rich and you have horses."

"Is that all?"

"Oh, no," he said. "Oh, no, indeed. You have a lot of assets, Princess."

When Jay got up a few minutes later to go to the bathroom, Marina looked at me and shrugged those beautiful broad shoulders. "I think this is madness, don't you?"

"I never make judgments, Princess, about how people choose to live their lives, as long as they hurt no one."

"Then you think that Jay and I are suited to each other?"

"I don't know about that," I said. "You see, Princess, to him the track is like going to the office is for other people. It's what he does best."

"So?"

"So I think that in his world you represent a hazard."

"Really?"

"Yes, really. You see, what Jay does requires a degree of monastic concentration achieved only by important mystics."

"Oh, dear," she said. "And I thought we were only going to have the fun this summer."

FOUR

The Big Horse

WE DROVE OUT to Oakview Downs the following Tuesday, six days after our first meeting with Marina. It was the only day we could go, because Del Mar isn't open on Tuesdays and we'd have plenty of time to enjoy the drive and no pressure of a call to the post to compel us to rush back. We left after breakfast, just as the sun had begun to burn off the early-morning cloud cover that had made getting out of bed the last few days a little bit harder than usual. Marina had even suggested postponing the trip. "It's going to be a simply magnificent morning," she observed over coffee on our tiny balcony overlooking the track. "Perhaps we should go another day."

"Come on, Princess," Jay said, "don't you want us to see your big horse?"

"Well, of course," she answered. "That is the whole idea."

"The beach will still be here when we get back in the early afternoon."

"Of course," she agreed. "Are you certain you know the way? I have a map."

"We don't need a map," Jay said. "I know exactly where we're going."

"That is what Dino always said to me about everything," she observed. "We were always lost."

We made the trip in Marina's Mercedes 450 SL convertible, with the top down and the wind blowing in our faces. Jay drove and we took our time, staying off the freeway and sticking to back roads that meandered through the dusty-looking California hills, patched here and there by groves of eucalyptus and sycamore trees, occasional lone oaks and, every now and then, citrus groves laid out in long, straight rows of lemon and orange trees bulging with fruit. Horses grazed on the upper slopes and ranch houses nestled behind greenery, almost hidden from our view as we sped past. The sun beat down on us, baking the unwatered hillsides brown and reminding me forcibly once again of the basic savagery of this natural desert landscape. It accounted for so much that happened here every year, from the brush fires that seared the hillsides clean in the hot, dry months of summer and fall, blasting away houses and trees with the ruthless, cleansing efficiency of an angry pagan deity, to the ensuing mud slides that swept down the newly barren slopes during the winter rains, burying houses and vehicles under tons of ooze. As a native Easterner, born and raised on the North Shore of Long island, I'd always been astonished at the severity of every untoward occurrence in California, where the weather, with its sudden passionate extremes, seemed to set the tone for a society in which moderation was conspicuous by its absence. Marina, I think, shared my feelings, because on the drive she reacted with distaste to the spectacle before her. "It is so—so untamed," she said at one point, as we passed a row of stony hills piled like bric-a-brac on the tabletop of a flat, yellow plain of dead grass. "It is like the surface of the moon, as if we do not belong here."

"We don't," Jay cheerfully agreed. "Without the water we stole from everybody else, nobody could live here. This is basically a desert, you know."

"It is frightening, I think," she said. "In France, you see, the countryside is much more charming, more civilized. This is like—like a pampa."

"Ah, France," Jay sighed. "Someday you'll take me there, Princess."

"Yes, perhaps," she agreed, smiling and reaching up to scratch at the nape of his neck. "If you are very sweet to me."

I tried not to pay too much attention now to this conversation. I loved the way Marina talked. Her English was very precise, the product of many years of study in some ferocious foreign school system, but her accent softened its grammatical exactitude, her throaty gargled *r*'s rolling out from behind her nose, and her *i*'s and *e*'s long and flattened, in the best professional Casino de Paris style. With her superb body and elegant gestures, she seemed to me the embodiment of everything I'd ever dreamed about in a beautiful European woman and I was riddled with envy that she had hit it off so explosively well with Jay and not with me. After all, I was the one with the right credentials for her—a reasonably good education, a fairly sophisticated background, some knowledge of the outside world beyond the confines of a grandstand. But she had picked Jay, a provincial California ex-jock with no ambitions, no culture, and no future. I got a little sick every time I thought about the two of them locked in each other's arms and thrashing around on an expanse of rumpled, sweaty sheets. Sometimes I had to shut my eyes at the vision I kept having of her, with those long, perfect legs locked behind the small of his back and the thrust of her body up to meet him as he drove into her. I began to think I was falling for her myself; so now, whenever they touched each other, I'd quickly look away. It was too painful to tolerate.

"Here we are," Marina said. "The barn area is behind the main house."

I had been looking out the side of the car at the hills and missed the entrance to Oakview Downs, a white corral gate and a gravelly dirt road that led straight up a slight incline between rows of sycamores to a rambling house and outbuildings clustered on the highest point of the property. To our left, green fields, fenced off into sections, stretched for a mile or so toward a ridge of rocky hills; to our right, a fenced half-mile training track was in full use, with several horses and riders galloping over it. One animal, probably a two-year-old, was working fast along the inner rail, the exercise boy hunched low over his shoulders and clucking encouragement to his mount. At the end of a short chute just behind a six-stall starting gate, a middle-aged man in boots, jeans and a pink cowboy shirt stood watching the workout, stopwatch in hand.

We parked by the fence and took it all in. After a half-mile, one full turn around the track, the rider stood up in the stirrups and allowed the horse to gallop out, then turned him and brought him back along the outside rail, the animal's neck bowed, his feet still full of run, as if he couldn't understand why he'd been eased up and not allowed to push himself to the limit. "Good move, Harv," the man with the stopwatch called out. "I got him in forty-eight and three, perfect. Get him cooled out now and we'll call it a day here."

Marina waved and the man with the stopwatch ambled over to us. He was a lean, weathered cowboy of about five-six or so, probably older-looking than his years, with curly gray hair, deep lines around his eyes, furrowed cheeks and impenetrable black eyes. As he came toward us, he touched two fingers to the brim of his hat, a battered-looking black Stetson, and nodded to Marina. "Howdy, ma'am," he said, with no trace of emotion in his voice. "Did you see the work?"

"The last part of it," Marina said. "Who was that?"

"That Piquant, that young colt of yours," he said, pronouncing it Pee-cant. "Pretty nice work."

"Oh," Marina answered, looking puzzled. "I thought he was at Del Mar."

"He was," the man said, "but Bert thought he needed a little settling down. He wasn't doing too good at the track. Too much excitement for a young horse, maybe. Also, we need to work him all the time out of the gate now. He didn't break too good his first start, Bert tells me."

"He didn't break at all," Jay said. "I guess you're waiting for a mile or more, right?"

Marina introduced us. "This is Bud Grover," she explained to us. "He's Bert's right hand. He has been with him for many years."

Grover favored us with a wintry half-smile, about as close as he probably permitted himself to outright merriment. "And what do you gentlemen do?" he asked.

"We're just friends of Marina's," Jay said. "Driving around on a nice day with nothing to bet on."

"I thought I would show them around," Marina said. "Will that be all right?"

"Sure," the cowboy said. "Not much to see here but horses, if you call that looking around."

Marina waved goodbye and we drove up toward the main house, then around to the back where three rows of sheds and about a dozen pens lay under the shadows of a cluster of oaks, eucalyptus and palms. Horses stared dumbly at us over the pen railings as we got out of the car and walked toward the far end of the nearest barn. The air was soft with the warm, musky smell of animals and hay; a flock of pecking chickens scattered before us. The tack room was empty and no one seemed to be about, so Marina turned and led us along the row of stalls. "I think he is back here," she said, stopping now in front of a stall and peering inside. "Yes, I am certain this is Balthazar." She clucked to the horse. "Hello, *chéri, comment ça va?*"

"I thought you told me the horse came from Argentina," Jay said. "You'd better talk to him in Spanish."

"Horses, *mon cher*, understand your tone of voice, not the words you speak to them."

"Horses understand very little, babe," Jay said. "That's the trouble with them."

We peered into the recesses of the stall where a huge chestnut colt stood with his rump to us and his head down, probably asleep. He ignored our presence completely. "He is beautiful, no?" Marina observed, smiling. "He looks splendid, *n'est-ce pas?*"

"He looks more like a cow than a racehorse," Jay ventured. "I'd be happier if he were trying to kick us or bite. That way I'd know he's a thoroughbred."

"I don't understand you."

"It's the mean and feisty ones that can run, Princess," Jay explained. "This beast doesn't give a shit about us."

"But he is resting," she said. "Don't be foolish, darling."

We couldn't really see very much of Marina's champion and

I suppose at that point we'd have left, but a small, wiry, olive-skinned man suddenly popped around the corner of the barn and came up to us. He was in his fifties, dressed in sneakers, manure-stained white cotton pants and a blue shirt, and he smiled and nodded to Marina as he joined the group. "Oh, Eduardo," Marina said, "these are my friends. This is Eduardo. He works here. I'm afraid he speaks very little English." She pointed to the horse. "Eduardo, how is he?"

"He is?" Eduardo answered us, as if to echo her question. "Ah," he then exclaimed and shook his head. "Is not good, no."

"No? What is wrong?"

Eduardo shook his head again but offered nothing more. He merely shuffled from foot to foot, made uncomfortable, perhaps, by the concern Marina was manifesting at his answer. "Perhaps we could see him?" Marina asked.

"Ah, *sí*," Eduardo said, smiling again. He opened the stall door and went inside, where he slapped the big horse on the rump and began to talk to him in Spanish. He slipped a halter over the animal's head, then backed him out of the stall and led him out into the sunlight where we could get a good look at him. He made an impressive sight, all right.

"He's big enough," Jay said. "What is he? Seventeen hands?"

"Not quite," Marina answered, her eyes glued on the horse. "About sixteen and a half, I think. That is why he was lightly raced, you see. He was still growing."

"What was his record?"

"He lost his first two races, which were at brief distances," Marina explained. "Then he won his next three, all at thirteen hundred or fourteen hundred meters. What is that here?"

"Six and a half furlongs and seven furlongs," I told her.

"Ah, yes," she said, "and he won a big race for young horses there. We bought him last winter."

"Who's we?" Jay asked.

"Dino and I, through Bert. Then when we separated, I kept all the horses."

"It sounds like you got the worst of the deal, to judge by Eduardo," I said. "What's wrong with this horse?"

"I don't know," Marina said. "He looks beautiful, doesn't he?"

Almost all racehorses look beautiful to me, since I have a hard time distinguishing between a champion and an ordinary animal just on looks, but I had to agree with Marina. Balthazar really looked spectacular. He stood quietly in the sunlight, his coat gleaming and the muscles of his legs and shoulders rippling impressively under the skin. He turned his head to look at us and I noticed the white blaze that ran from just above his eyes down almost to the tip of his nose. "Sure looks like he could run some," Jay observed. "So what's wrong with him?"

Marina concentrated hard for a minute or so, then spouted what sounded like pidgin Spanish at the groom. I caught only a few words, but it was clear to me that she was inquiring on the state of Balthazar's progress. Eduardo heard her out, then shrugged. He looked away for a second, then answered in a few quick sentences that seemed to puzzle Marina.

"What's he say?" Jay asked.

"That he is not himself yet," Marina said. "At least I think that's what he means."

"It takes foreign horses a while to adjust, I guess."

"That is what Bert has explained to me."

"You'd think Eduardo would know that."

"Yes."

"How long has he been around racehorses?"

"I don't know," Marina said. "A long time, I suppose."

"Where's he from?" I asked.

"Chile, I think."

"Well, if he knew so much, he wouldn't still be just a groom, would he?" Jay observed.

"Hey! What the hell are you doing?" The voice, as hard as an iron spike, seemed to transfix us. We turned and stared. Bud Grover had come around the corner of the stable and was moving toward us as if about to commit an act of violence. His face was red with anger and his fists were clenched. "What the hell's going on here? Who told you to move that horse?"

Eduardo looked alarmed; his eyes beseeched Marina. "I told him to take the horse out," she said quietly. "I'm sorry. We wanted to look at him."

Grover didn't answer right away. He stared hard at the groom, then turned to us. "You shouldn't have done that, Ma'am," he said. "Nobody does nothing around here without Bert's or my say-so and this boy knows that." The cowboy was obviously making an effort to be at least polite, but it wasn't coming easily to him. He flicked a hand toward Eduardo as if he meant to throw it at him. The groom silently led the horse back into his stall.

"Please, Bud," Marina said, "it really is our fault."

"It's okay, forget it," Grover said. "It's just that if an animal gets hurt, I'm responsible."

"I understand. I am so sorry."

"It's okay." The foreman turned and started for the tack room.

"What's wrong with the horse?" Jay asked.

"Wrong?" Grover whirled on us. "Who said there was something wrong?"

"The groom. He said it."

"He meant the horse was not feeling well, perhaps," Marina explained.

"Ain't nothing wrong with that horse," Grover said. "That boy don't know shit." He resumed his determined stride toward the tack room, went inside and slammed the door behind him.

"Charming," I said.

Marina looked distressed. "Oh, dear, I think we have done a wrong." She went into the barn to console Eduardo, who was standing by the horse's head as he removed the bridle. When she came back, she looked shaken. "That man has the most awful temper," she said. "I think we should go, no?"

"Yes," Jay agreed.

We walked back to the car and Marina turned for one last

look, but Eduardo was not to be seen. "I hope he is all right," she murmured.

"He'll be okay," Jay said. "Come on, we're wasting good beach time."

We saw Eduardo again five days later, when Piquant was entered in the fourth race of the day, another sprint, and we all went down to the paddock to look at him. The horse had drawn a slightly better post position this time, the six hole in a seven-horse field, but it was obviously a no-go as far as betting on him. Buckingham had nominated a jockey named Lonny Richards to ride him, which, as far as we were concerned, almost certainly meant a stiff job. Richards had once been a top rider, but although he was still only in his early forties, a year or two younger than Bill Scarpe, Buckingham's favorite jockey, he was deemed to be pretty much washed up. A rider of enormous natural ability, he had acquired over the years a reputation for leaving horses in the gate, a favorite method of making sure the animal couldn't win. The fact that he did this over and over with favorites in races for the smaller purses had led to a certain amount of suspicion about him on the part of such observers of form as Sour Sam and the other pros. "The only time to bet that bum," Sam once said, "is when he's an overlay in an exacta race. Then he'll ride like a demon for you." It was Sam who had hung the nickname of the Undertaker on him. Richards reportedly also had a drinking problem that had diminished his skills over the past few years and he wasn't getting the mounts anymore. Buckingham and a few other trainers continued to use him from time to time, but he no longer rode important horses for anyone and had been limited to one or two rides a day, usually on longshots. His presence on the back of a Buckingham maiden was the equivalent of a declaration that the horse had not been entered to win.

By this time Jay had succeeded in persuading Marina not to bet on her horse. We stood on the lush, green grass of the paddock and watched the animals come out from under the overhang of the saddling shed. Marina immediately spotted

Eduardo, who was leading Piquant into the ring. The thin little man smiled tentatively and nodded to her. When Buckingham appeared with Richards in tow, we gathered around to hear his instructions, but this time he didn't give any; he simply gave the jockey a leg up and watched the horse head out for the track. "Is he going to run any faster this time?" Marina asked.

Buckingham grunted. "I don't know," he said. "He'll break faster out of the gate, that's for sure, but he's still a little green."

"What is Eduardo doing here? I thought he was taking care of Balthazar."

"He goes back and forth," the trainer explained. "He's pretty good with young horses and this one usually needs settling down when you start to saddle him."

The two-year-old ran better this time. As Buckingham had predicted, he broke well out of the gate and ran up with the leaders for a half-mile, then dropped back and finished out evenly, about eight lengths off the winner. Marina was disconsolate. "He ran worse than last time," she moaned.

"Wrong, Princess," Jay said cheerfully. "Wait till he stretches out to a distance. What I think we just saw was the million-dollar move."

"What is that? I do not understand."

"I can't explain it to you right now," Jay said. "Wait till next time. Then I can show you in the *Form* what I mean."

The rest of the afternoon went well. Sam came up with a dead crab in the ninth race, in the shape of a horse that one of the clockers had told him couldn't lose and we all cashed tickets on him at odds of better than four to one. Marina didn't know what the term "dead crab" meant either, but nobody had the time that day to explain it to her, though it was one of my favorite Jay Fox tales. One reason we had no time was that she had told Jay earlier in the day that she had to drive up to L.A. immediately after the races. She had an appointment with her lawyer at nine o'clock the next morning on old business with Dino, so she left right after the ninth, also with money in her purse from Sam's good thing.

She was supposed to return the next afternoon or call Jay, but he didn't hear from her. Or maybe she did call and missed him. We had had another good winning day and all went out to dinner together, not getting in until pretty late, by which time she had undoubtedly given up. Jay fell on his bed like a tree trunk and passed out, still fully dressed.

Early the next morning, I was on the terrace sipping my second cup of coffee and getting ready to practice some new illusions I was working on, when Jay suddenly appeared, bleary-eyed and unshaven in the doorway. He looked strange, as if someone had woken him up by putting an ice cube against the back of his neck. "What's wrong?" I asked. "You look terrible."

"Marina just called," he said. "She's really upset."

"What about?"

"That groom, Eduardo, the one we met at Oakview . . ."

"What about him?"

"He was killed night before last."

"What? How?"

"A sheriff's car found him by the side of a road, near Rancho Santa Fe."

"Hit by a car?"

"That's what they thought at first. No, he was shot several times, apparently. That's what killed him. He was run over, too, but he was probably dead by then."

"Jesus, what for?"

"Robbery, I guess. His wallet was gone, also his jewelry. He wore a gold chain and a medallion around his neck."

"How did Marina find out?"

"Somebody called her. She's really upset."

"I guess she must have known him pretty well."

"I guess. He took care of her big horse. Seemed like a nice little guy, didn't he?"

FIVE

Single-o in Vegas

MARINA DID NOT come back from L.A. for several days and hadn't returned by the time I had to leave for Las Vegas. Ordinarily, I always planned my year so that I never had to work during Del Mar, but this trip was in the nature of an emergency. My friend Vince Michaels, who is the finest close-up magician I know, had come down with some sort of bug and had telephoned, asking me to work for him that weekend. Vince was resident conjuror at the Xanadu, one of those gambling palaces on the Strip, and he'd made himself a fixture in the Emerald Room, where he went from table to table performing his wonderful illusions. He is the best man with Cups and Balls and Ring on the Stick I've ever seen and he has a quiet, understated, sly sense of humor that has always made him a favorite wherever he works. I couldn't refuse Vince. When I first came to L.A. twelve years ago, Vince took me in, got me a job in a magic store on Hollywood Boulevard and gave me an intro to the Magic Castle, where I got my first local work. More important, he taught me a lot, not so much about magic (I'm probably better with cards than he is) but about how to talk to the customers, how to work an audience so that you had them eating out of your hands. We used to spend one night a week just dropping into various bars and restaurants in the San Fernando Valley, where Vince then lived, and doing a little magic. He had made it possible for me to perfect and enlarge my repertory in public, so I couldn't refuse to fill in for him now.

I went right from the airport to his apartment. He lived in a small duplex east of the Strip, surrounded by his cartons of books on magic and the paraphernalia of his trade. On the walls were framed reproductions and prints of such scenes as "The Conjuror," by Hieronymous Bosch, and "Sleight of Hand," by the American artist Willian V. Birney. You didn't have to hang around Vince very long before you began to realize he was a man obsessed. The front door was open and I stood in the hallway and called out his name.

He was upstairs in bed, a tiny gnome of a man with spiky black hair and glittering eyes, propped up against a wad of pillows and leafing through an *Encyclopedia of Sleeving*. He grinned at me and riffled through a deck of cards. "My favorite card cheat," he said. "Sit down, Shifty. Tell me about life."

"What's wrong with you?" I asked, perching on a corner of the king-sized bed. "You've probably got the clap."

"No such luck," he answered. "The last lady I had in here fled in terror when I woke her up at three A.M. and asked her to take a card. What's new? How are the horses treating you?"

"Pretty good. Jay's in fine form. So what *have* you got?"

"A virus, I guess. I'm feeling better, but the local quack says to take it easy for a week or so."

"I can only stay the weekend," I said. "You're screwing up my vacation."

"What vacation? You're always on vacation," he snapped. "If you worked at your magic as hard as you work at the horses, you'd be the best magician in the world. Tell me about yourself."

We talked magic for a couple of hours and I showed Vince some new ways of shuffling I'd been working on, so that I could cut the middle three cards out of any deck with no risk of being caught even by an expert spotter, and the time flew. "It just shows you how easy it is to cheat people," Vince observed. "You could always get work here as a mechanic in a casino."

"If I cheat," I said, "it's not going to be for the house."

"That's the trouble with you, Anderson. You have ethical standards. How do you expect to get anywhere in life?" Vince asked.

"I don't, but I have fall-back positions."

"You still like the cards, that's good."

Vince knew me so well. I could never get enough of cards and in my younger days I used to collect moves the way other people collect stamps. I could deal from the bottom, the middle of the deck and second from the top. I could palm, sleeve, crimp, jog, blind-deal, fake-cut, do just about anything with a good deck that could be done. I could also work coins, sponges, string, pencils, rings, thimbles, cups, rubber balls, bottle caps, handkerchiefs and other bits of social debris, but with cards I was the best and I knew it. I'd never be the magician Vince was, because I didn't have his drive or his touch with people, but with cards I was as much of an artist as he was. I'd have backed Vince head to head, trick for trick against any other magician in the world, but at cards I'd have had to back myself against anyone. If Vince was to parlor magic what Horowitz was to piano-playing, then with cards I was Rubinstein.

"You'd better get ready," Vince finally said to me. "You got to be there at six. People eat early in this town. Did you bring clothes?"

"My one three-piece suit and my only tie. That all right?"

"Yeah."

"I'll get dressed." At the head of the stairs I called back to him. "Oh, say, how's Dawn?"

"I thought you'd never ask," he shouted. "She's at the Stardust, on the early night shift. She'll be surprised to see you."

"I'll bet."

"Whatever happened to you two?"

"I wish I knew," I said. "Inertia, maybe."

I went downstairs and got ready. When I had washed up and was fully dressed, I stuffed more than I thought I'd need for the night into my pockets—a steel nut, a piece of string, some threads, a box of matches, a colored handkerchief, some sponge-rubber balls, a couple of pencils, several cigarettes, some bottle caps, several envelopes, a small glass, a few coins, and, of course, a pack of cards. When I was all set to go, I called up the stairs. "You need anything, Vince? I'm going."

"I'm okay," Vince called back. "Just going nuts from boredom. See you later."

"If you're asleep, I'll talk to you in the morning."

"You can stay here, if you want to, or at the hotel. Have you checked in?"

"I'll do it now."

"Going to see Dawn?"

"Maybe. I don't know yet."

"She still looks great."

I didn't answer. I simply let myself out, climbed into Vince's car, a blue Toyota sedan, and drove about half a mile to the Xanadu, a huge, pink-and-blue terraced tower sandwiched between two garish slot emporiums. I was feeling pretty good about working again, and not even missing Del Mar too much, as I parked, walked inside and headed across the casino floor, a wading pool of craps and blackjack tables surrounded by slots, to the Emerald Room.

The place had a reputation for decent Chinese food, which made it practically a gourmet restaurant by Vegas standards, and it was a pleasant ambiance for a magician. Decorated in neo-Victorian style, with lots of dark wood paneling and colored glass, the room was divided into booths that offered a good deal of privacy and also helped keep the noise level down. I introduced myself to the maître d', an affable middle-aged Italian-American named Renato, gulped down a little sweet-and-sour pork, cased the premises and was at work by a little after seven.

The place was about two-thirds full and I picked a booth occupied by an older couple and two younger ones, probably a family grouping from somewhere in the Midwest. They all looked a little alarmed when I showed up by their table, but I quickly established my credentials and offered to show them something unusual. I decided to start, as I often do, with coins, because everybody's interested in money. I made three quarters vanish, change hands, become half-dollars and turn red, by which time I had their undivided attention. Furthermore, the group proved to be nice people and I really enjoyed myself. "Can you make our check disappear?" the old man asked, after the waiter arrived with the bill.

"No, but I can double it," I told them.

"Can you make my wife disappear?"

"Sure. With your wallet."

We laughed a lot and I left them five minutes later, after one of my better card numbers, the one in which I spread the deck out, snap it shut, shuffle it and then turn the cards blank. They applauded and I took a break, feeling very good about myself.

The rest of my gig went smoothly enough. I had a great time with some young college people and also a dentist and his wife, who both came from a small town near Green Bay, Wisconsin, and who loved my patter even better than my sleight of hand. I got a laugh with my opener, "Either I'm going to fool you or you're going to be fooled by me," and when I stopped in the middle of Ring on a Stick, reached into my pocket for a pair of glasses, stuck them on my nose and said, "Oh, I want to see this one," I thought the dentist's wife would swallow her molars. "You're terrific!" she gushed at me, as I said good night. "Where did you learn to do all that?"

"From my brother," I explained, "who's very clever with his hand. He has only two more years to do and then he'll be out." She and the dentist fell into each other's arms laughing, but then some people are very easy to amuse.

My only unpleasant turn came toward the end of the evening, when Renato came over and suggested I entertain a large dinner party occupying the best corner booth. The host of this group was a small, dapper-looking man in dark glasses who looked as if he had been sculpted into his suit.

He wore a dark-red silk tie, a white silk shirt and his wrists and hands sparkled with jewelry. When he laughed, which he did frequently—and always at his own jokes—his teeth flashed as if they had been lacquered. He had a thick head of black hair and looked about thirty-five, though I guessed he was older. His party consisted of several well-groomed middle-aged men and three women who looked like ruined fashion models. The tall blonde sitting next to him had a spectacular bosom, most of which she had taken no trouble to conceal. The minute I came up to their table, the host let me have it. "You are a magician?" he said, in some sort of Latin accent. "Ah, then you can make yourself disappear, no?"

"Certainly," I said and began to leave.

"Hey, do some tricks," the man called out. "Show us something."

I started conventionally enough with coins, but this group talked all through my first illusion. I concentrated on the blonde and made a sponge ball vanish from my hand to hers, then I watched her smilingly drop it into her blouse. "Can you get it now?" she asked sweetly.

"I'll find it," the man next to her said, "if you give me twenty minutes."

I asked her to remove the ball, which she did. No sooner had she given it back to me than I made it disappear, then I looked at her. "Well?"

"Well, what?"

"Where's my other ball?"

"Even magicians got two of them," her companion said.

I decided to ignore this boor. "Well?" I repeated, concentrating on her.

"What other ball?" she asked.

"You have another one in there."

Surprised in spite of herself, the girl reached into her blouse again and produced a second ball. After that, I had them, at least for a few minutes, but I was eager to finish up and get away from them. Their boorishness annoyed me and I didn't want to jeopardize Vince's status at the hotel by saying anything to irritate them. So I did three of my best card tricks and wound up with my favorite classic, Cups and Balls. Using their coffee cups, rolled-up dollar bills, and a table knife for a wand, I made the balls vanish from my hands, reappear under the cups, change denominations, penetrate the cups, multiply, and finally metamorphose into an apple, a lemon and a peach. It's a pretty hard act to top, but this group paid very little attention. When I had finished, the host held out a crisp twenty-dollar bill to me as if extending his hand to be kissed. "That's okay," I said, "I work for the fun of it."

"Take the money or you make me angry," the man said.

I hesitated, then took it, nodded and left. "Who are those people?" I asked Renato a few minutes later.

"I don't know the others," Renato said, "but the guy is an Italian movie producer. He's here quite a bit. His name's Caretoni."

"Dino Caretoni?"

"Yeah, that's it."

"He's a charmer."

"Big tipper. He's in here maybe two, three times a month."

"What for?"

"A big gambler, I hear. Baccarat, roulette, poker, you name it."

"I know his wife."

"Yeah? I never seen her. He always comes in here with a big party, always a lot of broads, hookers mostly. I hear he can't ever go back to Italy."

"No? Why not?"

"Taxes or something. He don't pay 'em."

"It doesn't surprise me." I looked at my watch. "It's about midnight. Think I can leave?"

"Sure," Renato said. "It's a fairly slow night. How's Vince?"

"Suffering, but he'll be all right."

"Tell him I said hello. He's the greatest, that guy. I had my wife and kids in here last week and he killed them. You seen what he does with that ring on a pencil bit?"

"Yes," I said, "it's one of his great moves."

"You got some nice moves yourself, I notice."

"I try hard," I said. "Good night, Renato. I'll see you to-morrow."

I drove to the Stardust, only five or six blocks away, and arrived just as the second show in the main lounge was getting under way. The lobby was half empty and I had no trouble spotting Dawn, who was dealing at one of the tables nearest the front desk. I walked over and eased myself onto a corner stool. Two seats away, the other players, a young couple betting a dollar each at a time, were trying to decide whether to hit or stand against Dawn's up card, a seven. "Draw," I said. "She'll have a four in the hole. I know this lady."

Dawn was startled to see me, but she did her best to hide it. "Well, look what the desert wind blew in," she said. "A tumbleweed all the way from the beach. What's happening, Shifty?"

"Not much," I said. "I'm subbing for Vince Michaels at the Xanadu for a couple of nights. He's got a virus or something."

"Yeah," Dawn said, "I hear there's something going around."

"We'll each take a card," the young man said. Dawn busted him with a king, then dealt his bride a twenty-one. They split when Dawn had to stand on her seventeen and the boy grimaced at me. "She's murder," he said. "She never goes bust."

"Give us a break," I said to Dawn.

She smiled wickedly at me. "Are you playing, sir?" she asked very sweetly.

I bought dollar chips with Caretoni's twenty and pushed a single chip out in front of me. Dawn dealt me a sixteen and I stood, after which she busted her own hand and paid us all off. "See?" I told the couple. "She does have a heart."

"It was broken years ago," Dawn said, flicking out the cards with casual, professional grace. "Some guy went right through me and smashed up everything inside. Now I deal cards and try to bust everyone. Isn't that right, sir?" And she smiled at me.

"Something like that," I said, picking up my hole card, a six under a queen. "You haven't mellowed a bit, I can tell."

It took about forty minutes for Dawn to beat me out of my twenty, by which time the kids beside me had gone and we were alone. "When do you get off?" I asked.

"Four o'clock." I groaned and she smiled. "I suppose you think you can just blow in here unannounced two or three times a year and ravish my fair white body at your convenience," she continued.

"Something like that," I answered, "only it's not quite as coarse as you make it sound. I'd have called you, but I literally flew in here on two hours' notice."

"And you don't have my phone number."

"That's true, I don't."

"It's real slow tonight," she said. "Reaganomics is killing us. Maybe I can get off a couple of hours early."

"Wonderful. I really just want to talk to you."

"Oh, sure you do," she said. "That would be something new."

A heavyset middle-aged man wearing a plaid leisure suit and a golf cap sat down at our table and dropped a wad of hundred-dollar bills in front of him. "Let's play some cards, honey," he said. "I feel real lucky."

"Do you?" Dawn told him, favoring him with her finest barracuda smile. "Then we'll have to do something about that."

"Look out for her," I said. "She's a master of the Erdnase Shift."

"Huh?" The man stared at me as if I had exposed myself to him. "What the hell you talking about?"

"It's all right, sir," Dawn reassured him. "He's just talking cards. He's the magician from over at the Xanadu."

"Yeah?" the leisure suit said. "Honey, just deal. We'll let the cards talk for themselves, okay?"

I eased myself out and went into the coffee shop. I looked at my watch and saw that it was nearly one A.M. now, but I wasn't at all tired. I was still charged up from having worked and I was pleased at my performance. Like all close-up magicians, I'd always operated single-o, as they say, and the bad nights were always those in which you blew some move or other or failed somehow to please your audience; the good nights were like good sex, because, for me, close-up magic is the only other human activity that depends upon achieving intimacy with at least one other human being. I think that's why it had attracted me in the first place, way back then, when I was fourteen and growing up on Long Island and had a bad complexion and stammered and couldn't make any of my high-school athletic teams. Magic had provided an avenue for me and, while I hadn't exactly made of it what I had originally planned to, it had smoothed my way out of an unhappy childhood and given me confidence in myself as well as a trade, a skill I could always fall back on, no matter what happened.

I sat down and sipped a cup of coffee while I waited for my eggs over easy and I began to think about Dawn Caputo. I'd met her five years before at a poker parlor in Gardena, where she was then employed as a cashier. What had happened to us? We had liked each other at once and moved in together and for nearly a year everything had worked out very well. She had been married once and had an eight-year-old boy named Ronnie who was a nice, quiet kid, away at school most of the time, and we had hit it off just fine. But somehow it had all begun to unravel without our ever being aware of it until one afternoon I had just packed up and moved out. We had never even quarreled, but I did remember one thing Dawn had said to me one night, a few weeks before our breakup. "You work single-o and you live single-o," she'd said very quietly, almost sweetly, as she watched me work on some of my moves with cards. "You're a nice guy, but I can't reach you, Lou."

I hadn't paid too much attention then, but those words had come back to haunt me very often since. Now I closed my eyes and tried again to pinpoint exactly when it was that our relationship had begun to come apart and I still couldn't quite figure it out. Maybe I shouldn't have bothered. Now, whenever I saw her, we could be friends, we could even make love, and for a few hours at least it would be as it had been, warm and caring and, yes, exciting, too.

She came into the coffee shop a little after two and slipped into the booth with me. "Hi," she said. "I'm off. Where are you staying?"

"Vince got me a room at the Xanadu."

"Good. I can't take you home. Ronnie's here on vacation."

"I thought he might be."

She leaned over and kissed me. "Am I still the best casual lay you know?"

"I don't know about casual," I said. "Nothing about you is casual. But we could find out. It's been too long."

Making love to her that night put a cap on a really terrific evening. Dawn was in her mid-thirties and looked every day of it around the eyes, almost certainly because she had seen a little too much and lived a little too hard a little too early, but she had a wonderful body, soft and smooth to the touch, full-breasted, firm in all the right places, and her legs were long and strong. Best of all, she made love in a giving, generous way, uninhibited and concerned for me. I almost fell in love with her all over again and I told her so.

"Bullshit," she said, sitting up and reaching for a cigarette. "Let's not mistake a little friendly fucking for the real article."

"Sweetly put," I answered. "You always had a way with language."

"No, that was your talent, Lou," she said. "You could talk a snake into shedding its skin." She swung her legs out of bed. "I've got to go."

"What for?"

"Ronnie wakes up early. He knows I'm not a virgin, but I don't want him to think I'm a slut either, and I don't think he'd understand about you. He was more upset than I was when you moved out."

"That was quite a while ago."

"Funny thing about kids," she said. "They don't forget or forgive as easily as we do."

It was a wonderful, creative two days. I spent most of the next morning and early afternoon talking magic with Vince and looking at some new moves he'd worked out that I thought were nothing short of sensational. His temperature was down and he was obviously looking forward to going back to work on Tuesday, so I made plane reservations for San Diego that Monday afternoon. I had wavered, wanting suddenly to spend more time with Dawn, but I could tell that she was anxious for me to leave. We had meant too much to each other in the past to be able to risk a renewal of our affair now and I was determined to cause her no more pain.

I arranged to have a farewell drink with her my second night, just before I had to go to work. She came by the hotel and we met in one of the downstairs bars, as far away from a loud jazz trio as I could get her. "You don't want to come up to my room?" I asked. "It's awfully noisy down here."

"No, thanks. We'd only wind up in bed again and that's no way for old wounds to heal, is it?"

"Fair enough." We chatted about this and that and I could tell that she was nervous, increasingly anxious for me to be off. After perhaps an hour of inconsequential chatter, I paid the tab and escorted her out through the lobby. She wouldn't let me go with her to her car but turned suddenly and kissed me. "What happened, Dawn?" I asked.

"Don't ask me," she said. "You always had your mind on other matters."

"I do care for you."

"Yes, but you don't love me. Not enough, anyway." She patted my cheek as if I were a furry pet of some kind. "Good-bye, Lou. Call the next time you're in town."

I watched her walk away from me, then turned to go back inside; it was nearly time for me to go to work. A large black Rolls now pulled up to the curb and Dino Caretoni emerged from it, looking as trim and sleek as a small killing animal. I stepped aside and watched, guided by some impulse I can't recall, perhaps merely curiosity. He was followed out of the car by one of the men I had seen with him in the Emerald

Room, who now turned to offer his hand to another passenger. To my amazement, it turned out to be Marina. She was dressed in a white off-the-shoulder evening gown, with her hair piled up on her head and a double strand of very authentic-looking pearls draped around her long, handsome neck. She looked absolutely terrific, but very tense, her mouth set in a cold, hard line. I waited for her to see me, but she marched inside looking straight ahead, as if headed for a rendezvous with a tax auditor.

I followed them in and watched them cross the lobby toward the elevator bank at the far end, then disappear. Later that evening I again asked Renato about Caretoni. "I don't know," the maître d' said. "There's some talk of him making a movie here, but it's mostly rumors. Like I told you, he's a big plunger."

"How big?"

"Very. He plays in the private penthouse upstairs, him and some other high rollers and a bunch of Arabs. Big money. They got chips up there that look like small breakfast trays."

"He was with his wife tonight."

"Yeah? That's a change. He likes hookers, mostly."

"They're separated or divorced, she says."

"I wouldn't know," Renato said. "They got a lot of funny games going on in this town and there's hardly anybody that ain't for sale sometime. His wife, huh? Maybe she likes the big bucks. Dino is big bucks, believe me. They flow like water all around him and he's like a whirlpool, it sucks everybody in."

SIX

Sources of Rapture

JAY and I were standing under our favorite grandstand television monitor on Saturday, watching a rerun of Wednesday's feature race, when I ran into Bunny Lehrman again. Actually, she accosted me, which was a surprise, as I hadn't seen her since the night I'd unraveled in Bully's and spirited myself away with her. It was an evening I had done my very best to forget, but life, I've discovered, has an unwholesome habit of dredging up the past and swamping you with it. We all pay for our sins, my father used to tell me, sooner or later, even if in unpredictable ways and when we least expect it.

Anyway, Jay was expressing a certain amount of outrage at what he thought was the incompetent ride some normally skillful jockey had given his horse and was making notes on it, when I felt a flutter of cold fingers on my arm. "Hi," this squeaky little voice piped up behind my ear. "Winning any money?"

I turned and found myself confronted by Bunny's bucktoothed grin. She was wearing tight corduroys, sandals and a thin blue T-shirt with a Malibu logo imprinted over an unfettered bosom that was clearly threatening to cascade out of the cloth and smother somebody. Her corn-yellow hair lay piled up on top of her head Medusa-style and her pale blue eyes seemed as blankly indifferent as those of a sunfish. "You winning?" she asked.

"No, not today," I said. "What are you doing here?"

"Oh, I sometimes come to the track," she said. "Maybe two or three times a summer. Kretch usually brings me."

"Kretch. Is he here now?"

"Oh, no. He went up to L.A. again for a couple of days. But I told him I'd give you the message."

"What message?"

"See, I told him all about you."

"You what? I thought you said he'd kill us both."

"I didn't tell him we got it on, stupid. My God, he'd cream us. I told him about the magic, the cards, *you* know." She giggled nervously, like a schoolgirl surprised with a copy of *Playgirl* under her pillow. "I mean, Jesus, Lou . . . He, you must think I got a death wish or something."

"Or something."

"But, boy, I've never seen anybody do cards like you. I mean, like you're *great*. So I told him about you, about how you came into the bar a few nights ago and did all these great tricks and like that, see?"

"I guess."

"So he wants to meet you, that's all. I told him I'd tell you, if I was to see you somewheres. He'll be back tonight. You gonna stop by, maybe?"

"I don't know."

"It's okay, honest. He don't suspect."

"Well, I was planning to drop in, as a matter of fact. Jay here—"

"Oh, is this the Jay you was telling me about?" Bunny asked, as Fox turned toward us, now that the rerun was over. "Boy, I heard a lot about you."

Jay looked blankly at her, his mind obviously still focused on the atrocity he had just witnessed that had cost us both money. "What?"

"Jay, this is Bunny," I said. "She works at Bully's."

"Huh? Oh, yeah. Did you see what that little monkey did?" he asked me. "First he goes five wide on the turn and then cuts inside and gets himself boxed. All he's got to do is get clear by the eighth pole, the jerk, and he wins easy. He had a ton of animal under him. Next time out the horse'll be one to two and we'll have to sit on our money. Goddamn."

"It's over," I said. "Next problem."

"You lost, huh?" Bunny observed. "Gee, that's too bad. I had the winner." She held up a two-dollar ticket on the six-to-five-shot that had won the race by a neck from our selection, which would have paid off at better than five to one.

Jay stared at her with cold contempt. "The Dummy God is in session," he said. "All's well for the innocent of wallet." And he left us abruptly to return to his seat.

Bunny blinked at me. "Who's he calling a dummy? Does he always talk like that?"

"Sometimes. He's having a bad day," I explained. "He's lost two photos and now he gets a terrible ride from Chris, which is not a usual thing."

"I just bet colors," Bunny said. "Like today was green and gold day."

"That sounds like a terrific system. Listen, Bunny—"

"Yeah?"

"Why does Kretch want to meet me, then?"

"I told you. I told him about your magic tricks."

"He's a magic fan?"

"I don't know."

"What does Kretch do, Bunny, when he isn't creaming people?"

"I ain't sure. We met here, you know, last summer. He plays cards a lot." She frowned, as if trying to piece a complicated puzzle together in her head. "We been together a while."

"You moved to L.A.?"

"No. On the weekends and Mondays, Kretch is here. Sometimes I go up to see him, but not during the racing season."

"Where does he live?"

"Gardena. Kretch likes to play poker. They got clubs there where you can play legal."

"I know."

"Then he's got his own game. Two or three nights a week he does something else."

"Like what?"

"I don't know, Lou. All I know is he takes good care of me."

"He does?"

"Yeah, he treats me nice. Most of the time." She blinked sorrowfully at me, like a small Disney animal confronted by Snow White. "He's got a terrible temper, though. I mean, you don't want to cross him or nothin' like that."

"Look, tell him you didn't run into me."

"I don't think I can do that, Lou."

"No? Why not?"

"Because he won't believe me and then he might get mad. I mean, I told him where you was at the track and all, so he'll think I didn't try, see?" she explained, those pale blue eyes widening in alarm. "Please, Lou. He don't suspect nothin', honest. He will if we try to play games. Anyway, he'll find you for sure."

"Bunny, you have a sizeable mouth."

"Tell me about it, Lou, tell me about it."

She looked almost ready to burst into tears, so I patted her reassuringly on the shoulder. "It's okay, Bunny," I said. "I'll probably drop in tonight. Jay and I were talking about having dinner there. You can introduce me to Kretch then, okay?"

"Yeah. Thanks, honey."

"Are the steaks still good this year?"

"You ate one the other night."

"Who remembers the other night?"

"Yeah, you was something, all right," she said. "The meat's good, like always."

I heard the bugle signaling the departure of the ninth-race entries from the paddock. "All right, Bunny, I'll see you, huh?"

When I got back to our box, I found Jay glancing through tomorrow's *Form*, which he had run down and bought while I was concluding what passed for a conversation with Bunny.

"Hey, look," he said, tapping at the entries for the fourth race with his index finger, "look here."

I looked and saw nothing significant.

"This horse here, Gran Velero," he said. "The owner."

I looked more closely. Gran Velero was a four-year-old maiden trained by Wilbert Buckingham and owned by Marina de Nevers. "Oh, I guess she ought to be back tonight then."

"Yeah, so she said," Jay answered. "Though it won't be because of this animal."

"No good?"

"He's run four times this year," Jay said, "and he's never been closer than ten lengths to the winner. You add the four bad races this year to the four bad ones he ran last year and that makes eight lousy races in a row. An established bum."

"He *is* dropping in class," I observed. "It's the first time he's running for a tag. You can buy him for only forty grand."

"He isn't worth a dime," Jay snapped.

"What does Marina say?"

He shrugged. "She's never mentioned him at all, but then why would she? He's got to be the worst horse in her string. Some pig old Wilbert got her to buy on breeding, maybe, who's turned out to be nothing. Happens all the time." He sighed. "I wish I had just ten percent of all the money Buckingham and these other trainers have pocketed under the table over the years for getting their owners to buy stiffs like these from people. I could have my own stable."

The horses in the ninth race, a sprint for cheapos, now appeared out on the track and began to file past us. I picked up my glasses and focused them on the one horse, Hullabaloo, an old gelding with ancient class who had seen better days. Nevertheless, I had figured he could pop up here at a price; the old boy was eight to one on the line and might go off as an overlay, I reasoned. I mentioned him as a possibility to Jay, who also had his binoculars trained on the post parade. "I don't think so," he said. "He doesn't look right."

"What's wrong with him?" I asked. "His last race, at Hollywood Park three weeks ago, Wharton got him fanned on the turn. He must have lost five, six lengths, and he only got beat about two."

Jay shook his head and glanced quickly down at his notations on the race. "He's eight years old," he said, "and he's lost his speed out of the gate."

"He's got class," I objected. "He's dropping into a race against nothing. And he goes from Wharton, who's just another jock, to Tim McArdle." McArdle and Luis Pelé, two of the best jockeys in the world, were tied at the top of the rider standings with twelve wins apiece.

"I'm going to pass, Shifty," Jay said, snapping his notebook shut and leaning back in his seat. "I'll take my loss like a man today and wait for tomorrow. There's always tomorrow."

"We keep going like we have the last couple of days and there may be no tomorrow."

"Oh, ye of little faith," said Jay. "Never fear, there's always tomorrow."

I picked up Hullabaloo in my glasses again as he came jogging past on his way to the starting gate. He had his ears pricked and looked full of run, with McArdle sitting confidently in the saddle. As I watched, and without any urging from the jock, the old boy suddenly broke into an easy, fluid-looking canter. McArdle stood halfway up in the stirrups to slow him down. I got up. "Where are you going?" Jay asked.

"I like the looks of him," I said. "I'm going to bet him. McArdle doesn't ride cripples."

"From the inside he's going to need more speed than he's got," Jay warned.

"I don't care," I said. "Maybe I'll get lucky. Tim will get him out and the price is right." I glanced at the board just as it blinked and Hullabaloo's odds dipped from nine to one to six to one. "Oh oh," I said, "somebody sees what I see."

"They always bet McArdle down, if his mount even looks alive. This is no dead crab."

I didn't answer but made my way to the betting lines. I'd

been standing in one for about three minutes and knew I'd get my wager down in time when Sam approached me. "Here," he growled, handing me a fifty-dollar bill, "bet this on the one horse."

"You like him, too, huh?"

"I like the action on him," Sam said. "He took a good bet early, then they left him alone, and now he's getting hit again."

Sam had it right. The odds on Hullabaloo had dropped to nine to two. With two minutes or so before the race got off, he'd probably drop some more, maybe to three to one, now that the lemmings were flocking to him. I hoped we wouldn't all go over the cliff together.

I got to the window just as the horses reached the gate and bet seventy dollars on Hullabaloo to win, fifty of it for Sam. I couldn't get back to my seat before the race went off, so I watched it on the monitor with him. Sure enough, the odds on our champion dropped to three to one at post time, making him the second choice in the race. McArdle got him out of the gate alertly and had him laying about fourth as they hit the turn. He kept him on the rail, waiting for an opening, then, at the head of the stretch, he tapped the old boy once and he shot through a tiny gap between the front-runners to open up two lengths on the field. A smart, daring ride. Hullabaloo won handily by three, even though he pulled up soon after the finish and eased up very sore. "Nice hit, Sam," I said.

He almost smiled. "Only bet I made all day," he said. "How'd you do?"

"This got me out," I told him. "Jay got buried. He didn't like Hullabaloo."

"That's okay," Sam observed. "One thing about the Fox, if he doesn't like an animal, he won't play him. And he don't chase his money. He's still ahead for the meet, isn't he?"

"Yeah, sure, but he's getting chopped down some."

"The vicissitudes of fortune," Sam said. "I read that somewhere."

"I'll bet you did, Sam."

I met Jay out in the parking lot and he looked glum. "I could have risked a few bucks," he said, "but the front bandages stopped me. He came back real sore, too. He probably hasn't got another race in him and he got claimed. By Larry Talbot, I think. That bum couldn't train a canary to sing."

On the drive home, I did not engage Jay in idle chatter. Whan a man is hurting at the betting windows as the result mainly of losing two photos and being given a horrible ride in another race, it is wiser to remain discreetly silent, especially about one's own successful coup, until the pain has been partly dulled, at least, by time, a hot shower and the first stiff drink of the evening.

Jay went to see Marina that night. She had not answered his phone call from the house, but he was convinced she had returned, so he dropped me off at Bully's and proceeded up the beach to her waterfront mansion. He planned to rejoin me for dinner if she weren't there, or at least make arrangements to pick me up later if she were. The Datsun had popped a splint or something equally mysterious to me and was being serviced. It would not be ready until the following afternoon, which had left me without wheels for the whole day. In Southern California, this is equivalent to being sentenced to house arrest, since what passes for public transportation in our fair state is essentially to service ethnic minority groups and the poor and to keep this rabble isolated in its ghettos. There are very few poor or minority groups in the North County area of San Diego, consequently almost no bus service of any kind.

It was well after seven when I walked into Bully's and the place, a dark, smoky emporium with a dozen or so dining booths in the main room and a long bar against one wall, was already crowded. I left my name with the hostess, an angular brunette who informed me in a cheerful nasal scream that I'd have to wait an hour to get seated, and made my way to the bar. From my post at the near corner, I spotted Bunny, who waved cheerfully at me and disappeared with a loaded tray of food out toward the back patio, where you could eat in the open under Del Mar's often clammy night sky. I took a sip of my first margarita and hoped fervently that Kretch would fail to show up.

"Look at that little bum," a voice next to me observed. "His goddamn face ought to be on every post office wall in the country, the fuckin' thief."

"Who's that?" I asked, glancing up from my drink to find myself in conversation with Bet-a-Million, an overweight loser of about fifty with the red face of a paranoid in a permanent state of outrage. He was famous in our set for heavy action on odds-on favorites, a guaranteed method for assuring insolvency; how he stayed in action year after year and where the money came from was one of those mysteries in which the track abounds.

"The Undertaker," Bet-a-Million said, glancing toward the far end of the bar where Lonny Richards sat, surrounded by two or three seedy-looking backstretch cronies. "Did you see him leave that horse in the gate in the second? He should have won by ten."

"The horse has a habit of breaking slowly," I said. "Why would you bet him, with Richards up?"

"'Cause he was underlaid," Bet-a-Million explained, in the strangled tones of a man smothering a fearful fire within. "I figured they had one going."

"Who's 'they'?" I asked.

"You know, him and the crooks with him."

"Seven to five is not Lonny's price," I observed. "You made a risky bet, friend."

"Ah, what do you know?" Bet-a-Million answered. "If I ever get the bum alone in a room somewhere, I'll kill him."

The conversation saddened me, so I decided not to pursue it. I shut out Bet-a-Million's garbled complaints, now being directed at the startled young couple to his left, who evidently knew nothing about horse racing and had no idea what this wild man's rantings could possibly refer to, and nursed my margarita through another half hour of din and despair. Just as my name was paged, Jay came through the door; he was alone. "Good timing," I said. "Where's Marina?"

"She's here, but she doesn't want to eat," he said. "So I told her I'd drop you off after dinner and come back. That all right with you?"

"Sure." We followed the hostess to our booth, in the far corner of the room, and sat down. I already knew what I wanted to eat, a New York steak, rare, with fries, so I sat back and cased the locale while Jay studied the menu. I hadn't informed him about seeing the Princess in Las Vegas with her ex-husband, because I was wondering whether Marina herself would tell him. Also, I was jealous of Jay at that point and I was hoping my secret would somehow give me some sort of advantage in regard to Marina. If she wasn't going to be on the level with the man she was having an affair with, then that would be a useful bit of insight into her for me. At least, that was the way I rationalized my silence at the time.

"So how is Marina?" I asked.

"She's all right," he said. "A little down."

"About what?"

"Some money problems with old Dino," he said. "The guy's erratic, I guess."

"So I hear? Where is he?"

"New York, I think. Anyway, she was holed up with her lawyer half the time just trying to get things straight with him," Jay explained. "That's depressing enough, you know. Then the little guy, that groom she liked, got killed and that upset her. Mainly, she's tired."

"Did she see Dino?"

"How could she? I told you, he was in New York."

"Did she say anything about Gran Velero tomorrow?"

"Are you kidding?" Jay said. "I didn't even ask her. The horse has no chance. Did you see who's riding?"

"No."

"Richards."

"He's here tonight," I said. "Over there."

"He's here every night," Jay said. "He's a lush."

"You could ask him," I said, grinning, because I knew exactly what the response to that suggestion would be.

"Jesus, Shifty, sometimes I wonder how you survive at the track," he said. "I explain everything to you, but you don't listen."

"I'm not a figure man," I said, "you are. That's the difference."

He sighed. "Come on, let's eat. You're beginning to worry me."

Jay and I spent the next hour and a half talking horses and betting strategy over our steaks and a good bottle of California zinfandel. This is as interesting a way of passing time as any I know, mainly because Jay is so knowledgeable about his craft and because we are dealing here with one of the great, enduring mysteries of existence—the isolation of winners from the great snarl of often conflicting statistics that shroud the average horse race. Compared to it, deciphering cuneiform script is mere child's play, no more than the filling in of blanks in an admittedly complicated crossword puzzle. No chess master or bridge expert faces a more formidable daily task than the skilled handicapper, with the added difference that the solution to the puzzle pays off in very tangible rewards. Only magic holds the same thrill for me, but its demands are different, essentially physical and disciplinary, whereas the mystery of a horse race is in direct touch with still unsolved, untapped sources of energy that radiate from some dark, eternal force at the center of life. When I try to explain this feeling I often have to people who may never have seen a thoroughbred run, I am usually met either by polite incredulity or the tolerant smile of the average honest citizen for the hopeless addict. I don't try to rationalize it away or fight to explain it anymore. To those outside the charmed circle, the game seems mere folly, a useless and wasteful consumption of precious time; to those of us within it, the hours spent locked in mortal combat with the enigma are essentially devoted to what amounts to a grapple for a sliver of immortality. It is made all the more relevant and poignant by the fact that the mystery is not susceptible to dogma. Each race and each moment of each race, like the fusion that releases energy into the atmosphere, remains a conundrum. The acts are performed, often with the aid these days of such sophisticated tools as the computer, but the riddle at the heart remains, no more susceptible to pure logic that the annual liquefying of the blood of San Gennaro in Naples. Trying to pick winners is an act of faith in the human condition, nothing more nor less.

Jay doesn't like to hear me talk like that, so I don't argue with him anymore. To him there is no mystery that cannot be solved, no irrationality that cannot be contained within the perimeters of known fact. The attitude is admirable, because it seeks only to bend the mystery to his will, but it removes him from the one source of rapture that to me makes the game worthwhile—the sudden, unexpected flash of blinding inspiration, free of all logic and rationalization, that occasionally illuminates the darkest corners of existence. How else to explain the inexplicable, in the form, sometimes, of the hopeless long shot that crashes the sound barrier of the finish line at unheard-of odds? That is the intangible Jay chooses to ignore, to him simply another sickening manifestation of the Dummy God in session, but to me it is a glimpse not into an abyss, as it is for Jay and Sam and all the other logicians, but the fleeting revelation of the still unsolved conundrum that ridicules the theoretical posturings of the absolutists. Talk like that offends Jay so I usually content myself by basking in his solid, factual knowledge; the unseen forces I tap into on my own.

The time passed very quickly, as it always does in these circumstances, and I had forgotten all about the possible impending appearance of Bunny's massive swain. We had paid our tab and were on our way out to the street, when a body the size of a pilot whale detached itself from the crush at the bar and swam ponderously after us. "Hey, Anderson," a gravelly voice hammered at our banks. "I gotta talk to you."

Out on the sidewalk, I turned and found myself confronted by Kretch. He was wearing baggy gray slacks, loafers, a herringbone sports jacket and a tie that looked like someone's entrails splashed across his chest. A single dark eyebrow cut a straight line above the bridge of a great beak of a nose that made him look like a huge carrion bird. He made an altogether unreassuring picture, but not one to be easily dismissed from one's consciousness. I felt myself rise on the balls of my feet, poised instinctively for serious evasive action.

"I'm Sol Kretchmer," he said, making no effort to shake hands, which was all right with me, because I valued the continued health of my fingertips. "Bunny told you I had to talk to you, right?"

"Right."

"How about tomorrow?" Jay suggested. "I have a date."

"I don't need to talk to you," Kretch said. "Beat it."

"Wait a minute," Jay began, bristling, but I cut him off.

"You got wheels?" I asked.

"Sure."

"Then you can drop me off, right?"

"Yeah. Come on, I can tell you in the car. It won't take long."

Jay looked a little worried, but I felt reasonably sure this monster was not about to dismember me—not that night, anyway—so I left Jay to his late rendezvous with the Princess and followed Kretch around the corner to his car, the big silver-gray Cadillac I had glimpsed the morning of his return from L.A. "This won't take long," he said, opening the door on the driver's side. "I got a problem maybe you can help with."

I gave him directions to our place and on the way Kretch outlined his small dilemma. "I run poker games," he said, "me and a couple of other guys. For big stakes, you understand?"

I nodded. "Kretch, I don't deal," I said, "I'm—"

"Shut up and listen," he interrupted. "I ain't askin' you to, am I?"

"Not yet."

"Right. Now here's the problem," he resumed and went on to explain that one of the games he was operating took place right there in Del Mar during the summer race meet. He'd been running it for several years, every Monday night, in a condo he rented from some friends of his at La Costa, the resort development and spa ten miles north up the freeway. "It's a legit game, see?"

"I believe you, Kretch."

"Five-dollar ante, table stakes and dealer's choice, only no wild cards or crazy games," he explained, "and no high-low. High or low only. You got that?"

"Sure. So?"

"Somebody's ripping the game off," he said. "I know who it is, but I don't know exactly how he's doing it, see? That's where you come in."

"How?"

"Bunny tells me there ain't nothin' you can't do with a pack of cards, right? She says you're the best she's ever seen. Now, she's one dumb broad, but on this I believe her. I checked you out."

"Really? How?"

"I called around. I know about you."

"You must have called the Magic Castle, then. They know me there."

"Yeah, there and a couple of other places. So here's what I want you to do," he continued. "I want you to sit in next Monday. I'll introduce you as a friend of mine from back East and I'll back your action."

"What if one of these guys recognizes me?"

"Don't worry about it. They're all from out of town, only here for the summer. You ever go in the Turf Club?"

"No."

"These guys is all high rollers, millionaires. They don't

know from magic or shit like that. You ever play cards for big money around here?"

"No."

Kretch now eased the big car up to the sidewalk outside our condo and turned the engine off. "All you got to do is tell me how the guy is cheating, see? But I got to know how before I make a move."

"What kind of move, Kretch?"

"Probably nothing. Anyway, that ain't nothin' for you to worry about, Anderson. I'll take care of that end. You just tell me how it works. Okay?"

"What if I lose your money?"

"Can you play the game?"

"Yes. I'm pretty good, in fact, but I can't afford to play for myself."

"So this time you can play. If you win, you can keep three hundred bucks for your time. Only don't get into no hands where this guy is cheating."

"If I spot him."

"You'll spot him."

"And if I lose?"

"Tough shit. What do you want, a guarantee?"

"Yes," I said, amazed at my own effrontery. "I'm a magician, not a card shark. Three hundred dollars is my fee, win or lose, Kretch."

He grunted noncommittally. "You're a gambler, ain't ya?"

"No, I'm a horseplayer. There's a difference, Kretch. And I don't gamble when it comes to what I do for living," I said. "I can be hired, Kretch, but I have to be paid for my time. I want three hundred dollars and that's it."

"Okay, you got it," he said. "Next Monday night, eight o'clock. I'll give you all the dope later. You got any sharp clothes?"

"One suit, two sports jackets, three pairs of slacks. What do I need?"

"Don't show up looking like a bum," he said as I stepped out of the car. "You're supposed to be a rich asshole from the East, you got that?"

"Well, I was born on Long Island, but the unfashionable part of it. Do I need a monocle or something?"

"Don't make a fuckin' joke of this," he said. "I don't like jokes where I'm making money, you got that?"

Before I could answer, he swung the car away from the curb and disappeared into the night, like Moby Dick sounding.

SEVEN

A Million-Dollar Move

"WHAT IS THIS that you are always calling by this funny name?" Marina asked, settling herself comfortably into the sand beside us. "I have heard you use it several times now. What does it mean, this 'dead crab'?"

"Vespucci here began using it as a term after we came back from Kenya that summer," Jay explained. "Tell her, Sam."

Sam permitted himself the tiny grimace that passes for a smile with him and shrugged. "It's your story," he said. "You tell it."

"Why do you not remove your clothes?" Marina asked him. "You would be more comfortable."

"He might be more comfortable," Jay said, "but what about us? Can you imagine Sam exposed to sunlight? We'd need special goggles, like the kind they use in welding."

"Terrific," Sam said. "Hilarious."

We were, of course, at our usual post on the beach. Jay and I were sitting on the blanket, with Sam perched precariously on a rickety wooden beach chair and Marina, having completed her morning romp, stretched gloriously out on her towel. Sam was, as usual, attired for the sidewalks of New York, in shoes, socks, pants and a short-sleeved shirt, his now disgustingly dirty gray porkpie resting on his head like a battered tin pan on a soccer ball. His resistance to the outdoors was gallant in its consistency, immune, as ever, to the slightest hint of compromise.

I looked at Marina. She was even more beautiful than the first time I'd ever seen her, and she seemed to be herself again. I wondered if she had yet, or would ever, tell Jay about her trip to Las Vegas, but I had decided I was making too much of the whole thing. It made perfect sense that she would have to go there and see Dino, if they had important matters to discuss and he was too caught up in his heavy action at the tables to want to break away. She would have gone, all right, and it could not have been a pleasant experience for her, which would have accounted for the tight, angry expression I had seen on her face as she entered the hotel that night. I would never mention the incident to Jay. I was fascinated by the Princess and already more than half in love with her myself, but I was not going to betray my best friend or cause trouble between them simply to get to her.

"Please, I must know," Marina said. "You have used this term again, when I joined you."

"It's a horse, Princess," Jay explained.

"It is a bad horse?"

Jay laughed. "Just the opposite. It's what we used to call a mortal lock."

"Please?"

"An animal that cannot lose the race," Sam said. "Of which there ain't any such animals."

"Then why do you say so yourself?"

"Ah, it's a way of talking, that's all. It don't mean a thing, except to indicate a beast that should win by ten lengths."

"Oh, I see," Marina said, looking slightly bewildered. "That is, I think I see."

I decided to come to her rescue. "Four years ago, if you can believe this," I explained, "Jay went on safari to Africa."

"So? I have done that myself."

"Yes, but this was during the Hollywood meet," I elaborated. "Horses to bet on were running five days a week as always and Jay actually went on safari. You don't grasp the enormity of that fact? Even now, as I think back on it, I find it mind-boggling."

Marina laughed. "It is funny to hear you talk, Lou," she said. "You are always so funny."

"*Toujours gai, toujours amusant,*" I agreed.

"What is this shit?" Sam asked. "You talking frog?"

"Sam, don't be a boor," Jay said. "Shifty here has been everywhere. He picks up bits of this and that wherever he goes. Right, Shifty?"

"Right. Only I have not been to Africa."

"Tell the Princess the story. You tell it better than anybody."

I did. The only time Jay had ever permitted himself to wander beyond the continental boundaries of the United States, I told her, was four years ago, toward the end of the Hollywood meet. He had had a terrific spring and was up over ten thousand dollars on his own action alone, but he had begun to tail off and he needed freshening before moving down to Del Mar for the summer. He had considered going up to San Francisco, a town he enjoyed mainly for its restaurants, but he knew he'd wind up chasing horses again at one of the nearby fair meets. What he wanted was a complete hiatus, a clearing of the mind that would bring him back to the wars at Del Mar ready to win big again and feeling fit for the struggle. "I was like a classy old plater, still full of run but obviously in need of a rest," Jay explained. "Handicappers are just like horses; they need to be turned out somewhere two or three times a year."

It was at this point in his fortunes that Fido suggested a solution. Through a friend in a travel agency who had cashed a couple of big bets on his tout sheet's releases, Fido came up with a couple of bargain-rate empty seats on a two-week package tour of African game preserves. Ordinarily, Jay wouldn't have dreamed of squandering folding green on such a frivolity, but for some reason the prospect seemed attractive to him at that particular moment. The clincher had been Fido's assurance that the tour was sure to include a sprinkling at least of bare-breasted Amazons, the kind of readily available human game that crops up in magazine ads for French vacation playgrounds on tropical islands.

This had turned out, like so many of Fido's predictions at the track and elsewhere, to be mere wishful thinking. After having been persuaded to part with eighteen hundred dollars each, Jay and Fido found themselves embedded in a phalanx of about thirty middle-aged American tourists being hustled from one dusty African outpost to another to stare at herds of galloping gazelles. "Some of those beasts could run a little," Jay conceded, "but you couldn't put saddles on their backs."

"Who's telling this story?" I asked.

"You are, Shifty, but I have to be allowed an occasional editorial comment," Jay objected. "I'm the one who survived the trip."

By the time Jay and Fido had reached Mombasa, a center of native culture Jay had described as a sinkhole on the east coast of Kenya, they had both had it with wild animals and Africa generally. "If I want to see game, I can go to the zoo," Jay explained. "Africa is no girls, no TV, no action, nothing. The only thing that saved me from going nuts was this tip we got on a dead crab."

The tour had been booked into the Hotel Nepenthe, a decent enough hostelry with clean beds and room service. Jay and Fido were just lying around at about seven o'clock Saturday night, sipping vodka-and-tonics and trying to figure out how to kill the rest of the evening, when some noise outside lured them to the terrace of their second-floor windows. Their room, like those of the rest of their party, overlooked an inner courtyard, where about half a dozen black men were engaged in setting up a racecourse of sorts. "Can I tell this part?" Jay interrupted.

"Why not? It's your story."

"They'd roped off a circle about four feet in diameter," he continued, "with a kind of cage in the middle in which they had all these little crabs with colored numbers painted on their backs. One guy made the odds on this blackboard, another one took the bets from the public watching at the terrace railings, two or three others ran the races off."

"But it is mad," Marina observed. "It is insane."

"They'd lift up the cage and the crabs would scuttle away to get the hell out of there," Jay resumed. "The winner was the first one to get to the outer rim of the circle. I mean, it was crazy, all these little crabs scurrying around all over the place with people shouting at them, but it was the only action in town."

Jay and Fido, deprived of workouts and past-performance charts, wagered cautiously until the fifth and last race on the card, which included a so-called exotic bet paying off at five to one. "You had to figure out which crab would be the last one out," Jay explained.

As they were standing there on their balcony and studying the dozen or so entries in the starting cage, their waiter, a cheerful ancient with a smile like a sunrise, came up beside them. "I think, sir," he whispered, "that the number four is very sick." They studied the number four carefully for a couple of minutes through their racetrack binoculars. "Sick?" Fido said. "I think the sonofabitch is dead."

"We looked at him some more and he didn't even twitch an antenna," Jay recalled, "so I said to Fido, 'He *is* dead.'"

Just before post time, Jay and Fido bet the equivalent of twenty dollars apiece on the four, a bit of action that closed off the betting and sent the starter rushing to the cage.

"And did you win?" Marina asked.

"Sure," Jay said, smiling. "All the other crabs scrambled out of there but the four. He *was* dead. Stone cold."

"I think it is a very strange story," Marina said.

"That's the last winning tip I can ever remember getting," Jay said.

"And I think it's entirely appropriate that it came on a moribund crustacean," I commented.

"So that is what you mean when you say that something is dead," Marina said. "I understand."

"A dead crab, not just dead, Princess," Jay corrected her. "A sure winner. Sam thinks we have one today."

"Not Gran Velero, I think."

"Oh, no, Princess, not Gran Velero."

"It's an animal in the fifth, name of Bouncing Peter," Sam explained. "This beast was stiffed by Bill Scarpe in his last race at six furlongs and now he's coming back at a distance with Scarpe up again. He cannot lose."

"But will not everyone bet on him?" Marina asked.

"We don't think so," Jay said. "There's no trouble line on the horse in the *Form* and it's only his second outing in six months. The trainer, Ted Farnsworth, is competent, but he has only a few horses and doesn't win very often. There are two obvious favorites in the race, both coming off good efforts and ridden by McArdle and Pelé, top jockeys. We should be third choice, at maybe seven to two or four to one."

"You are certain he will win?" Marina asked.

"He's a dead crab, Princess," Jay told her.

"Then you must bet on him for me," Marina said. "I will give you the money. I cannot see the race, as I will be with my horse, who is in the next race."

"Gran Velero is not a dead crab," Jay said, "Don't bet on him."

Marina laughed. "Oh, I always risk something on my own horses," she said, "even Gran Velero. I do think he will run better this time."

"What makes you think so?" I asked.

"I don't know, just a feeling I have, that is all."

"Save your money," Jay told her. "Gran Velero's an EB."

"A what?"

"Established bum."

"Oh, dear," Marina said, turning over on her back with a small giggle, "that is very unfeeling of you, Jay. He is such a *nice* horse, sweet and gentle, like a big dog."

"He *is* a dog," Sam said, forcing himself to his feet and jamming his *Racing Form* into his back pocket. "I'm going inside. I can't take this sun no more. See you at the windows, gents."

"You stepping out today, Sam?"

"My biggest wager of the meet," he answered, pounding

heavily off through the soft, hot sand toward the safety of the great indoors.

I don't know now exactly why I decided to go down to the paddock for Gran Velero's race. Perhaps I was a little disgusted with myself and needed to get away from Jay and the others after the previous contest. Bouncing Peter had come in first at nearly three-to-one odds, exactly as Sam and Jay had predicted, and by an easy two lengths wire to wire, but I had cut my bet in half on him when he had shown up on the track in bandages for the first time. I have an aversion to betting on horses with bandaged front legs unless I have seen them run in them or the trainer has a history of putting bandages on his charges, which a few of them will do, usually for protective purposes. Wraps on cheap horses too often indicate bowed tendons or other serious ailments and/or that the trainers of these animals are hiding something. Over the years, I think I've saved myself money by being cautious in this area, but this time I had been wrong. Farnsworth, Bouncing Peter's trainer, had probably put the wraps on to scare off bettors like me, as well as any possible claims for his animal. The technique had worked. No one had taken Bouncing Peter and he had won like a good thing, which had enriched both Sam and Jay; they had bet a couple of hundred apiece on him. I had risked only forty dollars and was feeling foolish, so I had quietly risen from my seat and headed for the paddock area, leaving Sam and Jay to bask in their victory.

The first thing that struck me about Gran Velero was his looks. I was standing against the railing of the walking ring near the gap where the horses file out toward the track, when Bud Grover led him in. Gran Velero had drawn the nine hole, one of the outside posts, so that he was the next-to-last entry in the ten-horse field to enter the paddock, but he looked immediately outstanding. He was a big chestnut colt, with no distinguishing marks, and he seemed to be full of himself. He looked alert, his ears pricked and his legs full of bounce. Like all of Buckingham's classy horses, he was obviously fit and healthy, with a coat that gleamed in the sunlight. He was very much on the muscle, a phrase that simply indicates an animal is ready to run his best race. As he was being walked around the ring with the other entries in the contest, I fished the *Form* out of my back pocket and took another look at his record.

It was not reassuring. In fact, except for his apparently excellent breeding, there was nothing in the numbers to recommend him. Even his four listed workouts since his previous race, at Hollywood Park early in the spring meet, were undistinguished. I could have discounted those, because I knew that Buckingham never asked his charges for much speed in the early mornings, but the dull times, combined with the horse's dismal record, made him impossible to bet on. This estimate of his abilities was shared by the *Form*'s handicappers, none of whom had picked him even for third, as well as the track's morning line, which listed him at fifteen to one. As far as I was concerned, he should have been fifty to one. But I had never seen a horse look better before a race and I began to have a feeling that for some reason he might run well today. Some young horses are slow to develop, I told myself, and I knew that Gran Velero's trainer was one of the best at not rushing an animal, allowing him to find himself and develop on his own time. Horses are dumb beasts. Some of them don't know they're supposed to go out there and run their eyeballs out every time that starting gate pops open.

I glanced up at the tote board just as the odds changed. Gran Velero dropped from sixteen to one to twelve to one in a single blink. I stuck my *Form* back in my pocket, leaned my elbows on the rail and really began to look hard at the little group of people around Marina, who were now waiting for the paddock judge to get the festivities under way.

First of all, I asked myself, what was Bud Grover doing there, and especially in the role of groom? And why was he all dressed up for the occasion? As for the other people there, only Buckingham was a professional. I recognized two or three others as friends of Marina's from her Turf Club set, but there was another man I had seen before whom I couldn't quite place. He had bright pink cheeks and light sandy hair and looked about thirty or so, though he could have been older. He had a tight, thin-lipped smile and kept his hands resolutely in his pockets. Where had I seen him before?

"Go to your horses, riders!" the paddock judge called out in a high, nasal twang.

Lonny Richards, sporting Marina's distinctive pink-and-blue silks, detached himself from the group around her and walked toward his mount. The trainer was waiting for him and now leaned over to say something to him. Richards' head jerked upward in what seemed to be amazement.

"Riders up!" the paddock judge sang out.

Buckingham offered his arm and gave his rider a leg up. As the jockey settled into the saddle, he turned and stared at the trainer, who spoke to him again, then walked away. The horses began to file out of the ring toward the main track. Grover led Gran Velero past me and I had another opportunity to take a good look now at the rider's face. Richards seemed a little perplexed, as if doing his best to assimilate a bit of unexpected news. As he rode out, I saw him lean over and give Gran Velero's neck a pat, but then again perhaps he was having one last word with Bud Grover.

I glanced up at the board. Gran Velero's price had risen to eighteen to one, no help there. Except for that one dip in the odds, no one was betting him. It looked as if he'd go off at better than twenty to one. In the crowd ahead of me, I caught sight of Marina in an elegant green pants suit and I hurried to catch up to her before she could disappear into the Turf Club, where I couldn't follow her.

"Marina!" I called, as she reached the entrance.

She glanced back, smiled and waved. "Luigi!" she exclaimed.

I saw now that she was with the sandy-haired man. He had her by the arm and was trying to hurry her inside, but she said something to him. He let her go and went off without her, just as I came up beside them. "Hey," I said, "what's going on?"

"Oh, doesn't he look wonderful," she said. "Gran Velero, I mean."

"If I didn't know better, I'd say he couldn't lose."

"Bert believes that he will run well today."

"What makes him think that?"

"How do I know, *mon cher*? I only know what he has told me. He has a wonderful way with horses."

"Yes, he does," I agreed. "Are you betting on him?"

"But of course," she said. "You know that I always bet on my own horses."

"I promise not to tell Jay."

"It does not matter what you tell him," she said, detaching herself from me. "It would not make any difference, would it?" With a smile and a quick wave, she disappeared up the stairs into the Turf Club.

I went back to our box, arriving just in time to see Gran Velero gallop past on his way to the starting gate. "He looks terrific," I said, focusing my glasses on the horse.

Jay had his head buried in his charts. "Who?" he asked, without looking up.

"Marina's horse."

"Gran Velero?" Jay laughed but did not look up. He was making a notation on something that had caught his eye among the haze of numbers spread out on his lap. "If looks could run . . ."

We were alone in the box. I didn't answer, but kept my eyes on the long, ground-eating stride of Marina's established bum. Richards was standing up in the stirrups with an easy hold, then he settled down on the animal's back as they rounded the clubhouse turn. I put my glasses down and looked at the board. Gran Velero was nineteen to one. I stood up.

"Where are you going?" Jay asked. "You're not going to bet real money on that stiff, are you?"

"Buckingham told Marina the horse would run much better today."

"Trainers always say that to their clients, Shifty. What's the matter with you?"

"Five dollars, that's all."

"Give me the money," he said, in disgust. "Save yourself a trip."

"It could cost you. He's going to be twenty to one."

"The horse has no chance. What are you, sick?"

He almost had me convinced, but now the tote board blinked again. Instead of rising, Gran Velero's odds dipped abruptly from nineteen to fourteen to one. Somebody had obviously just made a solid wager. "Jay," I said, "something's going on." I told him about the two jolts the horse had taken at the windows. "It wouldn't be the first time this kind of thing has happened, especially with a maiden."

"Well, you've got a point," Jay agreed. "But it's not old Bert's style. He doesn't need to do this kind of thing. Secondly, he rarely fires at six furlongs. Thirdly, this horse has had eight races and never showed a lick of speed."

"I'm going to bet ten dollars on him."

"Well, it's your money."

The horses had turned back and were nearing the starting gate. I hurried away toward the betting windows and stood in the line reserved for the big players, so I'd be sure not to be shut out. I realized that what Jay had said was correct. Buckingham occasionally liked to bet on his own horses, but he had always been fairly open about his action. His usual style was to run a young and untried charge in a couple of sprints just to season him. The idea was to get a couple of races into him in which he'd get the feel of competition, get jostled and bumped and hit in the face with dirt clods and whacked with the whip, the sort of invaluable experience impossible to achieve in the more leisurely training moves of the early mornings. Then, when he felt the horse was ready, he'd enter him in a race at a mile or more, put Bill Scarpe or some other top jockey on him, and fire. This pattern had become such a recognizable part of Buckingham's style that his budding maidens rarely went off at high odds and often won handily. The sort of maneuvering I had suggested to Jay was going on with Gran Velero was much more typical of several other trainers we knew, mostly men with small stables and cheap horses who depended on the occasional betting coup to stay alive. Nevertheless, I had a gut feeling this time that something was up. And what was I risking? Ten dollars. I also had the idea that Jay and his numbers could be wrong from time to time.

As I reached the window, the announcer called out post time. The odds blinked and Gran Velero dipped to twelve to one. "Ten dollars to win on the nine," I said.

"This is a hundred-dollar window, buddy," the clerk said, looking at me in disgust.

"What's the matter, you don't want my money?"

"Don't be a wise guy."

I had to run into a bureaucrat. I shut my eyes and forced myself not to unload on this cretin. "Look, I'm sorry," I said. "I made a mistake. Please let me have my ticket."

"Hey," the guy in back of me said, "let's move it. We're going to get shut out."

The clerk growled, but at least he did take my money. Ticket in hand, I rushed away from the window and emerged into the grandstand area just as the horses came out of the starting gate. At first I couldn't see anything, as the view was blocked by the rows of standees behind our seats, but I managed to get to our box in time to note that Gran Velero was not among the leaders. "The Undertaker up to his old tricks," was Jay's comment, as I searched for Marina's silks among the pack behind the frontrunners. "It wouldn't make any difference. The horse has no speed, anyway."

No sooner were these words out of Jay's mouth than I spotted Gran Velero. He was running easily on the outside, seven or eight lengths off the pace, but not making up any ground. As the horses hit the turn for home, I had just about given up on him, when he suddenly started to move. His head dipped, his stride lengthened and, still on the outside, he began to pick up the leaders with such astonishing ease that they looked as if they were floundering in quicksand. Between the three-eighths pole and the head of the stretch, he quite simply looped his field, which is not easy to do at Del Mar, a mile track with sharp, poorly banked turns that favor speed horses on the inside. "Look at that move!" I shouted, standing up to get a better view of it "He's coming through the parking lot!"

"What are they doing?" Jay asked the world at large. "What do they think they're doing?"

I knew the question was rhetorical, so I didn't bother to answer him. I kept my glasses glued on Gran Velero, who by this time had opened up two lengths on the field as the horses reached the head of the stretch, less than an eighth of a mile from the finish line. Richards made no effort even to tap the horse with his whip but simply hand-rode him home. Just past the sixteenth pole, he took a backward look, saw that nobody was gaining on him and eased up. By the time Gran Velero swept past us at the wire, he was four lengths in front and merely galloping, with his jockey practically upright in the saddle.

"Did you see what I just saw?" Jay asked. "Do you believe that?"

"I told you," I said. "I had ten dollars on him. I wish now I'd bet a hundred."

"Come on, Shifty, you can't handicap a race like this," Jay retorted angrily. "You're going to tell me they didn't pull off something here?"

"Marina said he'd run better."

"Marina doesn't know anything," Jay insisted. "They put one over here. That horse ran like a goddamn Secretariat. The stewards will have to ask some questions on this one."

"Wilbert Buckingham? He's the most respected trainer in California," I objected. "They'll investigate *nada*."

I watched Gran Velero trot back toward the winner's circle; the horse wasn't even damp. In fact, he looked as if he'd only been out for a light morning gallop. He had his ears pricked and was looking around at his unfamiliar surroundings as the winner with what I took to be an air of mild *noblesse oblige*. Richards was grinning widely and nodding his head to the trainer, who had come out to say something to him and give the horse's neck a satisfied, proprietary pat. Bud Grover now took the animal by the bridle and led him toward the winner's circle for the usual obligatory photographs. In the group waiting for the picture was Marina, of course, and her now ecstatic Turf Club friends, all of whom must have bet the horse, but I didn't see the sandy-haired man. As I looked, Marina glanced up toward our box and waved. I waved back, but Jay simply sat there, arms folded, an expression on his face like that of a man who had just swallowed a live frog and was trying to keep his composure while it jumped about inside him.

After Richards had dismounted, shaken hands all around, been kissed on the cheek by Marina and weighed in with his tack before walking back toward the jockey room, the race was declared official and the tote board lit up with the payoff prices. Gran Velero's were extraordinary. His win price was $22.80 for a two-dollar ticket, but he also paid $16.40 to place and an astounding $12.20 to show. In other words, he had been hit hard in the win pool and gone off at slightly over ten to one, but had hardly been touched in the place and show betting. The other two horses to finish in the money behind him had been the two favorites in the race, which meant that, if Gran Velero had been bet normally, his place and show prices in relation to his win price would have been much lower. Whoever had wagered heavily on the horse was so confident of winning that he or they had not bothered to land on the place and show pools but had simply chucked it on him to finish first. I had to agree with Jay; Buckingham and his cronies, or at least someone who knew him very well, had put one over. Not for years had I seen a horse as well hidden from the form and speed handicappers, the real pros like Jay and company, as Gran Velero. I wondered what, if anything, Marina would have to say to him later about it.

"I still can't believe this," was all Jay said now. "I still can't believe they did this and we didn't sniff it out."

"Do you think Marina knew? She did say—"

"Forget it, Shifty," Jay cut me off. "She didn't really know anything except what Buckingham told her, that the horse would run better, the old bullshit all these trainers feed their clients. Do you know how much money they ran through the windows here on this race? They had thousands on this horse. Somebody made a killing. That pig made the biggest million-dollar move I've seen all year between the half and the eighth pole. Unbelievable."

"His final time wasn't that fast."

"Final time means shit, you know that. It's fractional time that counts."

"He could have won by ten," I had to admit.

"Ten? Try twenty." Jay stood up in disgust. "I need a beer."

Sam came up behind us, his face a grim mask. "So?" he said. "You still think you can read Buckingham's action? You like that race? What I saw I still don't believe."

"I believe," I said, getting up with what must have been to these two old friends of mine the most infuriating grin of the year. "I'm going to cash my ticket now."

"Fuck you," Sam said, "and may all your wells be poisoned, your camels barren and your goats homosexual."

"We had what you call a dead crab," Marina said, "no?"

"No," Jay told her. "A dead crab, Marina, is a horse that cannot lose. Gran Velero was a horse that could not win. There is a difference."

They were sitting in a corner table at Sans Souci, a new French bistro some enterprising devotee of *nouvelle cuisine* had opened on the old Pacific Coast Highway near La Costa, about ten miles north of Del Mar. Jay later told me that Marina had invited him to dinner this time and they had just ordered a hundred dollars' worth of edibles and a forty-dollar bottle of very dry champagne to celebrate Gran Velero's astonishing victory. Jay had still not recovered from it, because it outraged him and made him almost physically ill when he could not account for the outcome of the puzzle he was spending his life trying to solve.

Marina, of course, noted the darkness in him. "But why are you so angry?" she asked. "Why are you not happy for me? Only because you did not bet on him, that is no reason—"

"I know, I know, Princess," he replied. "It has nothing to do with you. It's just that I can't stand their putting one over on me. It offends me."

"How strange you are." She squeezed his hand under the table and kissed him quickly on the neck. "I will make it up to you."

"Is that a promise?"

"But of course, my darling. And I always keep my promises."

The champagne arrived, was duly poured and the bottle tucked away into an ice bucket. Jay raised his glass. "To you, Princess."

"To both of us," she said, squeezing his thigh under the table as they drank.

"Careful," he warned her, "I'll ravish you right here."

She laughed. "I think I would like that. What would people say?"

"It would give the place a reputation, at least," Jay said. "The joint's half empty."

Jay did not mention Gran Velero again until after the main course, when they were nibbling lethargically away at an endive-and-walnut salad and letting the food and champagne smooth out the wrinkles in the evening. When he did, the remark was casual, as if he were discussing only the obvious. "What did Bert give the horse to make him run like that?" he asked, toying with the stem of his wine glass.

"I beg your pardon?"

He repeated the question. "Marina," he added, "horses don't suddenly run like champions after having solidly established themselves as bums. What did Bert do to this horse to make him run like that?"

"I don't know, Jay," she said, "I never ask him those questions."

"Why not?"

"Because he is my trainer and I have to trust him," she explained. "He is the best, is he not?" Jay nodded. "Then I must trust him to *do* his best, that is all. He did not tell me why and I did not ask him. He did say that Gran Velero would run better than last time."

"Better? That's a wild understatement. That horse showed us a million-dollar move, sweetheart. Don't you understand?"

"If you say so, my darling."

"Let me explain it to you," he continued. "You do want to hear this?"

"Certainly, if it gives you pleasure."

"Most horses can only run top speed for about half a mile," Jay explained. "Some horses will use this speed early, then rely on their stamina and gameness to withstand late challenges in order to win. Others have no real quickness out of the gate and take time to find their best stride. They reserve their speed for the latter stages of a race. I'm oversimplifying here, but it's important that you understand these things."

"If you insist, *mon cher.*"

"I do. Now, the classic million-dollar move is a horse breaking fast out of the gate to be up on or near the lead. He stays on top for a half-mile or so, then drops suddenly back to mid-pack and remains there for the rest of the race, not gaining but not losing any more ground either. Is that clear so far?"

"Perfectly. Let's have some more champagne, all right?"

Jay nodded, refusing to be distracted from his dogmatic elucidation of the mystery. "What this shows very often," he continued, "is a horse that has much ability but is not yet in condition. He is being raced into form and is still one or two races away from his best. Now, Gran Velero won, but he beat nothing. He ran a very dull first quarter and an even last one, but on the turn he ran like an express train. He showed us he is another class of horse entirely in terms of basic ability. You see what I'm driving at?"

"Partly. But why is this thing called a million-dollar movement?" she asked.

"Because you bet the horse next time it runs," Jay announced. "The crowd ignores him, because, to the uninformed dummies out there, he shows nothing obvious to bet on. You cash in big. The million-dollar figure is a metaphor."

"That is very sweet. But Gran Velero won, didn't he?"

"Yes, but it's still potentially a million-dollar move."

"Why?"

"It depends on where your trainer runs him next time. If he jumps him up three or four notches in class, he'll be a big price again." Jay shook his head and stared moodily into his now empty champagne glass. "The million-dollar question is why." He blinked angrily at Marina. "He's as rich as God and he's the top trainer in the West, one of the three or four best in the whole country. Why is he doing this?"

"It is not cheating, is it?"

"Yes, it is," Jay admonished her. "Yes, it is. You watch. The stewards will call him in for an explanation. That kind of form reversal is too extreme not to demand some sort of inquiry, even if it is Buckingham. Though I'm sure he'll have an answer. They always do, these guys," he added glumly.

"You are funny," Marina said, "yes, you are. There is probably some very simple explanation. I will ask Bert."

"He won't tell you anything."

"He will, if I ask him. Trust me." She reached over, grabbed his ears with both hands and kissed him on the mouth this time. "Now, my darling, we will talk no more about it tonight, or I will let you pay this dinner bill."

That shut Jay up about horses for the rest of the evening. He reaped his reward, however, when they got back to Marina's place. It was a warm, moonless night and she insisted on making love out on the patio facing the beach. She was wild, like an animal in heat, and she clung to him, pressing him into her as she climaxed and digging her nails into his back until he had to ask her to ease up. When they had finished with each other, they sat, still naked, out under the stars, swam in the surf and sipped Armagnac until the first early-morning jogger came thumping by on the hard-packed sand at the water's edge. They went inside and slept quietly in each other's arms until nearly eleven.

What astonished me most about the whole episode was that he failed to do his work that morning and actually passed up going to the track at all. "I need the day off," he said, as if this sort of thing had happened often to him before. "I'm going to just lie in the sun and snooze."

I knew better. I knew he was in danger of falling in love with his Princess. And, by that time, so was I.

EIGHT

The Cooler

THE NEXT MORNING, Marina came up with an explanation for Gran Velero's sudden form reversal. She and Jay were walking hand in hand by the water's edge and splashing idly along on their way to her house, when she commented, apropos of nothing at all, "Darling, it was *le sexe*."

"I know it was," Jay told her. "I didn't mistake it for ping-pong."

She laughed. "Not us, *amour*—the horse. It was *le sexe*."

"What are you talking about?" Jay asked, turning to look at her in amazement. "They didn't cut him, did they? Gran Velero, I mean? He's listed as a colt on the program, as well as in the *Form*."

"I do not understand you."

"I thought you were trying to tell me that Gran Velero was gelded and that's why he ran well," Jay explained. "Sometimes colts have ability but won't run because they've got their tiny minds on other matters, such as getting laid. You can settle them down by gelding them."

"Would that help with you?"

"I don't think it would help either of us," Jay said. "If a horse has a terrific pedigree, nobody wants to cut him, because there goes the stud value. Breeding is where the big money is in racing, but you know that. So what's this about sex?"

"*Le sexe*," she insisted. "I went to the stable area early this morning for breakfast and spoke to Bert. He says they gave the horse *le sexe*. He is explaining it to the stewards this morning, but they know, he told me."

"Of course! Lasix! My God, he was a bleeder!" Jay exclaimed, almost jumping with glee at the news. "That accounts for it."

"It is a drug, no?"

"It is a drug, yes," Jay said. "I looked into it a few years ago, when they began using it a lot here in California. It's a diuretic."

"*Pardon?*"

"It's given to humans to drain excess fluids from the system," Jay explained. "It also constricts the blood vessels. It's given to horses who are known bleeders."

"*Mon Dieu,*" Marina exclaimed. "Bleed? Where?"

"In the lungs, Princess," Jay explained. "It's quite common and the only treatment for it is Lasix. It's not legal in all states, but it is in California. That's why some horses that can't run back East are shipped out here, where certain drugs, like Lasix and Butazolidin, are legal."

"It makes a big difference, then?"

"A big difference. Marina, Lasix can move a horse up ten lengths. That would account for Gran Velero's form reversal. Why didn't Buckingham tell you before the race?"

"*Mon cher,* it is not like Bert to think of such things," she said. "He tells me very little."

"Like all trainers, the bastards."

"It is serious, this bleeding?"

"Can be. Usually, it can be controlled. What happens is, a horse gets to running, he bleeds, his lungs fill up and he slows down or stops." Jay paused to think the matter through. "They're not obligated to list a horse who's getting Lasix for the first time, though they ought to be. It's a crucial piece of information. Sometimes Fido hears about it, or Sam, from one of the clockers. Otherwise, there's no way of knowing. It's more important than any equipment change, like adding blinkers or more weight, and the public ought to be told. But there's a whole racing establishment, you know, that doesn't care about the public. People who still think it's a game for the rich and their friends."

"Isn't it?"

Jay laughed. "Without us and all those poor dummies out there pouring their money through the betting windows nine races a day, where would this so-called sport be, huh?" he asked.

"You are so idealistic, my darling."

"You know, what I still don't understand," Jay said later, as they sipped iced coffee on her patio and watched the surf roll majestically in, "is why your trainer waited so long."

"Waited for what?"

"When a horse runs as badly as Gran Velero did for so long, you'd try to find out why," Jay explained, "especially if he's as well bred as you tell me he is. One of the first things you'd do is scope him."

"*Quoi*? Scoop?"

"No. It's an instrument called an endoscope. It'll tell you if the horse is bleeding or not. Only rarely will a horse bleed badly enough so you see blood in his mouth."

"Darling, I did not know you were an expert."

"I have to be, Princess. I try to make my living out there," he said. "I need all the edge I can get."

"Well, Bert knows what he is doing."

"Trainers are not world-class contenders in the IQ department," Jay argued. "A normally intelligent person could pass as a genius in those ranks."

"You are so cynical, my darling." She stood up and stripped in front of him, then stretched and began oiling herself for a session of total tanning. Jay watched her with undisguised wonder. "Stop staring," she ordered him. "It is rude."

"I could never stop staring at you, Princess," Jay said. "You're the finest foreign site I've ever toured."

Bunny Lehrman opened the door and let me into the apartment unit that night. She was dressed in a virginal-looking simple black outfit with a single strand of pearls around her neck and golden hoop earrings, with her hair combed and pulled back into a ponytail. She looked like a wicked nun. "Kretch was worried about you," she said.

"I'll bet he was."

"Where were you? You're late."

"I took a wrong turn past the freeway exit," I explained. "All these condominium developments look the same to me. They started yet?"

"Just about to. Go on in."

"What are you doing here?"

"I'm off Mondays, so sometimes Kretch has me run the bar here. Didn't he tell you?"

"No, but then why would he?"

I walked into the living room where five men sat around a poker table under bright neon lamps. One of them had a deck of cards in his hand and was about to deal. Kretch, a huge shadow in one corner, near the curtained glass doors presumably leading to a terrace, detached himself from the darkness and greeted me. "Mr. Anderson, you're just in time," he said, in an incredibly phony accent he must have acquired from watching old thirties movies on TV; his idea of respectability, no doubt. "We was wondering if you was lost."

"I were," I admitted. "Sorry."

One of the other men laughed, but luckily Kretch didn't get it. "Gents," he said, "this here is Mr. Lewis Anderson from New York. Introduce yourselves." He pointed to the only empty chair at the table. "Over here, sir. You know the rules of this game, I presume, from our previous conversation, right?"

"Right."

"Perhaps you'd like to cut the cards?" the dealer asked. "It's five-card stud."

"No need," I said, sitting down.

"Your chips," Kretch said, dropping a stack of them in

front of me. "The whites are ten, reds twenty, blues fifty. You got a thousand dollars there. You need more, you ask me. We settle up after the last hand."

"Thanks."

"Also, I cut the pot. You know the rate?"

"Yes, sure."

"My name's Jed Gordon," the man on my left said. "This is Henry Arthur and over there's—"

"Come on, let's play cards," the man on the right of the dealer said. "We're wasting time."

It was the sandy-haired man I had seen with Marina on the day of Gran Velero's big race. I could tell now, under this harsh white light, that he was older than he looked, perhaps in his early forties. His skin was very fair and he had a cherubic countenance, but in close-up there were nests of fine lines around his eyes and mouth, which was small, thin-lipped, a bit petulant. He was dressed expensively in a cashmere sports coat and Dior shirt with gold cuff links. His small, round face peered at us over a green silk foulard like a disagreeable owl from the hollow of a tree stump. I took an instant dislike to him, not surprising in view of his rudeness, but I decided to do my best not to make myself too noticeable to him. I had also just remembered where I had seen him before. He had been at Dino Caretoni's dinner table that night in Las Vegas and then the next day with Marina and her ex-husband, when I had seen them enter the hotel after I had said goodbye to Dawn. He gave no sign of remembering me at all, for which I was thankful. His first name, I soon found out, was Guy, which he pronounced in the French manner, although he spoke unaccented, obviously well-educated East Coast American. From the way he seemed to harbor a small potato up behind his nasal passages, I suspected he had attended some Eastern prep school named after one of the less flamboyant saints.

I drew a two in the hole and a four on the first hand, so I folded and spent the time trying to size up the other players. Jed Gordon, I knew, was a TV movie director, but I had no idea who any of the others were. After an hour of playing cards with them, however, I had a pretty good feel for their abilities. Gordon was an excellent poker player, great at dissembling, a ruthless sandbagger, altogether a winner. None of the others was quite up to him, but there were no real patsies in the game.

Guy was an enigma. He seemed to know what he was doing, but he liked to bluff and Gordon caught him at it twice. About a third of the way into the evening, Guy and I were the only losers, down about six hundred apiece, with Gordon the only real winner; he was about a thousand ahead. So far I had spotted no cheating, but then none of the hands had been fiercely contested either.

Halfway through the evening, when Bunny came around to take a drink order, I found out Guy's last name. It was Harrison and I immediately realized I had heard of him. He was the scapegrace younger son of a very rich, old-money banking tycoon who had disinherited him years before, after a divorce scandal in Palm Beach, Florida, involving Harrison, his wife, the wife's lesbian lover and a major drug dealer. I couldn't remember any of the details, only that they had been deliciously sleazy, gourmet fodder for the *National Enquirer*. I began to watch him with real interest just as he got the deal again and called for a hand of seven-card stud.

Three minutes later, I knew who the cheater was. Harrison had gathered up the cards and spotted three kings at the bottom of the deck, then shuffled while keeping them there, offered a cut, after which he'd restored the top part of the deck to its original position. He was going to deal off the bottom to himself or to a possible confederate. So despite the fact that I found myself with jacks wired, I quickly dropped out of the hand. This evidently surprised Harrison and I realized I was the one he had set up for the kill this time; I should have remained in action longer, so as not to arouse his suspicions. "Boy," I said, "I don't have any confidence." I stretched and excused myself to go to the bathroom. "You guys are tough."

Harrison grunted and dealt to Gordon and Arthur, the only other two players to stay in the hand. I lingered just long enough to watch the first of his kings surface and left the room. I passed Kretch in the corridor on my way back and smiled at him. "Obvious," I whispered and went back to the table, where Harrison and Arthur were now locked head to head. The pot got up to twelve hundred dollars, with Harrison forcing the bidding, and, sure enough, he emerged with a full house, kings up, to Arthur's club flush. Harrison had lucked into a nice little score. "See what I mean?" I said, smiling and sitting down again. "I'd have gotten killed."

"How do you know?" Harrison asked. "You might have been lucky."

"Not that lucky," I said. "I just have this gut feeling tonight's not my night."

"That's a hell of an attitude to bring to a poker table," Gordon said.

"You're right. I probably should have stayed in my room at La Costa and sent out for a nubile hooker," I said. "It would have cost me less."

"What exactly do you do?" Henry Arthur asked, watching glumly as Harrison raked in the pot and began stacking his chips.

"Investments," I answered. "Mostly software."

"Cagey, too," Arthur said, with a sigh. "All right, let's play poker."

During the next hour and a half, I watched Harrison pull his maneuver off again trapping both Arthur and Gordon this time, and picking up another twenty-six hundred dollars. I was surprised. It takes years to master most card manipulations and this particular swindle, although simpler than most and effective in a low-stakes game, was being clumsily handled. No top player would have been fooled by it and I wondered how long Harrison imagined he could get away with it. The mere fact that his winning pots always came on his own deals should have been enough of a tipoff to experienced players like this and I did notice that Jed Gordon had become ominously quiet as his own winnings had begun to dwindle. Obviously, Harrison would have done better to involve a confederate at this point, if he was planning to stay in the game all through the rest of the summer. At the very least, he would now have to cool it and sit on his winnings until the last round started at one A.M., as agreed upon earlier.

For nearly two hours Harrison dropped out of nearly every deal, which made Gordon turn sour. "If you're going to sit all night on your goddamn money," he growled, "what the hell's the point of playing?"

"My dear fellow, I can't play if I don't have the cards, can I?" Harrison answered. "I certainly am not going to *give* you back the money."

"That's obvious," the director said.

"You're pretty lucky, Guy," one of the other two players noted. "You seem to get those big hands when you need them."

"Yes, I have been lucky," Harrison agreed. "But that can change."

"It better," Gordon observed. "Otherwise I'll begin to believe you know how to play this game."

By this time I was down over eight hundred of Kretch's dollars, a fact he reminded me of when I emerged again from the bathroom and found him waiting for me in the corridor, a huge and menacing figure with a deep scowl on his face. "You're costing me a fuckin' fortune," he said.

"You want me to run a cooler in on him?"

"Yeah," he said hoarsely.

"Whatever I win, you can have it," I said. "All I want is my fee. All right?"

He nodded. I went back into the bathroom and took the deck of cards I always carry around with me out of my pocket. It was a standard poker deck of the kind used in American casinos and exactly like the two decks in action in the other room. I stacked it so that every player would come up with a good hand, especially Harrison, who would find himself with a cold full house, queens up. I dealt myself three sevens and put the fourth one on the bottom, from where I'd have no trouble at all dealing it to myself. The point about a cooler is that you only have to run it once into any game to clean up, because everybody stays in, bets heavily and helps to build up a tremendous pot. It's easy enough to get a cooler into play; the trick is to shuffle the deck without actually doing so, a maneuver only a broad-tosser as skillful as I am can get away with. I was fairly sure nobody in this game would be able to spot the maneuver, especially as no one had yet caught on to Harrison's much clumsier technique, so I was only a little on edge when I went back to the table and sat down again. After all, I reasoned, we were dealing with amateurs here, not the pros.

"We played a quick hand of five-card stud while you were out," Henry Arthur informed me.

"That's okay. Who won?"

"Jed. Who else?" Arthur said. He himself was down over a thousand, but he was being a good sport about it. I had fixed the cooler so he'd probably be the first to drop out, along with Gordon, who was too smart a player to risk savaging.

When I called for draw, jacks or better to open, and finally dealt the hand, toward the end of the evening, I watched Harrison carefully. His eyes widened, his face reddened and his fingers trembled slightly. Then, with an enormous effort at self-control, he set his hand facedown on the table and waited for an opening bet. Gordon, who had two small pairs, bet the whole pot, exactly sixty dollars, and waited confidently for some of us to drop out.

Nobody did. Before anyone asked for cards, the pot had reached thirty-two hundred dollars and everybody stayed in. Only Harrison stood pat; everyone else asked for one or two cards. I took two and dealt myself the fourth seven. I glanced at Harrison. He had begun to sweat like a fractious filly being led for the first time into the starting gate. I began to feel a warm glow all over from what I was going to do to this bastard.

Henry Arthur, who had not improved his hand, was the first to drop out. Gordon, with his three kings, stuck it out for one more round of betting, then folded, followed by the other two players, both of whom held flushes. Eventually, only Harrison and I were left, with a pot in front of us amounting now to over eleven thousand dollars. I was out of money by this time and asked for more credit, so I could match Harrison's final bet, the last nine hundred dollars he had in front of him.

"It's up to Mr. Harrison," Kretch said, hovering over the table now like a giant manta ray.

I looked at Harrison. I could see the greed in him spread like a cancer. "Certainly," he said, smiling at me with almost naked glee.

I decided then and there that he was a fool. I wrote a chit for another nine hundred dollars and pushed it into the pile of chips on the table to match Harrison's final bet. "Well, Guy," I asked uncertainly, "what have you got?"

"Full house, queens up," he said, his hands already hovering over the loot before him."

"Gee, I'm sorry," I said, turning over my four sevens.

The color drained out of his face and he jumped to his feet. "What?" he shouted. "You set me up!"

"Bullshit," Kretch snarled at him. "You just got beat."

"It was a hell of a hand, Guy," I said. "You didn't expect me to fold it, did you?"

Without another word, Harrison rushed out of the apartment, slamming the door after him. "Not a good loser, I'm afraid," I said. "That was some kind of hand, wasn't it? I've never had a hand like that before."

"I've never won one," Arthur said. "Well, that's it, I guess." He stood up to go. "Next Monday night, everyone?"

"Not me," Jed Gordon answered. "This game's become a little too rich for my blood. I'll pass." He pushed himself away from the table and looked at me, as if about to say something. But he must have thought better of it. I think now that he knew he'd been had, but he wasn't about to make waves, not with friendly old Kretch looking on in the background.

"I'm sorry," I said, quite truthfully. "I guess this game did get out of hand here. I was told it was a friendly game."

"Don't be sorry," Arthur said, affably enough. "Just come back next week and give us a crack at getting some of it back."

"There ain't gonna be no game next week," Kretch said. Nobody argued with him.

It was about one-thirty when I left Kretch's place and I should have been tired, but I wasn't. Poker, like anything to do with cards, stimulates me, even when I've lost. I wasn't ready for bed, so I drove a couple of miles back down the road and turned into the driveway of La Costa. I found a parking place not too far from the entrance to the main bar at the resort and went inside for a nightcap.

With less than fifteen minutes before the mandatory two A.M. closing time, California's only blue law, the place was emptying out. The band was thumping away at a medley of old show tunes and several middle-aged couples were still out there, bouncing about the dance floor in pre-rock belly-to-belly style. Perhaps half a dozen other small groups of celebrants were scattered about the tables and three grim-looking gray-haired women sporting furs and jewels held down one end of the circular bar, last survivors of the night's pickup action for the Geritol set. I moved up to the other end, ordered a brandy and soda and set about getting it down before they turned the taps off.

With about two minutes to go and one gulp left, I took another look around the room. Lonny Richards was sitting at a corner table near the door with a thin, dreamy-eyed little girl with orange hair who looked no more than sixteen years old. As I was idly staring at them, one of the bartenders called out, "Drink up, folks," and the band struck up "Good Night, Ladies." I swallowed the last of my brandy, picked up my change from the counter and got up to go home.

On the way out, purely on impulse, I stopped at Richards' table. He had his long, narrow nose and thin-lipped mouth buried temporarily in his date's neck, but she acknowledged my arrival with a weak little smile and a flutter of delicate, nail-chewed fingers. "Hi," she said. "Lonny's terrible. He thinks he's Count Dracula or something."

"I think he's displaying admirable taste," I answered. "You look scrumptious enough to nibble on."

"Yeah, I guess so," she said vaguely and I realized she had trouble sifting through the complexities of the English language. "Who are you?"

"An itinerant degenerate with a vested interest in necromancy."

"Weird," she said. "Far out. Like, heviosity."

Richards surfaced for air and blinked in mild surprise. "Huh?"

I leaned over the table. "Lonny, you don't know me—"

"I seen you around."

"Yes, anyway, I just wanted to congratulate you on that win the other day, Gran Velero's race," I said. "I cashed a nice ticket on you."

The jockey grinned. "Yeah, wasn't that something? Bert told me he'd run real good, but I didn't believe him."

"I hope you had something on him."

"Oh, yeah. The owners bet a hundred for me. Easiest grand I ever made."

"Lonny, I want to go home," the waif said. "It's late."

"Sure, okay." He patted her as if he were reassuring a small, nervous dog. Evidently the lady had a tiny attention span in matters that did not bear directly on her.

"He ran like a stakes horse," I said. "I had the feeling you could have won by twenty."

Richards laughed. "Yeah," he said, "that's what really surprised me. I mean, Bert told me in the paddock the horse would run good and to keep him on the outside so he wouldn't get into no trouble. And then he says to me, 'Don't win by more than three.'" I remembered the surprised jerk of the rider's head in the walking ring, which is when the trainer must have made that remark. "More than three?" the jockey continued. "Shit, I had to strangle him to keep him down to four. I had a fucking jet under me."

"You know they gave him Lasix," I said. "He's a bleeder."

Richards looked surprised. "No, they didn't tell me. But they often don't. Man, that sucker moved up thirty lengths. Ain't many horses can do that, I don't care what they give 'em."

"Lonny," the waif wailed, "you promised . . ."

"Yeah," he told her, "you're right, baby." He looked up at me again. "Nice talking to you."

"Hey, don't tell too many folks," the jockey called after me. "I'm gonna ride him back, I hope."

"I won't," I said. "Take it easy."

Outside the air was fresh and clean. I took several deep breaths and walked down to the nearest parking lot to find my car. I was ready for bed now and feeling very fine about my life in general. I had decided that it was turning out to be a summer full of promise.

NINE

Dawn

SHE TELEPHONED ME early Tuesday morning from Las Vegas. "Lou? It's Dawn. I'm sorry to call you so early. I got your number from Vince."

"It's okay," I said. "Listen, let me take it downstairs. I won't be a minute." I put on my robe and went down to the kitchen. "What's up?" I asked. I was standing at the stove by this time and trying to make coffee with my free hand. I knew that she had to be calling about something fairly serious at that hour, so I was certain I would not be getting back to bed.

"It's Ronnie."

"What happened? Is he okay?"

"He's pretty sick, Lou. I've got to take him to L.A. for a few days, at least." Her voice sounded shaky, which was understandable; the kid had become her whole life. "We've got him booked into UCLA medical center for tests."

"What's the matter with him? Any idea?"

"About ten days ago, he got hit in the groin with a baseball," she explained. "That night he was peeing some blood and he was hurting. You know Ronnie, he doesn't cry or complain much, so I got scared when I saw it was bad for him."

"I can believe it. What did the doctor say?"

"They did a whole bunch of tests here and they found a lot of extra white blood cells and his blood count was slightly anemic. They put him on antibiotics, some kind of sulfa drug, and sent him home. Only he got worse. His heart beat's a little irregular and he's running a temperature, not high or anything, but it isn't good. He may have some kind of kidney disease, Lou."

"That doesn't sound good." I got the coffee going and took the phone over to the couch and sat down.

"The doctor here told me I ought to take him to UCLA, where they've got the top pediatric kidney specialists," she continued. "He's going to have to have X-rays and what they call a monitored EKG—"

"I know what that is. For his heart."

"Yeah, and some other stuff done. Maybe a biopsy of his kidneys. They go in with a big needle."

"Sounds terrific. Listen, why don't you stay at my place?"

"That's what I was going to ask you. I've got medical insurance and the casino gave me a week off, but I can't afford a hotel bill."

"Sure thing. Listen, what time's your flight?"

"We get in at noon. I'll take Ronnie right to the hospital. Does somebody have a key to your place?"

"The manager. His name's Silverman, apartment seventeen-B. He's a nice old guy. I'll call him, in case you get there before I do."

"You don't have to come up, Lou."

"I want to, okay? And listen, it's no problem. I got a roll-out bed in the closet."

"It's all right, Lou. It won't be the first time we've shared a bed, will it?"

"It's up to you, Dawn, honest. I just want to help."

"You're a nice man, Lou," she said. "I don't want to pull you away from the horses."

"They don't run here on Tuesdays and I'd have come anyway."

"I guess I figured you would."

"I also want you to know that I'm seeing a psychiatrist about my addiction."

"You what?"

"Honest. And he's curing me. You remember how I used to go to the track every day?"

"Yes," she answered, suspicious I might be putting her on, but not quite certain of it yet.

"Well, now I only go when it's open," I said.

She said. "You're crazy."

"I like the sound of laughter," I told her. "I'll see you in a few hours. Ronnie's going to be okay, I know it. Say hello for me."

"I will. Thanks, Lou."

"For what?"

I hung up, poured myself a cup of hot, very black coffee and tried to shake the cobwebs loose. By the time I was into my second cup, Jay emerged to begin his day's search for the winners. I told him about Dawn's call and that I'd probably be up in L.A. for two or three days. "I'll leave you a couple of hundred," I said, "just in case you find us a dead crab while I'm gone. You see Marina last night?"

"Yeah, but she couldn't stay. Some big party she had to go to."

"Okay, Mellors, do your thing," I said, heading upstairs for a shower.

"Mellors? Who's that?"

"Lady Chatterley's lover," I explained. "You meet any of Marina's classy friends yet?"

"I don't really want to."

"That isn't the point. Has she invited you to?"

"No, so what?"

"Just curious. I met one of them last night. He was in Kretch's poker game. He's the one who was cheating."

"You're kidding."

"No, I'm not. His name's Harrison, Guy Harrison. He's a real scumbag."

"What did you do?"

"I ran a cooler into the game. I beat his brains out."

"Holy shit, what did you take him for?"

"Nearly eleven grand," I said. "That was the big pot, only Kretch got to keep the money. I got paid three hundred for the gig."

"Shifty, you need a good agent."

"You've seen Kretch, haven't you? Well, that's one man I want to keep happy." At the head of the stairs, I looked back at him. He was sitting over his charts at the dining table, coffee cup in hand, but he hadn't yet begun to work. He looked thoughtful. "Why don't you ask Marina about Harrison?" I said. "I'd like to know a little more about him."

"I may just do that."

"With friends like Guy Harrison, she won't need too many enemies."

I left Del Mar about the time Dawn was taking off and I had been home for about an hour when she finally showed up. She stood inside my doorway, suitcase in hand, and looked around. "Well," she said cheerfully, "same old shithole."

I laughed. "Same old foulmouthed broad," I said, taking her bag and dropping it on the bed. "Want some coffee or a drink? Have you eaten?"

"I grabbed a sandwich at the hospital," she said. "Sawdust on white with toothpaste and a rubber pickle." She fell back into my only armchair and sighed. "Honestly, Lou, you could at least improve the looks of this dump."

"Can't afford to," I said. "But cheer up, I'm failing at a higher level this year. And also paying more taxes."

"Are you winning?"

"Not enough to live on, but so far it's been a good summer."

"How's Jay? And Sam?"

"They're both still out there battling. How's Ronnie?"

"He's feeling a little better today, but he's tired from the trip, I guess. I like his doctor. He's a guy named Rosenthal, absolutely tops on kidney diseases, I'm told. He's not a bundle of cheer, exactly, but he's obviously a hell of a doctor.

We'll know more tonight and get a full diagnosis in two or three days. You're sure it's okay for me to stay here?"

"You know it is."

"Can I have a shower? I always feel grimy after a trip, even a short one."

"Of course. Your towels are the blue ones on the laundry hamper."

"You were always grubby, but neat," she said, coming over to give me a quick kiss before disappearing into the bathroom. I went into the alcove containing the two-burner gas range and miniature icebox that passed for my kitchen and made some fresh coffee. Then I sat on my bed, my back against the pillows, listening to the familiar domestic sounds of this woman I really liked in my bathroom, and tried to see myself and my surroundings through her mildly disapproving eyes.

I would be thirty-eight years old in two more weeks and this tiny studio flat in West Hollywood was all I really had to show for my whole life. It was on the ground floor, at the back of a two-story apartment building a couple of blocks below the Strip. The structure, built in California Tudor style, had a shabby elegance about it that suited me. It enclosed a communal patio and a small swimming pool dotted with the leaves and fronds that floated periodically down from an old oak and a couple of dusty palm trees flanking it. A few rickety aluminum beach chairs, lopsided from overuse and age, lay scattered here and there and an open barbecue, encrusted with the scraps of long-forgotten cookouts, squatted at one end, behind an ominously warped wooden diving board nobody had used for at least five years. Except for a couple of gay day-players, who shared a small duplex in one corner, and a young black actress who had just landed herself a running part in a moderately successful TV series, I was the youngest of the tenants. My neighbors were Hollywood losers—a retired gaffer and his wife, a couple of middle-aged extras, the faded widow of a vice-squad policeman gunned down ten years earlier in a bar shootout, a failed architect, an unsuccessful designer who had lost his shop in a foreclosure—the battered survivors of a town replete with shattered dreams. I had never thought of myself as one of them, but now, after Dawn's remark, I had to wonder.

I had moved in here six years ago and stayed, mainly because it was cheap and the landlord, an ex-actor, was a decent sort who was slow to make repairs but didn't believe in gouging his tenants. Consequently, his building rarely had an empty apartment for rent and most of the other occupants had been with him for over ten years. I had found the atmosphere, uncontaminated by acid rock, public quarrels and all-night parties, benevolent. The manager, Max Silverman, was a retired violinist and magic buff, on whom I could try out all my new moves and who also liked to talk about Russian literature, on which he was an expert. I had settled into my place like a homecoming swallow into its nest and had no plans ever to move, but I could see that for a woman it had its drawbacks.

Even during the time Dawn and I had lived together, at her much larger, airy apartment in Palms, I had kept this place. As what? A saver? I had told myself I needed a hideaway, where I could work the five or six hours a day I needed to devise and refine my craft. But that had been only a half-truth and Dawn must have known it from the beginning. After all, Ronnie had been away at school till midafternoon and Dawn slept till midday, so there had been little interference with my practice time. No, she had seen it as a lack of commitment on my part, a fallback position to which I could retreat from the untenable heights of love and sharing. No wonder our relationship had foundered, even though I had never tried to shut her out completely from my inner life. I had even brought her to my place several times for overnights and an occasional weekend, when Ronnie was away with friends. She had always seen it, however, as evidence of my bottom-line inability to yield what had to be yielded to make a relationship whole. Had she demanded too much? Obviously. Had I been wrong not to give it? I didn't know. I hadn't dared, perhaps, to ask myself that question before and I rejected it now.

I loved this little room. It had all of me in it, the essentials that mattered. Aside from my queen-sized bed, the one arm-chair, a kitchen table and a couple of stools, the furnishings and decor reflected only my personal obsessions. Photographs of great horses in moments of triumph swept like a cavalry charge across one whole wall. In a corner, stacks of old race programs soared waist-high, while two sets of racing silks I had picked up in a curio shop had been nailed over my headboard. On a large wooden table, below an array of framed posters of Houdini and several less celebrated but far more masterful prestidigitators, rested the small tools of my peculiar calling, including a dozen or so decks of cards and a row of magic catalogues and books on sleight of hand. The tiny area summed up my life, which, I realized, did not amount to much but was precious to me.

When Dawn finally emerged from the shower and came back into the bedroom, I had begun idly to riffle one of my decks of cards, sending the little boards skimming through the air from hand to hand with an ease that outsiders always found miraculous but which to me, of course, was child's play and a favorite way of relaxing; it helped me to think. "How do you play this game?" I asked, smiling.

"Don't ask me. I wouldn't play cards with you on a dare."

"How are you feeling?"

"Better, thanks."

We spent the next couple of hours lying on the bed and chatting, then we watched part of an old Bogart movie on one of the cable channels. At about five, we left to go and see how Ronnie was doing. On the way, as we inched along the boulevards in heavy rush-hour traffic, I told Dawn about running the cooler into Kretch's poker game. "My God, Lou," she said, "you're not dealing now?"

"No, no," I reassured her, then explained the circumstances of my participation. "I got paid a flat fee of three hundred bucks and it was fun, I have to admit."

"Don't get carried away," she warned me. "A lot of the guys who run these private games use mechanics. It's very risky, Lou. And once you get in with these people, you can't get out."

"Well, I could always use the money."

"Don't kid yourself," she said. "A dealer I know began to work a game for some heavy types across the country and then he tried to back out after a few months. They smashed his fingers."

"Don't worry. It's not going to happen to me. This guy Kretch is a monster, but I don't think he's syndicate. At least he's running an honest game down there. He also runs them in L.A. and maybe elsewhere, but it's small potatoes compared to the big games. And the deal passes. Otherwise, he wouldn't have needed me. He'd have had it set up to cheat from the beginning and he'd have had this guy Harrison taken care of."

"Who?"

"Harrison, the guy who was cheating. In fact, his name is Guy, only he pronounces it *ghee*, as in geek."

"I know him," she said, staring at me in amazement. "From Vegas. It's got to be the same man."

I described him to her and she nodded. "Where do you know him from?" I asked.

"He's a total creep," she said, "a hooked gambler of the worst kind. He used to come into the Stardust and play at my table. The first couple of nights he won big, and for a week or so he always asked for me. He lost a lot. He knows how to play the game, but he's the kind who doubles up when he starts to lose."

"Was he nasty to you?"

"Not at first. In fact, he asked me out. He can be very charming, if he wants to," she said. "I did go out with him."

"What happened?"

"Oh, he took me to dinner and then he tried to get into my pants."

"That shows good taste."

"No, Lou. He treated me like a piece of meat. He comes from family money somewhere."

I told Dawn what I knew about Harrison's background, especially about the scandal in Florida. "I don't remember the details, but they were juicy—drugs and group sex, good stuff."

"It figures. I don't know where he lives, but in Vegas he runs with a crowd of high rollers. He's around that movie producer Caretoni a lot. A couple of times he came into the casino with this really terrific-looking woman and they went and played baccarat, which is a real fast-money proposition."

"Who was the woman? Was she tall, with long reddish hair, about thirty?"

"No, no. This gal was about five-four or five, dark hair, somewhere in her early forties. But really gorgeous, like an ex-movie star or something."

"I wonder who that could be."

"Why?"

I told Dawn all about our relationship with the Princess and Jay's involvement with her, though I left out my own feelings about her. "The funny thing is, she won't introduce us to any of her friends," I concluded. "Or maybe that isn't so funny. We *are* a raunchy lot in our summer gear. But then this crowd she moves in isn't all that tony, judging by Harrison."

"I asked Charlie, one of my pit bosses, about this woman Harrison was with," Dawn said, as I finally squeezed off Wilshire and headed into the heart of Westwood. "She was some kind of actress, never a star or anything, but she married a horse trainer and she likes to gamble."

"A trainer? Who?"

"I don't know."

I had a dim recollection now of having heard something once about Wilbert Buckingham's second wife, that she had been an actress and was really hot stuff, but it was all pretty vague. "I wonder if Vince would know," I said.

"Why?"

"Just curious."

"You hear a lot about Caretoni," Dawn said. "He's another big plunger and he's in town a lot. He sort of shuffles back and forth to New York and L.A., but he's always around. He's supposed to be involved in some shady stuff."

"Like what?"

"Loan-sharking, stuff like that," she said. "There's supposed to be a connection to a bunch of hoods, one of whom owns the jewelry concession at the Xanadu. A lot of those places are fronts for the Mafia. There was an investigation last year and a couple of guys left town, but nothing much happened. They questioned Caretoni, but he just said he knew some of those guys from being around, you know. Anyway, nothing came of it."

"I know he's a big gambler. And he's got a reputation for stealing from his production budgets, but then everybody does that. Only he steals more than most, they say."

"Well, you hear a lot of things around town, but I don't pay too much attention. I just deal the cards and try to get along. You don't want to ask too many questions in Vegas."

"You probably get hustled a lot, huh?"

She laughed, a little hard dry sound at the back of her throat. "It's a hustler's town, Lou. You live with it, especially if you're a woman alone."

I let that one go by in silence and drove into the hospital parking lot.

Ronnie looked very small and frail in a big white bed by the window of his room and he seemed uninterested in my presence. His eyes had the withdrawn, frightened look of an animal caught in a trap and resigned to the worst. He had an IV pumping a colorless liquid into his left arm and the nails on the fingers of his right hand had been bitten down to the quick. His mother kissed him and went off in search of medical authority while I did my best to cheer him up. I told jokes and tried a couple of my latest moves on him, but nothing worked. He looked so pale and vulnerable I became alarmed for him. I was relieved when Dawn came back and I could excuse myself to find a men's room.

When I returned, she was out in the corridor in consultation with a tall, slightly stooped man of about fifty who was dressed in a white lab coat and had the long-nosed, suffering face of a kindly trash collector. His name was Sam Rosenthal and he spoke in a slow, deep voice, as if pronouncing the end of peace in our time. I wasn't sure about his bedside manner, which must have been equally funereal and depressed his sicker patients, but for some reason I had instant confidence in him. I could see that Dawn took heart simply from listening to his voice, with its tone of benevolent doom. "He'd need to be hospitalized for a week, perhaps," he was saying, as I joined them, "but the prognosis is fairly good. Of course, it's too early to be sure."

Dawn introduced me and said, "The doctor thinks it may be glomer—something. . . ."

"Glomerulonephritis," Rosenthal said. "It's a variety characterized by inflammation of the capillary loops in the glomeruli, or tubules, of the kidney."

"I'm glad you said that," I told him. "Otherwise I wouldn't have known what was wrong with him."

Rosenthal looked momentarily confused, then made a horrible effort to smile, like the grimace of a man trying to make the best of having swallowed raw octopus. "In layman's terms," he continued, "the boy is pretty sick and he'll probably have to be careful for the rest of his life about what he eats and drinks, but this disease is not fatal. He'll get much better and we can medicate it and keep it under control. He's young and has been pretty healthy."

"Well, that's good," I said. "Isn't it?"

Rosenthal looked miserable. "But, as I previously indicated, we need to complete our tests. We won't know anything for sure for at least a couple of days. I'll insist on a renal punch biopsy for a definitive diagnosis."

Dawn thanked him and I could tell she was relieved. Something in Rosenthal's lugubrious style was peculiarly and uniquely reassuring, but he was a setup for a comedian. "The only physical ailment I've ever had," I assured him, as we parted, "was a slight anterior disclocation of the epiphysis of the capitellum. It kept me from broad-tossing for a couple of months." Rosenthal eyed me in horror and fled, lurching off down the hallway like a two-toed sloth jogging in tight shoes.

"You're wicked," Dawn said, laughing.

"I know, always the hopeless clown. By the way, I did have that dislocation when I was a kid. It's in the elbow. I couldn't do magic, so I practiced medical terminology. That guy's got a great bedside manner. It would make you want to die."

"I like him," she said. "I trust him."

"So do I."

We spent the next hour or so with Ronnie, who began to brighten after Rosenthal's departure. He even began to respond to some of my better illusions and once or twice I made him laugh. When Dawn and I left, soon after seven o'clock, we were all feeling better about life in general. "That was sweet of you, Lou," Dawn said, taking my hand as we emerged from the elevator into the hospital parking lot. "Thanks."

"For what? I like Ronnie."

I drove west on Pico to Fernando's, a small, family-owned Mexican restaurant in Santa Monica that was one of my favorite hangouts. We drank a pitcher of margaritas between us, ate the house's special burrito, bantered with the amiable proprietor's seven teen-aged kids, all of whom worked in the place, then, exhausted by the day's stresses, got back to my place somewhere after ten.

All I could think about was going to bed. The small red light on my answering machine was blinking, however, an unusual occurrence during the Del Mar season, when most of my friends and my agent know I'm out of town. Dawn went into the bathroom, while I picked up my one message. It was from Jay. "Shifty, old sport, Piquant, Marina's two-year-old, is in tomorrow's sixth. It's a stretch-out to a mile,

122 / TIP ON A DEAD CRAB

he's drawn inside and all systems say go. If you are not coming back in time, give me a call and I'll get down for you. Say hello to Dawn."

I hadn't planned to go back so soon, but Jay's call made me itch. A lot of bettors were on to Buckingham's style with maidens, so I felt reasonably sure Piquant would pay no more than five to two or thereabouts, but I like to be on hand when a good thing is going. I don't like in general to bet on a horse when I'm not present; one of the things I'm in this for is the thrill of the event itself, not just the cashing of a winning ticket. I was sitting on the bed, not having quite made up my mind what to do, when Dawn rejoined me.

"I can see that look on your face," she said. "It's okay, Lou, you don't have to stay. I'm fine, really."

I smiled. "You can read me, can't you? I never was able to fool you."

"Only at magic, not in life."

"Well, I don't know what I'll do yet."

"All I'm telling you is, do what you want. I'm fine and I'm sure Ronnie's going to be all right."

"You can stay here as long as you like."

"I know. Thanks."

We slept peacefully and chastely in each other's arms that night. In the very early morning, I got up, made some coffee for both of us, drank a quick cup of it and tiptoed out the front door without waking her. By the time I hit the freeway going south, just below the airport, it had already begun to clog up considerably with cars bearing grim-faced workers to assignations with tedium. A dedicated drone, I gunned the Datsun past them to my own personal rendezvous with destiny, in the form of a four-legged beauty lunging for the finish line with my money riding on his soft nose.

In the Dark

I THINK I first began to understand Marina the night of Alex Boucher's annual beach party, which he threw the Friday night after my return from L.A. and Piquant's easy win the previous Wednesday. Jay had told Alex about the horse and the movie producer had bet a thousand dollars on him to win, at odds of slightly over three to five. Alex only liked to bet on obvious favorites and Jay had touted him onto the horse about twenty minutes before post time, when it had become obvious to all of us in the box that the colt would go off at too short a price for us to play him. Alex had been losing all day and had dropped by to get some help. He had not hesitated to put up his money, even though Jay had warned him that no animal in the world was worth betting on at those odds. I'll always remember Sam's pitying look and what he said, as Alex rushed away from us toward the betting windows: "That jerk thinks betting horses is like putting your money in the bank. If horses was boats, he'd have tapped out on the *Titanic*."

Ecstatic from his ridiculous win, Alex had invited all of us to his bash, a catered barbecue he threw every year on the beach below his condo, a couple of miles up the coast. (If he had lost the bet, he wouldn't have asked us; like so many of his colleagues in the so-called Industry, Alex is a weather vane. "He's got his nose up your ass if you're a winner," was the way Jay once put it, "but he'll kick you in the balls if you're down.") The fact that he even invited Sam, who could lower the tone of any gathering simply by being on the premises, was a tribute to how badly Alex had needed to be temporarily bailed out. Of course it wouldn't last. Alex Boucher had never had a winning year, at horses or anything else in life. Pudgy, dour, with gray curly hair, small black eyes and the pursed, fleshy lips of an habitual lemon-sucker, he survived on tidbits from the tables of the great and what is called "development money." He had not produced a picture, or even a TV commercial, in several years, but he had survived. And, I had noticed, he still wore cashmere sweaters, Gucci loafers and enough gold jewelry to stock a salesman's tray. "What do you see in that bum?" Sam had asked, as Alex rushed away that afternoon.

"I keep hoping that, if I cast enough bread upon the waters, someday a crust will come floating back," Jay explained. "It's become an endurance contest."

"Don't worry, Sam," I pointed out, "we don't tell him about the good bets, like Bouncing Peter. Just the ones we don't play."

"How about that?" Sam had commented. "I could have sworn we'd get a decent price on this pig. Is the public wising up to Buckingham or what?"

"They sure tipped their hand this time," Jay observed, grimacing with displeasure. "Scarpe strangled the horse last time. Now I got to sit here all day without making a single bet."

"Yeah? Why?" Whodoyalike asked eagerly from the aisle behind us.

"Because, dummy, there is nothing *to* bet," Jay told him, shooting him a glance of icy contempt.

"You don't like anything, really?"

Jay had not even bothered to reply, knowing that Whodoyalike would not linger long enough even to hear his answer. Of such desperate vignettes is our day compounded.

I arrived late the night of Alex's party. I parked illegally by a fire hydrant, so I wouldn't have to walk a mile through the sand, and joined the nearest food-and-booze line. Ten minutes later, with a lukewarm beer in one hand and a gritty hotdog in the other, I gingerly made my way through the sizeable group, few of whom I recognized, around the bonfire and sat at the edge of the outer circle, with my back to the sea. It was a dark night, with only a sliver of a moon, the only light coming from the fire and the kerosene lamps mounted on the long picnic tables set end to end just below the parking lot and the coast highway. The guests milled about the tables, sat in beach chairs or sprawled in small groups on blankets and towels in the sand.

I knew at least some of these people, from the track, mainly, but for some reason I felt distant, removed from contact with them. I hadn't cashed a winning ticket since I'd come back; maybe that was why I had no inclination to mingle. I was into my first losing streak in several months and misfortune tends to paralyze me, like a butterfly impaled, still fluttering but helpless, on somebody's pin.

"Shifty, you look so sad," the voice murmured in my ear. "You look lost, like a little boy in a wood."

"Marina," I said, turning to stare at her, "where's Jay?"

"I do not know where Jay is," she said. "We are not currently on good terms."

"Oh?"

"He is so boring, with his funny little newspapers and charts," she said. "And he is angry at me."

"Why?"

"Because I am tired of always waiting for him. Tonight I decided to come ahead without him," she said. "Honestly, he spends all morning with his silly papers and now part of the evening as well."

"We've been losing the last few days," I explained. "When things are going badly, Jay dips into his charts. Somewhere in there is the secret symbol that will unlock the jackpot."

"You at least make fun of it," she said. "He has become simply a bore."

Dressed in skimpy white shorts and a dark-blue man's

shirt, with a gold necklace gleaming against her skin, she was kneeling barefoot in the sand behind me. Her long golden-red hair tumbled loosely down to her shoulders. I ached to take her in my arms, but, of course, I resisted the impulse. "Have you eaten anything?" I asked instead. "Why don't you get a beer, come and join me?"

"I abominate beer," she said. "I had some ghastly wine and I am not hungry. Who are all these people?"

"Flotsam and jetsam," I said. "Do you know Alex?"

"Who?"

"Alex Boucher, our host. I thought you might know him. He's a movie producer."

"Really? What movies has he produced?"

"Nothing recently and nothing good ever. But he knows everyone. I'm sure he must know Dino."

She shrugged; the possibility did not interest her in the least. "Do you know that Jay blames me for Piquant?"

"I don't think he blames you, Marina. He was angry about the price. He thinks Buckingham blew it by tipping his hand."

"Bert says that Piquant is only a mediocre sort, you know."

"That's why Jay is angry," I explained. "It was a chance to make a bet, but he feels that your trainer practically took ads to tell the dummies he was going to win with him."

"Jay is still angry about Gran Velero," she said. "He keeps asking me about him. It is driving me mad."

"Well, that's Jay," I said. "He tends to judge his friends and contemporaries by their fortune or lack of it at the track."

"There are other things in life besides the track."

"Not for Jay," I countered. "It all begins and ends there for him. If you had four legs and a tail he'd marry you."

She laughed. "Come on, Luigi," she said, "walk me home."

"What, now? Down the beach? Where's your car?"

"I did not bring it. I walked up here. It's not far. I told Jay he'd find me here."

"And now you're leaving?"

"That is his misfortune. He was to have been here an hour ago. I am not going to wait for him. Come on."

"I'll come part of the way," I said, standing up and brushing the sand from my trousers.

We walked down to the water's edge and Marina took my hand. It was still very dark, but the lights of Del Mar and the other coastal towns to the north and south of us lay strung out against the empty landscape like bits of glass floating in ink. A soft offshore breeze caressed us and I found myself marvelling at Jay's carelessness with people. How often in one man's life does any woman appear as beautiful and desirable as this one? I held on to her hand as we set out for her house, hoping she would never disengage herself from me.

"Shifty?"

"What?"

"I think you like me."

"You know I do."

"Than why do you not do something about it?"

I stopped as if I had hit a pane of glass. We had gone about half a mile down the beach, Alex's party still visible as a distant, flickering fire against which shadows moved. Otherwise we were completely alone, with this extraordinary question of hers hanging in the night between us like an invitation to catastrophe. "What did you say, Marina?"

"Must I repeat myself?"

"I don't think I understood you, Princess."

"Yes, you do. Do you think I have not noticed?"

"Noticed what?"

"You want me. I see it in your eyes every time we meet. I saw it there that very first day, when you and Jay rescued me from the ocean."

"And Jay? What about you and Jay?"

"He is very beautiful, like a statue. I wanted to make love to him."

"That's all?"

"I thought there might be more, but now I do not believe there is. What do you think?"

"Princess, it isn't what I think—"

"Don't call me Princess," she said. "It is a way of avoiding me. Call me Marina. That is my name."

"Look, I'm not really very good at games—"

"You think this is a game?"

"I'm not sure what it is, Princess."

"Marina. Say it—Marina."

"Marina, Marina."

"Now please kiss me."

She moved to me and cradled my head with both hands. Her kiss was anything but friendly; it made me tremble like an aspen in a gust of wind. When she had finished with me, she stepped back and smiled. It was very dark, but her teeth gleamed and I had the strange feeling that she could look right through me. I had become as transparent in my desire for her as a teenager about to be touched by a rock star.

"Marina, I don't like this," I managed to say.

"You do not act as if you do not like it, *chéri*."

"Well, I do like it—"

"Ah, good."

"But it's Jay. I—"

"Oof," she exclaimed, "you Americans, with your guilt, your boring rules."

"Jay's a friend," I tried to explain. "We share an apartment down here. As far as I know, you're still his girl."

"I am no one's girl," she said, the smile gone, her face inscrutable in the shadows. "I am me, Marina. I belong to no one, Luigi. No one belongs to anyone. We belong to ourselves. You understand?"

"Jay yesterday. Me tonight. Who tomorrow?"

"Oh, you are a fool," she said. "I thought you are so intelligent. I thought you had another life besides the races. There is something, you know, besides horse races."

"There's magic," I said.

"Ah, yes, the magic. No, Luigi, there is life. There *is* a life out in the world."

"I'm aware of it."

She moved in close again, taking my hands in hers. "Then you must reach for it," she whispered. "What are you waiting for?"

"I guess I'm waiting for you, Marina."

"No, you must see what you want and you must go after it." She kissed me again, savagely this time, with my lower lip briefly between her teeth; I thought she might draw blood. When she broke away again, I was helpless with desire. "Don't be a child, Luigi," she said, "What do you wish? That the world will give you what you want for nothing? You will not get it."

Without another word, she turned and ran off into the night. I stood there for I don't know how long, paralyzed with indecision. I had never met a woman I wanted more, but the unexpectedness of her availability was, temporarily at least, far too much for me. Nothing in our previous relationship had prepared me for it either. I had been startled by her aggressiveness and a little put off by her indifference to any possible consequences as far as Jay and I were concerned, but I knew that I wanted her as much as I'd ever wanted anything in my life. I also knew that, no matter what might happen, I meant to have her. I was glad she had suddenly run away from me out there in the dark, because I would have taken up her offer and she must have known it. I was still shaking with desire.

When I returned to Alex's beach party, I went looking for another beer to calm myself. I was like a hot two-year-old ready to explode out of the starting gate and I needed desperately to be settled down. The gathering seemed to have thinned out somewhat, but there were still about thirty people milling about the picnic tables and at least that many more on the sand about the bonfire. Sam loomed out of the darkness, a great, waddling bulk clutching greasy spareribs in one hand and a beer in the other. "Where you been?" he asked. "We was looking for you."

"Jay here?"

"Naw. Never showed up. He ain't missing anything. Food's lousy."

"So who's we?"

"Marina and me. She was asking about you."

"She found me. I just walked her partway home."

"Trouble," Sam said, "the broad is trouble."

"Sam, you are a perambulating cliché."

"You know what a cliché is?" Sam said. "A cliché is a truth repeating itself, that's all. And let me tell you something else. If you want to win at the track, you have to have freedom from distraction. Women and horses do not make a good parlay, Shifty."

"I guess you're living proof of it."

Before he could answer me, Alex Boucher came up beside us, though he did his best to ignore Sam, whom he must have considered a walking insult to his concept of the stylish life. "Where's Jay?" he asked.

"Home, handicapping, I guess," I said. "We've had a shaky few days."

"Too bad," Alex said. "I saw his girl here."

"Yes. I walked her home."

"She's one great lay, I hear."

"Who would you hear that from, Alex?"

"Dino told me."

"That was classy of him. When?"

"Oh, years ago, when he first met her."

"Where was that?"

"Cannes, at the film festival."

"I didn't know she was an actress."

"She'd done some bit parts, in Italy, I think."

"So he picked her up somewhere?"

"Not exactly," Alex said. "He sent out for her."

"What are you talking about?"

"She was a high-priced hooker, Shifty. All you had to do to get her was pick up the phone."

"And he married her?" Sam asked.

"He had a great line about that," Alex said. "Somebody asked him why they got married and Dino said, 'Because it fits.' What's the matter, Shifty? Did I say something wrong? You look a little green."

"Alex, you are one miserable son of a bitch." I dropped my empty beer can on his feet and almost bolted away from him.

"Hey, what did I say?" he called after me. "What the hell's the matter with you?"

The phone was ringing as I walked in the door; it was Dawn, still in L.A. "Lou, I hope it's not too late."

"No no. Is Ronnie all right?"

"Oh, yes," she said. "He's going to be okay."

"That's a relief. Merry old Sam Rosenthal is going to make him whole again?"

"Yeah, he's great. Ronnie's got a bruised kidney and an infection in there but it's not the other disease he mentioned."

"Then he'll be cured?"

"Probably almost as good as new. I'm going to take him home in a couple of days."

"Terrific. I'm very happy for you."

"Listen, that's not the main reason I called. I was going to tell you in the morning about Ronnie, but Vince has been trying to get you. He couldn't find you in Del Mar, so he phoned me here on the off chance and got me."

"What's up?"

"Did you call him a couple of weeks ago?"

"Yes, from here. After I got back from L.A. I was trying to find out who this woman was Harrison was squiring around there. Did Vince tell you?"

"No, but he's asking around. Discreetly. You know Vegas."

"Sure."

"But you didn't hear about Harrison?"

"No. What about him?"

"He was seen a couple of days ago and then he disappeared. They found him this afternoon. He's dead, Lou. Somebody beat him to death."

"Good God! Who? Where?"

"They stuffed his body into the trunk of the car he rented here at the airport. That's where they found him, the airport. In one of the parking lots."

"Who found him?"

"The car rental people. Vince says they beat him to a pulp.

They couldn't even recognize him. They identified him later at the morgue. Somebody literally kicked his face in."

"Jesus." I sat down on the couch. I felt as I used to when I was a kid and had had a bad dream. I was cornered in the upstairs room of a big, empty house in the middle of nowhere and the monster was coming to get me. Moving slowly, taking his own sweet sadistic time about it.

"Lou, what are you going to do?"

"I'm not sure yet."

"Be careful, will you?"

"Dawn, if I had a bomb-proof shelter somewhere, I think I'd go crawl into it."

A key turned in the front door and I jumped a foot, holding the phone in one hand. I went into a crouch, ready to bolt out the back. It was Jay. He walked in and stared at me in amazement. "What's going on?"

"Lou, you all right?" Dawn shouted, her voice sounded as if it was escaping from between the cracks in the sofa cushions. "Lou? What's happening?"

"It's okay," I assured her, slumping back into my seat. "It's Jay. I heard somebody at the door and panicked."

"You're weird, you know that?" Jay said, walking past me on his way to the kitchen and fishing a beer out of the icebox. "You're as nervous as two-dollar bettor with his welfare money on the favorite. What the hell's the matter with you? Who'd you think it was, the neighborhood ax murderer?"

"Lou, you take care," Dawn said. "Vince is working tonight, in case you want to call him."

"Yeah, thanks."

I said goodbye and hung up. Jay snapped his beer can open and sat down at the dining table, his eyes already wandering restlessly over his charts and figures. I told him about Dawn's call and he shoved himself away from the table, folded his arms and stared thoughtfully at me. "Well, Shifty, obviously you think it was Kretch," he said.

"Who else?"

"Is Kretch around?"

"I'm sure going to find out. Lend me some paper, will you?"

"Help yourself," he said, indicating the stack of lined yellow pads he kept in one corner of his work area. "What are you going to do?"

"I'm writing my memoirs," I said. "They are to be published only in the event of my death or disappearance."

"Interesting," Jay answered. "Might make a best seller."

"By the way," I asked, "did you go to the party?"

"Nah. Marina and I are on the outs right now, and I didn't feel like it anyway. How was it?"

"Terrible, like last year. Lukewarm beer and undercooked hot dogs."

"That's Alex for you," Jay said, "a cheap plater. Was Marina there?"

"Yeah, briefly. When you didn't show, she went home. What's going on?"

"Nothing too serious," he said. "The Princess just doesn't understand about losing streaks. But then why should she? And there's another thing."

"What is it?"

"Every time I talk to her about her own horses, she shuts me off," he said. "It's strange, Shifty. It's like she's hiding something."

"What?"

"How do I know? She's got this total faith in Buckingham and I can't talk to her. It's weird, man."

I showed up at Bully's well after midnight to find the place still in its usual uproar. The hostess, exhausted from the evening's excesses, was slumped against the wall by the door, like an old broodmare in foal. I looked around the room, then went up to her and asked for Bunny. "She's in the back," the hostess said, blinking wearily. "You want to talk to her?"

I nodded and gave her my name. "I'll be at the bar."

I squeezed into a corner and turned so that my back was to

the wall, like a Mafia don, and I had a clear view of the room. Two seats over from me, a familiar voice cut harshly through the din and chatter and good times. "Let me tell you about Scarpe," it was saying. "Sure, he's ridden four thousand winners and maybe he'll go on and break Shoe's all-time record one day, but he already holds one record of his own. Nobody has stiffed more horses, believe me, nobody. At least twenty thousand losers he's put the arm on coming out of the gate. I hate the fuckin' bum. He and Richards, between them it's like betting on cancer. It's terminal, man, it's terminal." Bet-a-Million in his glory and full paranoid cry.

I nursed my last beer of the night for ten or fifteen minutes until Bunny finally appeared. She waved to me from the kitchen doorway and I pushed my way back toward her until I was able to take her arm and steer out into the patio, empty now in the chill late-night air. "Hey, Shifty," she said, "what is it? You're hurting my arm."

"I'm sorry," I said, letting go of her. "Where's Kretch?"

"He ain't here. He's up in L.A. Why?"

"Just wondering. When's he coming back?"

"Maybe tomorrow. Hey, he wants to talk to you. He's going to start up a new game, somewhere in L.A., when the meet's over. Only high rollers. He wants you to deal, he told me."

"You have to be mad," I said. "No way."

"Well, he said he's gonna talk to you about it."

"Forget it. Bunny, I want you to tell him something for me. Will you remember? It's important."

"Yeah, I'll remember."

"Just tell him that I wrote it all down."

"What?"

"Never mind what. He'll understand. I wrote it all down and it's in a safe place. You got that?"

"Well, sure but what does it mean?"

"You don't want to know, honey. Kretch'll know."

"Okay, but I don't get it."

"You don't have to, believe me. You want to repeat what I just said?"

"Jeez, Shifty—"

"Bunny, it's very important."

"All right. You wrote it all down and it's in a safe."

"A safe *place*, with a friend. You got that?"

"Yeah. I'll tell him. He'll be back tomorrow."

"I don't think so."

"What do you mean?"

"I mean I don't think so," I said. "But he'll probably call you, right?"

"Yeah, sometime."

"Okay, don't forget to tell him."

"Boy," she said, "you guys . . ."

I left her there, hoping she would remember at least the gist of my message, and went back inside. I was suddenly bone-tired and anxious to get home. On my way out, I passed Tap-Out and the Mole deep in elegant conversation. "Hey, Shifty," the Mole said, "guess what? They threw Tap-Out out of the track today. He was using all this foul language and they threw him out. How do you like that?" The Mole's wizened gray face squeezed out a smile and his thin, bony frame shook with suppressed laughter.

"Yeah, it was after the fifth," Tap-Out said. "You seen the ride that chickenshit McArdle put in? He don't wait for a hole to open up. No, he's gotta go eighteen wide through the parking lot to get beat. And I'm standing there with two bills on his pig, a sure winner, if he don't piss in his silks at the idea he might win by coming through horses instead of by way of China. Sure, I started to let him have it."

"A bunch of women in the next box complained," the Mole said, blinking with glee behind his bottle-bottom glasses. "They came and took him away. You like that?"

"I love it," I said.

"Fuckin' women don't even belong at the goddamn track," Tap-Out thundered on. "But I'll tell you something—when these assholes let me back in, I'm not comin'!"

"You like that?" the Mole said. "You like the sound of that?"

"If you believe it, Mole," I told him, "you'll believe anything."

ELEVEN
Revelations

"I AM GLAD you came," Marina said. "I was worried that perhaps you would not come."

"It was an invitation I couldn't refuse."

"Does Jay know you are here?"

"No, I didn't tell him."

"That was prudent of you."

"He tried to call you a couple of times. He thinks you're ducking him."

"I do not wish to see him right now."

She closed the front door and led the way down a long corridor into the main social area of the house, a large sunken living room with sliding glass doors opening out onto a walled patio and the beach. I had very little time to admire the view, because she immediately pulled drapes that shut it off and she took the further precaution of making sure the doors were locked. "It is better," she explained. "Jay might come up the beach to see if I'm home."

"Your car's in the driveway."

"Where is he?"

"Deciphering the riddle of the Universe," I said. "Where else would he be this early?"

"Of course."

"But he might show up later."

She shrugged and walked toward the bar in one corner of the room. "He will not break in, if I do not answer the door, will he?"

"I doubt it. It's not his style. But my own car is outside."

"I do not think he will come," she said, "not after what I said to him. Will you have a glass of wine?"

"No, thanks. It's a little early for me."

"Coffee, anything?"

"Coffee. Just black."

"I'll be right back."

She disappeared into the kitchen and I sat down on the sofa and looked around. It was a large, handsome room, normally full of light and open visually to the elements. The morning fog that often lies banked along this coastline even in the summer months had not yet burned off, however, so that the place basked in a mild twilight glow that blurred the scene for me, making it difficult to individualize it. Nothing in this room spoke to me of Marina or anyone else. The sofa I was sitting on was part of a vaguely modern Danish-style set that included four armchairs, end tables, a coffee table, two ottomans, and large cushions scattered on either side of a fireplace containing iron logs over a row of gas jets. The lamps, two floor models and several table ones, were large billowing affairs with three-way bulbs, and the walls were decorated with framed French lithographs and posters of the kind that can be bought cheaply in any art store. I had the distinct feeling of a room that could be rented for brief periods of time and in which no one ever lived. When Marina came back with my coffee, I asked her about it.

"Oh, it's ghastly," she said. "When Dino bought this house, he called up a decorator and had everything ordered wholesale. We were not even here. It is used only in the summer."

"Dino likes to spend money, obviously."

"He is extravagant," she said. "He has houses everywhere."

I took a sip of my coffee and waited for her to come to the point. Her voice on the phone had sounded falsely cheerful, pinched, a gallant front masking genuine distress. Now that I was actually present, her tone had changed. She seemed, as always, calm, assured, supremely self-confident. And, of course, dazzlingly beautiful. She was wearing sandals, tight white jeans and a light blue open-necked man's shirt. Her hair fell loosely around her shoulders and her face, un-altered by cosmetics except for a touch of lipstick, glowed with animal health. Desire for her made me weak. I sank into the couch as if I wanted it to swallow me and waited. She perched on the chair across from me and smiled. "You look uncomfortable," she said. "What is wrong?"

"I don't know why I'm here," I said. "You called me."

"Yes?"

"Well?"

She shrugged. "I wanted to see you."

"What about?"

"I have to ask you something."

"Go ahead."

"Not now," she said, standing up. "Come upstairs."

"What for?"

"You'll understand later. Please come upstairs."

Still holding my cup in one hand, I followed her up the steps to the second floor, which consisted of a single room nearly as large as the one downstairs and also with floor-to-ceiling glass affording an ocean view, cut off, in this case, by white Venetian blinds. An enormous circular bed, un-made, dominated the space, like the killing ground in an ancient arena. She gave me a moment or two to appreciate this setting, then turned to face me and slowly, deliberately kicked off her sandals.

"What are you doing?"

"Is it not obvious what I am doing?"

"Well, I'm getting an idea about it."

"Don't tire yourself with too much thinking, Luigi."

"I'm trying not to."

Her jeans fell to the floor and she stepped out of them. "Do you like my legs?" she asked.

"I am an unabashed admirer of your legs."

"You talk such a lot."

"The patter helps. It's a cover."

"A what?"

"A cover. Most magicians develop a good patter."

"I will never understand all that."

Her shirt now lay on top of the rest of her clothes, a small sacrificial bundle to lust. Her arms went up around my neck and she moved into me with the calm assurance of ownership. The blood rose in me like the surge of a tidal current, unseen until too late and sweeping away every obstruction in its path. We became a wild tangle of arms and legs, hands grasping, caressing, pinching, squeezing, two in one, one in two, a thrusting, yielding jumble of creative bestiality. I exploded, and in that moment cried out with such fulfilled ecstasy that her arms encircled me to keep me whole, to make me sane again. I knew now that I could have died (or killed) for her. Instead, I lay in her arms spent, my head on her breasts, and tried to become rational again.

Did I sleep? I don't think so, but I have no remembrance of time passing. Only that, when I looked up, she was sitting, still naked, at the foot of the bed and gazing at me with calm satisfaction.

"I knew it."

"Knew what?"

"What it would be like," she said. "What it would be like with you."

"You're not going to tell me the earth moved."

"What is that?"

"Another cover."

"Explain, please."

"In uncertainty, I fall back on irony."

"I do not understand you, Luigi."

"Why do you call me Luigi?"

"I don't know. It suits you, I suppose. Would you like more coffee?"

"I don't think I ever finished the first cup."

"I will get you a fresh one, all right?"

She slipped into a terrycloth robe, picked up my cup and headed for the stairs. "And then we will talk, Luigi," she said. "I must tell you something that is very important. Do you have time?"

"Of course. I've already practiced some moves today. What did you have in mind?"

"I thought we could take a drive somewhere and simply talk."

"Yes, why not? The way I've been going, I could skip a day at the track," I said. "I was sure you had an ulterior motive in luring me up here, but you know what? I don't care."

Jay made only two bets that afternoon. He liked the favorite in the first race and bought three fifty-dollar doubles from it to his top horses in the second. After he won that wager with his third choice and found himself nearly a thousand ahead, he left his notebooks in the box with Fido and Sam and headed for the paddock area, out behind the main grandstand. The only other horse he liked all day would not race until the ninth, a race for fillies and mares at a mile and one-eighth on the turf course, and he had some time to kill. He did not tell his friends exactly where he was going, merely that he needed to stretch his legs a bit. The only person he eventually told was me, but not until later that night.

Security at the California race tracks is not as tight as it is back East. Any presentable-looking individual who knows a few people and the local jargon pretty well can easily talk himself, at least briefly, into almost any area of the premises during the course of the working day. Jay, who had dressed fairly respectably for the occasion in brown polyester slacks, a sports shirt and a ten-year-old brown-striped seersucker jacket, had no trouble walking past the uniformed attendant at the paddock, who mistook him for a horse owner. Jay nodded his thanks and kept right on going, through the walking ring, past the saddling stalls and into the receiving barn behind them. The horses for the third race were being walked under the low, shedlike roof in a slow circle or tended to in the stalls by their grooms, while the horse identifier, a man named Walt Lewis, scurried from one animal to another, checking each of them out. Jay joined the half-dozen other people watching this procedure and waited until the horses were at last summoned to the paddock. After they had filed past, he followed Lewis into his office, a sour-smelling little room containing a battered old wooden desk, a swivel chair and several large filing cabinets.

"Mr. Lewis?"

"Yes, sir. What can I do for you?" He was a short, bowleg-ged man of about sixty with a round, beet-red face and nar-rowed, hard blue eyes that peered out at the world from under a banded straw hat that looked as if it had put down roots into his scalp. If Jay had called up Central Casting for an old horseman who couldn't have been mistaken for any-thing else, they would have sent him someone exactly like Walt Lewis.

Jay introduced himself as a reporter from a local newspa-per in La Mesa, a middle-class suburb of San Diego. "I thought I might do a feature about what you do in here," he told him. "It looks a little tricky to me. That all right?"

"Sure," Walt Lewis said, sitting down behind his desk and gazing up at Jay with mild interest. "This ain't the glamorous side of racing, you know. What did you say your name was?"

"Fox, Jay Fox."

"PR send you down?"

"That's right."

"Well now, what can I tell you?"

"Why don't we start at the beginning."

"Suits me." Walt Lewis got up and waddled out of his office. "Come on. We got a couple of schoolers in here and I can show you what we do better than I can tell you. Like I said, it ain't fancy and I don't see a story in it, but that's your business, ain't it?"

Without waiting for a reply, he led Jay to the far end of the receiving barn, where the schoolers, a couple of very green, unraced two-year-olds, were being trained to get used to their unfamiliar surroundings. One of them was taking it calmly enough, but the other was gazing wildly around, his feet nervously stamping the ground and his head jerking back against the lead in the hands of a young Mexican, who was nearly as frightened as his charge. "Here, come on now," Walt Lewis said, walking right up to the animal, patting its neck and beginning to talk reassuringly to it. "That ain't no way to act, Junior. You get yourself all worked up here for nothin'. Ain't hardly worth it. Now you just be a good boy and settle down here, ain't nobody gonna hurt ya. . . ."

Within a couple of minutes, the old horseman had the schooler calmed down, much to the relief of the young groom, who smiled and nodded as Lewis talked. "See?" the old man said. "Look, here's what we do." Jay walked up and watched as Lewis patted the horse's nose, kept one hand flat against its neck, then grabbed its upper lip and peeled it back to reveal a row of tattooed numbers. "Every racehorse in America has a number," he explained. "We check it out before every race, make sure we got the right horse running, don't ya know?"

"I wouldn't think it's a foolproof method," Jay commented.

"It ain't," the old man said. "There ain't much time to check them numbers out. Then some of them don't show up too good, neither. After a while, twos get to lookin' like sevens, fives get to lookin' like threes. The older the horse, the less them numbers show up good and clear."

"Could you make a mistake?"

"Hell yes, make 'em all the time. Ain't nothin' I'm perfect at except drinkin' good Kentucky sour mash whiskey. Otherwise I'm usually a dollar short and a day late." The old man laughed at his own joke. He was a character, all right, Jay decided, and all the more so because he worked so hard at it. "Sonny," Lewis continued, "you'd be surprised at the mistakes that get made around horses. That's why I gave up trainin' them sonsabitches. Got myself an easier way to make a livin' here. Ain't nothing' to it, really."

"You don't make it sound easy," Jay said, pretending to make notes in a small pad he'd brought along to lend himself an air of journalistic credibility. "When's the last time you made a bad mistake?"

"Make so many I can't even get insurance," Lewis said. "If I was an open field, they'd close me up as hazardous waste." He cackled again and slapped his hands together.

Jay smiled wanly and resisted an impulse to deck this unfunny old joker. "Seriously," he said, "what could happen if you were to make a mistake identifying a horse?"

"You mean, if someone was to try to run a ringer in on me?"

"Well . . . yes. I guess that's what I mean."

"It'd be easy enough," the old man said. "If it was just an honest mistake, I'd catch it. I could fuck up on them numbers, but I got a good eye for horses and a good memory. We got photographs on all these animals and a chart on which we list all the markings—color, conformation, distinguishing marks, the works, you name it. Mornings here, I fish out everythin' I got on a horse and look 'em over. Like I said, I got a good eye and a good memory."

"But you could make a mistake."

"Oh, sure, real easy. But it don't happen much, or at least I don't know about it." He chuckled.

"What about a ringer?"

"Well, they don't try that much anymore. Time was, down in some little bush track, they used to pull that shit all the time, probably still do," the old man said. "When I was trainin' down in Caliente, Mexico, back in the forties and fifties, they used to pull that stunt a lot. Usually management was in on it. Them crooked trainers would tip the Eyetalian boys that run that track back then, just so's they wouldn't get into trouble. Well, you'd see them odds drop down real sudden like and you knew somethin' was up. But nobody never said nothin'. Hell, the purses down there was peanuts and we was all tryin' to stay alive, you know. Some ten-to-one shot would wind up goin' off at even money and win easy. You couldn't get rich that way, but you could cash a bet and keep goin'. It'd be harder to do today, a lot harder."

"Why? More controls?"

"Sure," Lewis said. "Didn't have tattoos in them days. In fact, some places they still ain't got 'em."

"Yeah? Where?"

"South America. Don't use 'em there."

"What do they use?"

"Markings, pictures, conformation, I guess. There's only one sure way to tell."

"What's that?"

"Night eyes," Lewis said, leaning over and pointing to two little knobs high up inside the young colt's front legs. "Them little buttons is like fingerprints, no two alike. We're changing the system now. By next year maybe we'll have 'em all photographed and it'll be standard, instead of these here tattoos. Of course, it ain't foolproof neither."

"How's that?"

"All you gotta do is shave 'em down to alter 'em," Lewis explained. "Eventually they grow back out the way they was, but you might fool a man once or twice who's lookin' at ten or twelve animals nine times a day in here. That about it?"

"Yeah, thanks." Jay followed the old man back to his office. "What about these South American horses?"

"When they come into the country," Lewis said, "they got Jockey Club papers with 'em and we photograph 'em on arrival, make notes on all the markings, stuff like that. Want to see one?"

"Sure would."

They went into the old man's office and Lewis opened one of the filing cabinets, reached in and pulled out several large brown folders. He dropped them on his desk. "Here, take a look," he said. "It costs sixty dollars to register a horse and they got sixty days to get it done. Over sixty days, it costs 'em four hundred and we can decide not to register 'em at all. We assign 'em a number and we get 'em tattooed. Foreign horses get five numbers. It's all in there." He pointed to the files on his desk. "You wanna excuse me a minute, I gotta piss." He left the room and walked out into the barn area.

Jay glanced quickly through the folders on Lewis' desk, then pulled open the file drawers. The folders were alphabetically arranged and he quickly located the ones he was looking for, made notes on markings and numbers, then shut the drawer again. On his way out, he met Lewis coming back from the toilet and thanked him.

"Send me a copy of your story, when it comes out, all right?" the old man asked. "I want to show it to the missus."

"Be glad to, I'll drop it off."

"Don't forget now," Lewis called after him. "Nobody's interviewed me since I stopped trainin'. Hell, that was damn near thirty years ago. Maybe I'll get on the Johnny Carson show or somethin'."

"Or something," Jay said. "Thanks again."

When Jay got back to his seat, he found Sam, arms folded, listening placidly to Action Jackson's fevered account of mismanagement and disaster. They both ignored Jay, who had his mind on other matters anyway. "So I wheel the twelve horse in the double," Jackson was saying, "only he gets fanned on both turns and runs third."

"I don't play the double," Sam said.

"Then, in the second, I single the four in my Pick Six," Jackson said, "which is the key to my four-hundred-and-eighty-four-dollar ticket. So he gets left in the gate, rushes up on the inside, checks on the turn and still runs second. He should have won by five, only now I'm out of the Pick Six."

"I don't play the Pick Six," Sam said. "It's for bridge-jumpers and other crazies."

Undeterred, Action Jackson, tall as a cypress and jittery as a filly in season, plunged on. "In the third, I key the favorite and I take him back and forth to two long shots and I also baseball him with the third and fourth choices and what happens? The second choice runs second and I finish one-three-four-five. I'm snake-bitten."

"I don't play exactas," Sam said.

"You don't?"

"No. And I don't play quinellas or trifectas either."

"Why not?"

"It's hard enough to find one live horse," Sam said.

"Well, you know," Action Jackson pointed out, "we're all out here gambling."

"No, that's the difference between us," Sam said. "You're a gambler, I'm a horseplayer."

"No difference," Action Jackson said, rushing away to spread his tale of woe.

"That's what you think," Sam said, turning now to Jay. "Where have you been? You missed a real bad race."

Jay did not even hear him. He was glancing through the notes he had taken in the receiving barn, his analytical mind fully concentrated on the interesting list of facts he had accumulated during his research and what they might add up to in terms of dollars and cents.

Marina and I bought sandwiches and a bottle of very dry French Chablis, after which we drove up into the state park on the bluffs a few miles below Del Mar. We spread a blanket out on the grass and lay in the sun; we were partly sheltered by the overhanging boughs of a large pine tree. We could stare out over the ocean below and the white sails of a distant regatta, or lie on our backs and gaze up at the sky, where two daredevils in hang gliders hovered high above us in the prevailing thermal currents like huge, ungainly birds of prey. Oddly enough, I was completely at peace with myself, despite having just betrayed one of my best friends and knowing also that this woman I was with was almost certainly not the person she had so far pretended to be. I didn't care. I was drunk with love of her and my whole body still glowed with the feel of her in my arms, the scent of her bare skin.

"Are you hungry?" she asked.

"No," I said. I was lying on my back, eyes closed, completely at one with her and this scene.

"Some wine then?"

"That, yes."

I sat up and Marina poured the cold liquid into a couple of champagne glasses she had brought along. "À nous," she said, toasting me. "To us, Luigi."

"I like the sentiment," I said, taking my first sip.

"Now we must talk. Can we?" she asked.

"Of course," I said, "but please tell me only nice things."

"I will tell you the truth," she said. "It will not be very easy for me. There is much I must tell you. You will think badly of me."

"Try me," I said. "I'm prejudiced in your favor."

"That is what I wish to ask of you—a favor."

"Well, what is it?"

"I wish to give you some money."

"I like the sound of that."

"I wish you to take it for me to Las Vegas and give it to a person I know there."

"How much money?"

"Fifty thousand dollars."

I rested my back against the big pine and looked at her. She was staring at me like a nervous squirrel, ready to turn tail and scramble at the least sudden movement. "That's a goodly sum, Marina," I said. "What does it represent?"

"Pardon?"

"Please tell me a little more about it."

"It is the money I have won betting on Gran Velero."

I stared at her in amazement. "You bet five thousand dollars on that horse?"

She nodded. "I had to," she said. "I knew that he would win. It was all the money I could afford to bet."

"Then it was all an act."

"What?"

"That you don't know anything about horses and all that. Obviously, Buckingham told you."

"Yes, he did tell me. He is trying to help me." She looked away from me toward the horizon, where the white sails of the regatta peppered the dark blue sea like scraps of paper scattered over a carpet. "I am in money difficulties, Luigi. I am not rich."

Slowly, haltingly at first, but then with growing confidence, she began to talk about her past. She had met Dino in

Cannes, just as Alex Boucher had said, but on the beach there. She had been working in movies in Italy, mostly in what the Italians call *gialli* or "yellows," thrillers and cop films. She had been offered a lot of work in soft-core porn, but had always turned those jobs down. "Not easy, you know," she explained. "I was very hard up for money."

"I thought your family had money, in France," I commented.

"I exaggerated, Luigi," she answered with a smile. "My father manages a grocery store in Nice for a large chain of stores. I have invented a more glamorous background for myself, because it is always good publicity to be a rich, glamorous person, I think. The grocery man's daughter is not interesting."

"I suppose not, in that world."

"I went to Cannes with the man I was living with, who was an actor in a film to be shown there," she continued. "I was lying on the beach in the morning taking the sun when Dino walked up to me and introduced himself. Do you know Dino at all?"

"No."

"He is the most charming man in the world when he wishes to be," she said. "He absolutely devastated me. I had been fighting with Franco, my boyfriend, for weeks, so I was ready for something. Dino took me away from him. Suddenly I was in a world I had always dreamed about and never known, a world where money means nothing and where everything you want is available. You clap your hands and it is brought to you. I went insane, I suppose. I was very young and very naive in many ways. Dino bought me, like he bought everything and everyone he wants. He is truly almost irresistible. I was ambitious and lazy, a wonderful combination for such a moment and such a man."

It had been easy for her to give up her career. She had never had much talent anyway and all that acting in movies had ever meant to her was an escape from her humdrum background, which Dino now offered her. They had lived very high on the hog, traveled everywhere, seen and done everything. She had not, however, understood about his gambling. "The first night I was with him," she said, "we went to the casino in Monte Carlo and he won two million francs playing roulette and *chemin de fer*. I thought it was wonderful. I thought that it would always be like that. Oh, I knew that one could not always win, but I did not realize how much one could lose. Two years ago, Dino began to lose very much and always he gambled more and more heavily. The gambling became everything, more important even than his movies. He began to steal. He stole from his movie budgets so that he could gamble. It became so that we had no life together anymore that was not gambling. We did not even have sex anymore. So I decided to leave him. That was last year."

"And the horses? He also bets on the races, I gather."

She shook her head. "No, that was a diversion for me," she explained. "I have always loved horses, ever since I was a little girl. For some years, when I was very small, my family lived on a farm and we always had horses. In Rome, Dino took me to the Capannelle, the racetrack there, for the Italian Derby. I was so excited and I loved it so much that he bought me a horse. That was the beginning of it. Instead of jewels or furs, I asked him for horses. In three years we had a good stable. Last year, when we decided to separate, all I asked for was the horses." She smiled a little sadly. "It would have done no good to ask for anything else anyway, as he has nothing now. It is all gone in the gambling. He is having difficulty with the financing of his films because of the gambling. Everyone in the business knows about it, you see. It is a tragedy."

"I can think of worse ones."

"Yes, of course. But it *is* a disease, you know, like alcohol or drugs."

"I suffer from a touch of it myself."

"I know. That is why I thought you and Jay would understand."

"Have you told all this to Jay?"

"Some of it, yes," she said. "Not all."

"What didn't you tell him?"

"I did not tell him about the money."

"Why not?"

"I started to, but then he became so angry that I didn't inform him about Gran Velero. All he cares about, you see, is his betting."

"So you came to me. Why me, Marina?"

"Because you are different, Luigi. And because you know Las Vegas well and you have friends there."

"In other words, I'm the logical person to help you."

"Yes, that is so."

The implications of this conversation were becoming unpleasant. I stalled for time by pouring myself another glass of wine. I didn't doubt that Marina was telling me the truth, but I was no longer certain I wanted to hear it. I sipped at my wine and concentrated on the view. "I know what you are thinking," she said.

"What am I thinking?"

"That I made love to you for a purpose."

"Didn't you?"

"Yes, that was my intention, Luigi. I admit it. But something else has happened between us, do you not feel that?"

"I'm trying not to."

"Don't," she said. "Give in to it." She took my face in her hands and kissed me. "Believe in me, please. You do not have to help me if you do not wish to. I will find someone else. I do not wish to poison what we have found." And she kissed me again. "Let's not talk about it anymore."

"No, it's all right," I said. "I want to. We must talk about it. How much, exactly, does Jay know about all this? Does he know you bet a lot of money on the horse?"

"No, but he is very suspicious now. He kept asking about it. He asked all these questions, until I became so angry I was screaming at him. He is a gambler, too, you see, like Dino. I do not think I can trust him. And now he is angry at me. He believes that I refuse to tell him what I know."

"Well, you didn't, did you?"

"No," she said, with a short, hard laugh. "How could I, Luigi? Would he understand? To him it is purely and simply a gambling situation. To me it is everything I have."

"Tell me this, Marina," I said. "Why do you need me, or anyone, to take this money for you to Las Vegas?"

"Because it cannot be sent any other way," she explained. "Obviously I can't deposit it in a bank and it would be very risky for me to take it myself."

"Why?"

"Because I am being watched."

"By whom?"

"I am not certain. Perhaps the tax people. For over a year now Dino has been pursued by these people. They have tried to attach his property, all his bank accounts, his offices in New York, everything. They have even tried to seize the horses, but I have been able to stop them. They belong to me, not to Dino. The horses are all I have, Luigi."

"What are you going to do with the money, Marina?"

"I wish you to give it to this person in Las Vegas. He is a man I know there, a person I can trust. He is going to wager this money for me there."

"You're going to gamble with it?"

"Yes. I am going to bet this money on Gran Velero in his next race. It is my only chance. If I bet there, at the right time, you see, with the legal bookmakers, it will not affect the odds on the race. My friend there will know how to do this. His name is Angelo. He works in one of the casinos there."

"Why can't he come and get the money?"

She sighed. "Oh, Luigi, you ask so many questions. You are like Jay. Never mind—"

"Look, Marina," I protested, "be fair. If I'm going to do this for you, I have to know what I'm doing and why."

"Luigi, I need two hundred thousand dollars," she said. "I must have that money or I will lose everything. Gran Velero is my only chance. Bert tells me that he will run very well next time also, which will be in a race during the next three weeks."

"If you bet all that money on him in Las Vegas," I warned her, "the gamblers there will lay it off."

"Lay it off? What is that?"

"They'll bet some of it at the track to lower the odds on your horse," I explained. "The Vegas people have guys posted at all the major tracks whose job it is to do that."

"I know, Luigi," she answered. "That is why Angelo must do this for me. He will know how to bet the money correctly."

"Tell me about Angelo."

"He is not a very savory person, but he is a friend of Dino's and mine. Dino was helpful to him with the immigration people and he likes me."

"Can you trust him with that much money?"

"I must. I have no choice."

"Why two hundred thousand, Marina? Why so much?"

"Because that is what I need. Otherwise I must sell everything at a loss."

"What about Balthazar?"

"He is not ready to run," she said. "Bert says that he needs more time. He says that some horses from another country need a lot of time to adjust. Balthazar is one of those, I am afraid. He was a champion in South America, but he is nothing here, until he wins a big race. I cannot sell him now, because he is not worth much until that time. Luigi, this is my only chance, believe me. Will you help me?"

"Why don't you let me bet the money for you? I think I could."

"No. Angelo will do it. He has ways, so that the money will not show up. I will pay you a thousand dollars to do this for me, Luigi."

I reached over and took her hands. "Now look," I said, "you can pay my air ticket from San Diego and back and that's it. If I weren't losing so much this summer, I wouldn't even ask you to do that. I either do it on those terms or not at all, understand? I have a place to stay there, if I have to." I told her about Vince Michaels and my friendship with him. "So it's all set."

she let herself go into my arms. "Oh, God, thank you, thank you. It's my only hope."

Later, after we had finished the last of the wine, she lay very close to me on the blanket and put her arms around me. "Marina," I protested feebly, "somebody'll see us."

"Never mind, let them," she said. "It will be very beauti ful."

The horse Jay had picked out in the ninth was a five-year-old mare named Soubrette, a French-bred making her third start in this country and trained by Wilbert Buckingham. She had run twice on the dirt without much success but figured to do much better on the turf, where she had performed very creditably in Europe. Furthermore, Bill Scarpe was up and it was well-known among the regulars that he never stayed around to ride the ninth at Del Mar unless he was up on something live. Soubrette went off as the third choice, at nearly four to one, and Jay bet two hundred dollars for himself on her and six hundred for his syndicate.

The mare broke well and lay third, hugging the rail and saving ground, about two lengths off the pace until the quarter pole. Then Scarpe saw an opening between the tiring leaders and drove her through it. She opened up two lengths, with the odds-on favorite chasing her, and looked like a sure winner. "This one's easy," Sam said, lowering his binoculars as the horses neared the finish line and leaning back in his seat. "I wish they was all this easy."

No sooner had he spoken than Soubrette, with less than twenty yards to go, suddenly bolted to the inside. She plunged through the inner hedge, spilling her jockey into the grass in front of the tote board, and took off across the infield. "Oh, my God," Sam exclaimed, "I thought I'd seen it all."

Jay looked at him in disgust. "You had to open your big mouth."

"You're right, you're right," Sam wailed. "In racing, anything can happen. I once saw a horse do this at Hialeah and drown in the infield lake. I should have known."

"Did you see that?" Fido screamed, rushing up the aisle toward them. "I hope that fucking Scarpe broke every god-damn bone in his body!"

Jay watched the two outriders in pursuit of the mare finally catch up to her. "They got her," he said. "That's good."

"Good?" Fido shouted. "What's good about it?"

"Fido," Jay said, "if you're going to bet your money on horses, you have to be prepared for anything. Tonight I'm going to light a candle to the Dummy God."

"Amen," Sam said, with a sigh from inside the depths of his dark soul. "Amen."

TWELVE

Metamorphosis

MARINA AND I found a motel up the coast in Carlsbad, about twelve miles north of Del Mar. It was a small, shabby establishment consisting of a single row of dark, boxlike rooms, but it was within easy walking distance of the beach and completely isolated from the downtown area, with its restaurants and shopping malls. The proprietor was a deaf old widower who mistook us for a couple from the nearby Marine base at Camp Pendleton and beamed toothlessly at us from behind the screen door to his cubbyhole of an office every time he saw us, usually either as we were arriving or departing. It seemed unlikely that anyone could ever find us there, since the locale might as well have been on the moon, as far as the denizens of our normal summer lives were concerned.

I had stumbled onto the place quite by accident two days after we had first made love in Marina's house. "We must not meet here," she had said. "No one I know or who knows me must connect you to me now." For my part, I had not wanted Jay to catch on, so I had immediately gone looking and had luckily spotted the small sign, the only one anywhere nearby, at the end of the road branching off toward the water from the main highway. "Kozy Kabins" the sign had proclaimed, over an arrow tilted toward the sky. Perfect, I had thought, and so it was. The only other guests during the time we were to spend there were to be couples like ourselves, almost certainly illicit and equally anxious to avoid public scrutiny.

I rented the Kozy Kabin nearest the beach and we met up there every afternoon for more than a week. I would leave the track right after the eighth race and drive up the coast road, then quickly turn down our lane and park outside our front door. Usually, I would get there before her. By the time she arrived, never more than a half hour later, I would have some cold white wine waiting for her and we would quietly clink glasses, sip it and soon after descend on the bed like participants in a carnal rite of passage. I had never before had a woman like Marina, who used her miraculous-looking body with the freedom of an animal and the imagination of a complete hedonist. We almost literally devoured each other and nothing else mattered to me. I kept right on losing at the track day after day, but it had no effect on me. By midafternoon, the horses and the fate of my bets on them had ceased to count even slightly. The fever would rise in me like steam in a radiator and I would be champing to be gone long before the time finally came. The only vision I had was that of Marina naked on my sheets, waiting for me in lust like a pagan goddess.

Jay, of course, noticed not only my early departures and my absences from all our customary late-afternoon pursuits, but also the strange detachment with which I lost, as if the money no longer mattered to me in the least. "What's going on, Shifty?" he asked me, a few days after I had embarked upon this new routine. "Where the hell do you go every afternoon?"

"I've got someone," I told him. "She's married and this is the only time we can get together."

"And you're not going to tell your old buddy who it is?"

"No. She has a lot to lose, Jay. She has two kids, her husband's a schoolteacher and there isn't much money there," I improvised, marveling at my own spontaneous inventiveness. All magicians, I suppose, have a gift for duplicity. "Anyway, the horses are not being kind to me. I have to take my pleasures where I find them."

"Where'd you meet her?"

"On the beach, where else?" I said quite truthfully.

"Shifty, you're a cunning rogue.

"They don't call me Shifty because I'm a straight arrow."

"Sam said you had a lady stashed somewhere."

"Sam has a keen nose for potential disaster."

Anxious to cut this dangerous conversation short, I started for the door. "Where are you going now?" he asked.

"Upstairs, to shower. What's up?"

"I just wanted to tell you," Jay said, "I'm on to something really big. If I'm right about what I think is going on, we're going to make a tremendous score, old buddy."

"I certainly hope you're right," I said. "I could use one, or I'll have to go back to work before the summer's over."

"Tremendous," Jay repeated. "The biggest dead crab in history."

I was so involved with my secret life then, so enmeshed in the pleasures of the flesh with Marina, that I paid almost no attention to the implications of Jay's confidence; I certainly made no immediate connection to Marina.

Late one afternoon, a couple of days after the start of our affair, Marina told me about Guy Harrison. Incredibly, I had not yet asked her about him, even though I knew she would have every reason to know a great deal. Not that I connected her in any way to Harrison's murder, but, in my normal right senses, I would have asked her what she knew. Even with Solomon Kretchmer firmly implanted in my head as the executioner, I should have realized she not only must have known about Harrison's death, but would have an opinion at least on who might have killed him and why.

"Do you remember my friend Guy?" she asked one afternoon, after we had made love and were lying side by side, propped up against our pillows and finishing our wine.

"I'll never forget him. I once played poker with him."

"And he lost, of course." She sighed. "He always lost."

"He cheated," I told her. "I caught him at it."

"He was such a fool. He was desperate," she said. "Did you know that he was killed?" She proceeded to tell me about the discovery of Harrison's body in Las Vegas. "Somebody else must have caught him cheating, somebody not as nice as you."

I related the circumstances of my involvement in Kretch's weekly poker extravaganza. "I can't help but feel it was Kretch who beat him up," I concluded. "I'm not sure he wanted to kill him. Kretch doesn't know his own strength. He's a monster."

"And where is this man now?"

"I don't know. In hiding somewhere, I suspect. He hasn't been around here and I've read nothing further in the papers about Harrison." I turned over on my side and gazed down the seemingly endless length of Marina's incredible body. "What was Harrison to you, Marina?"

"Just an old friend," she said. "I met him years ago through Dino, in Cannes or Monte Carlo, I don't remember now. He was so sweet and charming then and such a good friend. He was homosexual, you know, so we were able to be pals. He worked for Dino in New York."

"Doing what?"

"Nothing important. He did things for Dino. Favors, presents, errands."

"Sounds like he was his gofer."

"Yes, I have heard the term. He was always around. Addicted, of course, like Dino."

"To what?"

"To gambling. That is what they had in common. Guy had once been rich and was from a very good family in Boston, I think, or Philadelphia. He lost everything at the tables, but he could not stay away from them. It was sad."

"Wasn't there some sort of scandal in Florida?"

"Oh, yes. Guy was involved with a very naughty group down there. He had gone down for the winter, I remember, to a cousin's house and he fell in with a very fast crowd—drugs, orgies, everything," she explained. "He fell in love with a Cuban waiter down there and wouldn't leave. When the scandal exploded, there was poor Guy in the middle of it all."

"From the little I've seen of him, I can't believe he was just an innocent bystander," I said. "I gathered he had an almost limitless capacity for foolishness."

"Very nicely stated, *chéri*. Is there any more wine?"

I poured the last of the Muscadet into her glass and watched her sip it. Her skin glowed in the dim light and I had to force myself not to touch her. "Why do you bring him up now?" I asked instead.

"I don't know," she answered. "I was thinking about him today." She looked at me and smiled. "I know it will sound funny to you because he cheated at cards, but I trusted Guy. He would have done anything for me. I would have asked him to take my money to Las Vegas, you know."

"Risky," I said. "He probably would have lost it at craps on the way in."

"Guy never played craps," she said. "He considered it a vulgar game. He loved baccarat and *chemin de fer* and roulette. Roulette was his great passion. He lost a fortune at roulette. But because of the two zeros in America, he would not play roulette in this country. He liked *vingt-et-un*, your blackjack, but he adored baccarat the most."

"You can't beat the casino vigorish, Marina," I said. "Sooner or later it grinds you to a pulp. I never play casino games. Well, hardly ever."

"You know, I think Guy must have gambled here with someone else's money," she said. "He lost and that is why they killed him."

"We'll probably never know, will we?"

"He owed money to many people. Poor Guy."

"Rumor has it he was squiring Buckingham's wife around the casinos," I said.

"Oh, yes," she answered calmly. "Gloria loves to gamble and Guy was the perfect man for her. He was not a threat, if you comprehend the meaning."

"Did Gloria gamble a lot?"

"I don't know, Luigi. I don't think so. She loves the slot machines."

"I heard she was at the heavy tables, too. Baccarat, mostly."

"Really? That's a surprise. I don't think Bert would like that," she said. "You know she is much younger than he is and he has difficulty keeping up with her at times. Oh, Guy probably lured her into it. Gloria is a little silly sometimes, but Bert keeps an eye on her, or tries to. No, I don't think she would lose very much, not like poor Guy."

"Whose money would Guy have gambled with here? Dino's?"

"Oh, no," Marina said quickly. "Dino would never *give* Guy money. He paid him for what he did for him, but he knew that Guy always lost. No, he would not give him money."

"Who would?"

"They have people who loan money," she said. "Perhaps one of them."

"A Vegas loan shark? Then one of those guys could have killed him. Did Guy know about Gran Velero?"

"Yes," she said. "I told him to bet on him."

"And he did?"

"I think he did, but not very much."

"Why not? If you knew the horse was going to win—"

"I know," she interrupted me, "I know. I should have told him everything, Luigi, but I was afraid he would bet too much. He was so reckless."

"And the price on the horse would have gone down."

"Yes." She looked at me with stricken eyes. "Perhaps if he had won a lot of money on Gran Velero, he would be alive. It is my fault? I have thought so much about it."

"Don't blame yourself," I said. "Losers always find a way to lose. Sooner or later, Marina, he'd have wound up the way he did."

"I am not so certain. I have thought a lot about it."

"Don't. You didn't kill Harrison," I reassured her. "He managed to get that done all by himself."

She shivered slightly and moved in close to me, her face resting against my chest. I held her in my arms and kissed her. Through the open window I could hear waves breaking on the rocks below and a breeze stirred the curtains. The blind eye of the television set on the bureau stared at us and the closet door yawned open, revealing a long row of wire hangers dangling dismally over the clothes we had kicked off in our haste to get to each other. A dismal scene, even squalid, but a small paradise to me.

Marina's arms wrapped themselves around me and her face now loomed above me. "Let's do it again," she whispered. "Let us make the beast with the two backs one more time today. . . ."

Jay drove quickly in through the gates of Oakview Downs that last Tuesday in August and parked near the main ranch buildings, above the sweep of fenced meadows where horses grazed and the now empty training track, a circle of dark-brown pounded earth in the prevailing dusty green, stared emptily upward like a huge eye. The sky was a transparent blue and the hot midday sun had baked the scene into immobility. From the barn area chickens clucked, a dog barked, horses coughed and stamped in the gloom of their individual stalls. Nothing of importance would start up again until late afternoon, after the heat began to die down and the animals revived from the torpor of the midday break.

Jay got out and looked around. Nobody appeared to greet him and he started for the front door of the main house, then thought better of it and strolled into the barn area, notebook in hand. A row of horses' heads peered at him from the half-open stall doors as he walked along the first shed row, stepping carefully around bags of grain, buckets, piles of rags and bandages, straw, bottles of liniment, muddy spots where earlier the animals had been cooled, groomed, combed and brushed until their coats gleamed. At the end of the row, on a pile of fresh straw outside the tack room, a young Mexican rested on his back, feet drawn up, a battered straw cowboy hat over his eyes. "Hey, *amigo*," Jay said, "where's Buckingham's string?"

The boy grunted, slid the hat off his face and looked up. An arm, fingers extended, shot out like a turn signal. *"Numero dos,"* he said. "No wan ees dere."

"That's okay. I'll find my way."

"*Mas tarde . . .*"

"It's okay, they know I'm here," Jay said.

The boy fell back under his hat and Jay walked past him to the next barn, where the number two had been painted in white over the front. The initials WB on a wooden placard hung above a blackboard beside the first stall. It listed the names, usually abbreviated, of the trainer's charges and what the status of each was. Next to the indication "Bal" someone had scribbled the notation "wlk & turn out." Jay looked around. A mangy dog poked his head around the corner, growled and retreated, whimpering. A goat at the end of a long tether looked up indifferently as he passed. Halfway down the row of stalls, Jay stopped and peered into the gloom. "Hey, big boy," he murmured softly, "turn around. Let's have a look at you."

The big horse did not move. He stood head down, with his huge rump facing the stall door. Jay spotted a sackful of carrots propped against a post two stalls away and grabbed several, then clucked softly to the animal. "Come on, fella, here—look!" The horse turned his head and peered back at him, his eye now fixed on the proffered delicacy in his visitor's outstretched hand. He moved clumsily toward it as Jay backed slowly away, forcing the beast to stick its head out of the stall in pursuit. His teeth grabbed one of the carrots by the end and yanked it out of Jay's hand. "Attaboy," Jay said, studying the animal closely. He patted his hand and rubbed his fingers along the horse's nose, from between the eyes nearly to his nostrils. He fed him a second carrot, then a third one, before strolling back along the shed row the way he had come, leaving Balthazar to munch away and peer after him in mild curiosity.

The Mexican boy was asleep under his hat. Jay walked out of the barn area and back toward the house, where his car sizzled in the sun. A large fat woman of about fifty in floppy dungarees emerged from behind the screen door and stared at him. "Lookin' for someone?" she asked.

"Not really," Jay said, introducing himself.

"Oh, you're the reporter. You called this morning."

"Yeah. Nobody was around, so I just gave myself a little tour."

"Ain't much to see this time of day," the woman said. "You should come by in the early morning."

"Well, I'll come back, maybe tomorrow," Jay said.

"Harry'll be here then or later today," she said. "He can tell you anything you want to know. He went to the track about an hour ago, said he'd be back by four. You want to wait?"

"I can't," Jay answered. "I got another story I'm working on, but I'll be back. Tomorrow, maybe. Would you inform Harry?"

"Sure. I guess he told you—"

"Oh, yeah. I just couldn't get free earlier," Jay said. "But I had a look. How many horses you got here?"

"Maybe seventy, if you include the foals," the woman said. "But Harry can tell you all that. I just do the cookin'."

"I see Buckingham has quite a few horses here," Jay said. "Is that foreman of his around?"

"Bud? No, he's at Del Mar most of the time now. You'll find him with Bert."

"Well, thanks," Jay said, heading again for his car.

"Sure. You come back, hear? Harry'll be glad to talk to you."

Jay nodded, waved, got into his car and drove away. He was so excited by what he had seen that, as he hit the main road, he threw his head back and shouted, shaking both fists over his head. The car stayed on course, but an older couple in a pickup truck coming in the opposite direction stared at him in horror and nearly ran up on the shoulder to get away from him. Jay waved gaily at them and drove on.

That same day, in midafternoon, I called Vince in Las Vegas. He was not surprised to hear from me. "I tried to get you a couple of times," he said. "Where have you been?"

"Around. I just haven't been home much. How's it going?"

"Fine. I had some news for you."

"Like what?"

'You asked me about that fellow Harrison and the woman?"

"Yeah."

"Well, you know about him, of course. Nobody's come up with anything yet, but there's a suspicion he was involved with Rinaldi."

"Who's that?"

"A very dubious type, Shifty, my friend," Vince said. "He's a hood who moved here from Chicago about five years ago. For a while he had a jewelry concession in the Xanadu, but they say it was a front for a lot of other stuff. He's also a pal of that producer's."

"Caretoni."

"Yes. They both come into the Emerald Room quite a bit, sometimes together. Caretoni eats there all the time now. About Rinaldi, every three or four months he's in the news here. They're always trying to get him on one charge or another, but they can never make anything stick and he's got some heavy lawyer representing him," Vince said. "The word is he killed a couple of people back East, but again it's all supposition. They forced him out of the Xanadu and barred him from the casinos, because he has a record and all that, but now he operates out of a travel agency downtown. Nobody seems to be able to touch him and everybody you talk to is scared of him."

"Sounds like you ought to be, too. Watch yourself, Vince."

"I will. Most of what I'm telling you is common knowledge, anyway. I guess you know most of it."

"Some of it. What else is there, Vince?"

"Well, the main reason I called is this woman Harrison was always with."

"Gloria Buckingham."

"Yes. Now this is rumors, understand?"

"Sure."

"The word around town is that she was involved with Rinaldi."

"Involved?"

"Yes, she apparently had an affair with him. She's a crazy, hooked gambler. She and Harrison lost a lot of money. Hundreds of thousands, they say. I mean, a lot. This was when she hooked up with Rinaldi. They say she's a beauty."

"Yes, I heard that."

"Rinaldi seems to be into a lot of things, everything from hookers to drugs. And he's connected with the mob, one of the Chicago families. The cops are trying to pin the Harrison killing on him, but he can prove he wasn't even in Vegas at the time. He was in New York."

"What about Gloria?"

"Apparently she was with him. She's left that trainer. Another thing Rinaldi is into here is loan-sharking. Any of this making sense?"

"Quite a lot of it," I said. "In fact, part of what you're telling me is a big relief."

"In what way, Lou?"

"I had my own ideas about who did Harrison in," I explained. "Now I'm breathing a little easier." I told Vince about the poker game in which I'd caught Harrison cheating. "I figured it must have been Kretch, probably because he was angry about Harrison breaking up his game down here and maybe for other reasons as well. The Harrisons of this world have a gift for trouble."

"How do you know it wasn't Crutch—"

"Kretch, with a K."

"Whatever. It could have been him, couldn't it? Rinaldi wasn't around."

"If Rinaldi is what you say he is, he wouldn't dirty his own hands on small fry like Harrison," I explained. "He'd have paid to have the job done."

"Shifty, you better watch yourself."

"Don't worry, I'm being careful," I assured him. "By the way, I'll be in Vegas very soon for a day or two."

"Great. You can stay here."

"No, Vince, but thanks. I'll get a room in a motel somewhere."

"Why? I've got lots of space."

"I know, but I don't want to involve you in any of this. You have to live there."

"Don't give me that. I'll expect you to stay here and that's it. But what exactly is going on, Shifty?"

"I'm not sure, Vince. I'm trying to do a friend a favor, but basically I'm not really mixed up in this."

"Well, keep it that way. And watch yourself. Rinaldi is pure poison."

"I'll ask about him around here. My friend would know something. What's his full name?"

"Angelo Rinaldi. They call him Angie the Pick, because the two people he's supposed to have killed back in Chicago or somewhere were stabbed with an ice pick."

"He sounds charming."

"Be careful, Shifty. You're out of your league there. You're supposed to be a magician, not a cop, and in Rinaldi's world, when they make you disappear, it's forever."

This conversation with Vince troubled me and I poured myself a pretty stiff bourbon and soda, then got into my bathing trunks and went out to the pool in back of the main building in our complex for a swim. Luckily, no one was around, so I breast-stroked four leisurely laps, then lay on my back in the tepid water and stared up at the sky. I wanted desperately to believe in my Princess, but I was absolutely certain now that she had not told me everything she knew and that I had no wish to put myself in jeopardy, even for her sake. Something was going on that maybe she herself knew little about, but it had become imperative that she tell me everything she did know. I felt I had to protect not only myself, but both of us.

Whatever it was, Buckingham, I was sure, was involved in it. The old horseman knew all the tricks and angles of his risky profession. In his time, in the early days before racing had become as strictly supervised and regulated as at present, he had by his own admission pulled off some fairly unsavory stunts, such as stiffing favorites, hiding and falsifying workouts, goosing up cheap speed horses to run like bullets on drugs or battery devices, unloading crippled animals on unsuspecting buyers, taking money under the table in cash on sales so as to circumvent the IRS, and any number of similar maneuvers to make a quick buck. "In those days, before we had these big purses and so much racing all over the country, it was the only way a man could stay alive," he had once told a reporter for *Sports Illustrated,* in a long, candid interview after his first Kentucky Derby winner back in the early sixties. He had come across in the piece, I remembered, as a sort of old rogue turned benevolent elder statesman, who portrayed his early life in horse crime as the peccadilloes of an ambitious young genius. "Of course now racing's much more honest," he had continued. "It has to be, and there isn't any reason to cheat, if you get good stock, rich owners and you know what you're doing." In other words, he had cheated only when he had to. But it's easy to be honest when it pays well, and every year Wilbert Buckingham stood among the top ten winners nationwide in the trainer standings. But if he'd been a crook once, why not again, if for any reason he was being forced to by his wife's involvement with a Mafia hood? The more I thought about it, lying there in the pool and then for half an hour on a mattress under the hot late-afternoon sun, the more concerned I became, both for myself and Marina. I made up my mind to talk to her about it; I needed to know everything, so I could keep both of us from harm.

An hour later, when I went back inside the house, Jay was sitting on the sofa. He was sipping a light beer and looked as if he had just swallowed the world's largest canary. "Hello, Shifty. Off to see your tootsie?"

"The time of trysting draws nigh," I answered, heading for the stairs. I was anxious, of course, to avoid any more questions along those lines. "How about you? Seen the Princess lately?"

"Nope. The Princess is resolutely avoiding me and, frankly, I could care less."

"No, you couldn't."

"Meaning what?"

"You *couldn't* care less," I explained, happy for this grammatical diversion. "If you could care less, then it still means something to you. I realize this is California, but English is still supposedly the language spoken here."

"Oh, God, you Eastern seaboard snob."

"Just trying to keep your mind from rotting in all this sunshine, that's all." I started up the stairs.

"Shifty," Jay asked, "what do they call that trick where they make one thing disappear and reappear in another place as something else?"

"We call that an illusion, not a trick," I said.

"Well, whatever. What do you call it?"

"There are an infinite number of variations," I explained. "Do you have a particular one in mind?"

"Nope."

"Well, the basic illusion is known as 'metamorphosis.'"

"Like changing a woman into a panther, then making them switch places and like that?"

"Yes, something like that."

"How about making a horse disappear and turn up somewhere else as another kind of horse?"

"Never seen it done," I said, "but it would qualify. What are you driving at?"

He gave a self-satisfied little giggle and took another sip of his drink. "Metamorphosis," he said. "I like the sound of that. It sounds very dark and terrifically mysterious."

"Jay, what's going on?"

"Wait," he said, "wait until tomorrow."

"What's tomorrow?"

"We'll study the *Racing Form* together, old buddy," he said, digesting his succulent bird, "and then *you* will tell *me*."

THIRTEEN

Tip on a Dead Crab

THE HEAT RISING off the desert was like a blow in the face. The window of my ground-floor motel room looked out on a parking lot in which several rows of cars baked blindingly in the pitiless sunshine. The hot outside air distorted the view, so that everything seemed to shimmer, as if seen through water. In the distance, the row of glittering casinos lining the Strip looked like huge mirages, the fantasies of some fevered dreamer stumbling across a wasteland. I lay in my underwear on the bed, listening to the high-pitched, frantic whine of my air conditioner and waiting to hear something. I had been there for over an hour already and I had begun to have a few second thoughts.

"Listen, I know it's a pull-out bed, but it's comfortable," Vince had said, on our way in from the airport. "I don't understand why you have to stay in some crummy motel."

"I don't want to get you involved in this, Vince," I explained. "I'm delivering something and getting out of town, that's all."

"Okay, so make your delivery and then come and stay with me."

"I've got to get back."

"You can get on the first flight out tomorrow. I want you to catch my act tonight," he insisted. "I've got a couple of moves you've never seen."

"Well . . ."

"Come on, you miserable degenerate. There's always another race, but there's only one Vince Michaels."

Against my better judgment, I had given in. Vince Michaels was the finest close-up artist I had ever known and I told myself I couldn't afford to pass up a chance to watch him work his miraculous effects. My greatest evening in the profession had been a night at the Magic Castle several years earlier when I had watched Vince, on a bet, work for four hours without ever repeating himself. He could have gone on another four at least, but the management had begged him to stop, because the close-up room only holds about fifty spectators, including standees, and no one would leave to make way for new arrivals. Most magicians today master ten or twelve effects, which they've probably stolen from somebody else, and repeat them endlessly. In magic, imitation is the sincerest form of stealing. Vince Michaels stole from nobody and was always inventing new moves or refining old ones. He was unique, so how could I turn down an invitation to watch him work again? I had agreed to stay. I would deliver my package for Marina and move out of this tawdry little place three blocks off the Strip, catch Vince's act that night, stay with him and get out on the first flight to L.A. in the morning. The race I had to get back for, in any case, was on Labor Day. It was only Thursday, so I had plenty of time. And my Princess would be waiting for me.

I got up and pulled the blinds, then lay down again. The manilla envelope containing fifty one-thousand-dollar bills lay out in the open on the table, along with my toilet articles and the magazines I had bought for the flight that morning in San Diego. No sense trying to hide it, I had figured; besides, it would be out of my hands soon enough. From the lobby I had made the call to the number Marina had given me, inquired about my travel reservations to Denver and been told to wait; someone by the name of Gold would get back to me. I had been asked not to leave my room until then, because Mr. Gold would be bringing my ticket personally and I was to pay him for it on the spot. I would have no trouble identifying him, I was told.

Nearly two hours had now passed. I lay on the bed in the twilight of the room and stared up at the ceiling. I had been thinking very hard about everything for days now, ever since Marina's revelations about herself, but there were so many areas I still didn't understand. If she had told me the truth, and I had to believe she had, then perhaps we stood to make a great deal of money. Of course, the horse might lose—all horses could lose—but it seemed unlikely to me that Buckingham could be wrong. And if Jay had analyzed the situation correctly, then our chances to win had become even greater. We would worry about the cheating aspects of it some other time. One thing I was sure of: Marina herself could not possibly be involved. She had almost come apart at the seams when I had told her about Jay's dead-crab theory. The still murky areas of the scheme seemed unimportant; they could be cleared up later. The crucial part was making sure the horse would win with our money on him.

I shut my eyes and thought very hard about what could possibly go wrong. A lot of things, I realized, but I had no choice. Everything Marina had in the world was at stake here and I had to help her. It would have been better if Jay had not entered the picture at all, but he could never have not involved himself, not after the entries for the Del Mar Handicap had been published in the *Form*. And anyway, whatever Jay wanted to bet on the horse would not make much of a dent in the odds, because his capital was limited and he would be very secretive about this one; I knew he would not even include his syndicate in the action. Dead crabs of such potential magnitude come along once in a lifetime, if at all, in racing. . . .

"So what do you think?" Jay had asked me, as I studied the *Form*.

"What am I supposed to think?" I replied.

"You haven't seen it, have you?"

"Seen what?"

"Shifty, get with it," he said. "Look at the entries for the

Del Mar Handicap. They're listed on the front page, lower right corner."

I looked. Sixteen horses had been entered, listed in the order of weights assigned to each animal by the racing secretary and track handicapper. I recognized most of the names, because they were those of the best older horses on the grounds, asked to compete here in the traditional Labor Day feature race for a purse of a hundred and fifty thousand dollars added. At the very bottom of the list, however, one name leaped up off the page at me, Gran Velero. He had been given a weight of a hundred and five pounds, which indicated he was being given almost no chance to win. "Incredible," I murmured.

"Read the story," Jay ordered.

The accompanying article, by one of the paper's feature writers, began by discussing the chances of the favorites in the race, Twilight Zone and Machismo, two of the West Coast's top handicap horses. A full paragraph was devoted to a New York invader named Cheapseat Charlie, a tough old gelding who had been voted Horse of the Year a couple of seasons back and was still a major threat. Four or five other contenders were dealt with at some length, after which the writer speculated on the absence from the race of Ruddigore, the undefeated English import trained by Wilbert Buckingham. Interviewed on the subject, Buckingham had declared that Ruddigore was being pointed either for a turf race at Santa Anita in the fall or the Jockey Club Gold Cup in New York. "It all depends on how he handles the dirt," the trainer had said. "All of his races in Europe have been on the grass and we just don't know how he'd take to our sandy surfaces out here. So we're going to take our time with him and race him where and when we feel sure he'll do his best. He's never lost and we don't want to get him beat first time out in this country."

This statement had surprised the writer, who pointed out that for several months, ever since the horse's arrival in the U.S., Buckingham had been talking about getting him ready for the Del Mar Handicap, *after* which he'd be going east for the fall classics in New York and a bid for an Eclipse Award as the best in his category, perhaps even selection as Horse of the Year. "This leaves Bert with only one entry, Gran Velero, in a race the trainer has dominated in recent years, winning five out of the last ten renewals," the writer concluded. "Gran Velero ran a vastly improved race to break his maiden in claiming ranks here three weeks ago, but to send him up now against the best in the West is equivalent to aiming a gun straight up in the air in the hope of hitting a duck. Lonny Richards has been named to ride."

I put the paper down and looked at Jay, who was sitting at his table and grinning broadly. "It's crazy," I said, meaning it.

"You know how crazy it is?" Jay said. "You'd think, with that weight assignment, that Buckingham would use an apprentice, who could make the weight, wouldn't you? Or he could have asked Scarpe to ride him. Scarpe doesn't have a mount in the race this year, with Ruddigore out. At least he doesn't have one yet, and he's the only journeyman jock around who can make a hundred and five pounds. Plus he owes Buckingham a favor, because he's ridden so many of his good horses over the years. No, he's got Richards on him, who, even on his best day, can't make one-fifteen. What does that tell you?"

"He's shooting for the moon," I said. "Or maybe he just wants to have an entry in the race because he always has one and it's become a tradition or something."

"You think Buckingham is a sentimental type?"

"No."

"Then it's bullshit," Jay said. "So what do you make of it, Shifty?"

"I don't know what to make of it," I said, quite truthfully. Although I knew perfectly well what Marina was up to, I hadn't even imagined the possibility of Gran Velero surfacing in the Del Mar Handicap, the biggest race of the whole meet. Marina's horse had looked impressive beating nothing in a sprint; now he was being asked to compete against the best older horses on the premises at a classic distance, the so-called Crosby Course, in which the horses break out of the starting gate at the chute to the left of the grandstand and make a full circle of the track, a distance of exactly a hundred and twenty feet less than a mile and a quarter. Only the very best horses can handle this kind of competition. I couldn't imagine Gran Velero being up to it, not this soon after the first good race ever in his brief career. I decided instantly that Marina would be a fool to bet any money on him at all and that I had to persuade her not to. She would have to get Bert to enter the horse in a race he could win easily, another sprint, say, against mediocre horses, or even at a mile or more against such animals. Otherwise she clearly risked losing everything.

"It's a dazzler, isn't it?" Jay said. "So what do you think?"

I told him what I thought. "One of us better tell Marina to take her horse out. Buckingham's on some kind of ego trip at her expense."

"Don't you believe it," Jay said. "That fucker's going to win the race."

"You're as nuts as they are."

Jay shook his head vigorously. "No. Now I want you to listen to me, Shifty, because I've done a lot of thinking about this and I've also done some investigating, okay?" He shuffled through the papers on his desk and found what he was looking for, a lined yellow pad with some notes and figures scribbled on it. "Now hear me out," he said. "Don't interrupt me until I've finished, okay? Then you can try and tell me I'm crazy and we'll talk about it. Okay?"

"Shoot."

Jay came out from behind his table and sat down in one of our armchairs, the yellow pad on his lap and one of his ball-point pens in his hand. As he talked, he used the pen as a sort of combination baton and lecturer's rod, beating time to his tale and tapping at his pad to emphasize various points. I had never seen him so excited and some of it, despite myself, began to rub off on me.

"I first began thinking about this weeks ago," he said, "before Marina and I had our big fight and split up. I'd ask her from time to time about her horses and she'd tell me what she knew. Only she never seemed to know very much. About her big horse, Balthazar, she knew nothing at all. She'd always give me the same answer, the one she first gave all of us. The horse hadn't adjusted yet, was off his feed, wasn't doing well, needed more time, blah blah blah. Right?"

"Right."

"What was funny, though, was not only that she didn't want to talk about the horse, but she'd get sore if you pressed her on it. I mean, he's supposed to be the best animal in her stable, everything kind of hinges on him, he's costing her a fortune and she doesn't know anything about him. Old Bert won't tell her anything, although he tells her plenty about every other horse she has. She can answer all kinds of questions about them. She even told us about Piquant, remember, only we didn't need to be told?"

"Go on."

"Well, I thought it was strange, especially about how she obviously just didn't want to discuss Balthazar with me, but I put it down to her natural reluctance to question her trainer. I mean, he's the best there is and you're supposed to trust these guys, because they know what they're doing. Then I overheard a phone call one night. It must have been her ex-husband, that Caretoni guy. She thought I was upstairs in the bedroom, but I'd come down to get a beer. She had also come down for something and had taken the call in the living room. She didn't see me, so I just stood there at the foot of the stairs and listened. The call had to do with some horse or other and I heard her say in Italian something that sounded like 'prossima volta, sicuro.' I couldn't make out anything else, but that phrase I remembered, because she repeated it twice, and later I wrote it down."

"Always looking for the edge, Jay."

"You got it. Actually, after she'd taken that call and I asked her who it was, she lied to me. She told me it was some friend of hers down here asking her to a party. Now I don't speak

Italian, but I know horse talk when I hear it. This was horse talk, but she didn't know I'd heard any of it. The next day I went to the library in Del Mar and looked up those three words I'd written down, which are a lot like Spanish. They mean 'the next time, for sure.' So I began thinking about that and two days later I thought I had the answer. She'd been talking about Piquant, who we all knew would run well first time out at a distance, right? Which figured to be the next time and was. That's when I called you in L.A. and you came back down and we couldn't bet the horse because the odds were too low. I figured Dino must have bet him pretty good and I mentioned it to Marina, but she denied it. In fact, she said she hadn't bet him either, only her usual fifty bucks because it was her horse. And I believed her. You with me so far?"

"Yeah, it makes sense."

"So I put all this out of my mind, until Gran Velero ran. I couldn't get to Marina the day before. She had just disappeared or she was ducking me. Then I saw her on the beach that day as usual and made nothing of it. I mean, we all knew the horse had no chance, because he was a bum. So he won and we discovered he'd been given Lasix because it turned out he was a bleeder and Lasix can make a dramatic difference in any bleeder, maybe ten lengths. But then I began thinking about Gran Velero's race and it didn't make sense. I mean, that one move he made was awesome. I went to my figures, which showed the horse in that one move had improved not ten lengths, but twenty or more. Nothing can account for that. And then I thought about how the odds had fluctuated during the betting and about the payoffs and I realized two things: whoever had bet on Gran Velero had bet a lot of money and had been so certain about the horse that he'd bet him only on the nose. Gran Velero went off at ten to one, but in the place and show pools he was more like a hundred-to-one shot."

"You and your numbers."

"Sure, I believe in them," he said. "I have to. I make my

living with the numbers. If the numbers are right, I do okay. It's when the numbers say one thing and events prove them not just wrong, but wildly, totally wrong—that's when I begin asking questions. I go back to the numbers and I look for answers the numbers have failed to give me. And suddenly, the more I thought about it, the surer I was I had a possible solution. Fantastic, but possible."

"What is it?"

"Wait. One step at a time. First I went to see this old duffer Walt Lewis, the horse identifier. I told him I was a reporter and asked him how it all worked. Then, when he was out of his office for a couple of minutes, I looked up the files on Balthazar and Gran Velero. Here, take a look at this." He got up and thrust the yellow pad under my nose, his ball-point tapping at two sets of numbers he had written down side by side, 22987 and 27937. "See those? What do they mean to you?"

"Not a thing. What are they, license numbers?"

"You're pretty dense today, Shifty," he said. "Those are the lip tattoos of Gran Velero and Balthazar, both of whom came into this country within three months of each other, one from Chile, the other from Argentina."

"Wait a minute—" I began, as I sensed the drift of his argument, but he cut me off with a wave of his hand.

"When I've finished, Shifty, like we agreed, okay?"

"Okay, but—"

"But nothing," he said, beginning to pace around the room now in his growing excitement. "The next thing I did was to go out to Oakview Downs," he continued. "I passed myself off as a reporter again and I got there at a time when I knew nobody would be around. The one guy I was anxious to avoid was Bud Grover, Buckingham's foreman, but I figured he'd be at Del Mar with the big horse and I was right."

"The big horse? Gran Velero?"

"Wait, wait," he cautioned me again. "I'm almost there."

"I know what you're driving at, but it's too far out."

"No, it isn't," he said. "Okay, so I found Balthazar's stall and I checked him out. First I noticed from the work sheet that they're not even galloping him. They take him out twice a day and walk him around the shed row and maybe turn him out in one of the corrals so he'll get some exercise, but they're not putting him out on the track where anybody could recognize him. Second, I rubbed his nose good and hard. The hairs along the whole length of it to just over his eyes are not quite as smooth as the rest of him. It's hard to pinpoint exactly, but there's a little kind of sticky feel. Now take a look at the notes on conformation." Again he thrust his yellow pad into my lap.

I studied the figures. "Jay, it can't be—" I began.

"Yes, it can," he almost shouted, sitting down opposite me and lunging forward in his chair to drive his points home. "I'm telling you they've pulled a switch," he said. "Look at the figures. Both these horses are built about the same. They're both big, about sixteen and a half hands, and they're both chestnuts. Balthazar has a white blaze and Gran Velero doesn't. The horse whose head I rubbed at Oakview has a white blaze, but I'd give you any amount of money it's been dyed. And I'll bet you they've done the same thing to the horse at Del Mar, too, only in his case it's a brown one. No sense trying to check that one out, Shifty, because they won't let you near him. That cowboy Grover is with him most of the time now."

"Wait a minute," I asked, "what about the tattoos?"

"Easy," Jay countered. "Twos look a lot like sevens and an eight can easily be made to look like a three and vice versa. A little blue or lavender ink applied just before the horses go to the receiving barn, that's all. The one thing they couldn't fix would be the night eyes, but they're not using those for routine identification yet and probably never will."

"The horses can't look exactly alike," I insisted. "Someone would spot the difference."

"Who?" Jay countered. "Nobody at the track has even seen Balthazar, except in his disguise as Gran Velero. Only somebody who knew both horses well could tell and there isn't anybody."

"There was. Eduardo."

"Who?"

"That groom who was there the day Marina drove us out to Oakview."

"Christ, you're right!" Jay exclaimed, snapping his fingers and beginning to pace around the room again. "They killed him. You remember how uneasy he was that day when we talked to him? And how pissed off Grover was when he saw us there? He must have figured the old guy had spotted it. Remember, he was from Chile. He may not have known Balthazar, but he probably recognized Gran Velero or knew they had made a switch. So they had him killed."

"Who, Grover?" I stared at Jay in disbelief. "Why would they do this?" I asked. "It doesn't make sense. If Buckingham were just some hard-up old gypsy trainer, I could accept this. But he's one of the best in the country. He doesn't have to pull off this kind of shit to make money."

"How do you know?"

"Like all trainers, he makes ten percent of every winning purse, in addition to his per diem for each animal in training," I pointed out. "How much did his horses earn last year?"

"Just under three million dollars," Jay said. "I looked it up."

"So that's three hundred thousand dollars, plus his commissions on sales and his shares in broodmares and stallions," I said. "You're talking about a man who earns maybe half a million dollars a year."

"All taxable, or most of it," Jay said. "So let's say he nets between a quarter of a million and three hundred thousand a year, all right?"

I nodded. "All right."

"If he can pull this off," Jay pointed out, "he can clear a hundred thousand easy on a bet, all of which he can hide from the IRS. At least a hundred grand. I mean, shit, this phony Gran Velero will be thirty to one at least in the morning. They can spread the money around on him so it won't all show up at once and not all in the tote. He'll be betting it in

Vegas and Reno and maybe even Atlantic City and Tijuana. They're out to put one over, Shifty."

"I still don't see why he'd do it," I said. "If they catch him, he's blown his whole career, everything, and he's looking at a prison term as well. Where's the motivation? The downside risk is terrific."

"You're right about that," Jay admitted, sinking back into his chair now. "I thought a lot about it, too. All I could come up with was this: we know the guy has no qualms about cheating, because in the early days, by his own admission, he used to do it all the time; and he *must* need the money. That last one I have to take on faith."

"That's not like you, Jay," I argued. "You're a figure man. You don't step out unless the numbers are right. You're going to start betting on faith now?"

"No," he said. "It's the only negative, one red line in a sea of green ones. I'll let it affect my bet to a certain extent, but at ten or fifteen or twenty to one, which this horse is going to be, I have to bet on him. Now, if I could find out Buckingham does need the money, I'd bet every penny I've got on the horse."

"Remember Sam's golden rule," I said. "All horses can lose."

"Shifty, my friend, how often at the track does a huge dead crab stare you in the face?" Jay said. "You think I'm going to back off because he might lose? My whole life is predicated on the premise that somewhere, sometime I can come up with a betting proposition like this one. You can take it from me, Shifty, this is a tip on a dead crab you can't afford to ignore."

I didn't answer him right away. I sank deep into my chair and tried to think. Jay fished out a couple of beers and tossed me one. "It's going to be champagne very soon," he said, "and maybe a little caviar thrown in."

I pried the lid off my can and took a sip. "What about Marina?" I asked him.

"What about her?"

"You going to tell her?"

"No," he said. "I can't find her, that's for openers. She's ducking me, I'm sure. Then why should I tell her? Maybe she's in on it."

"You think so?"

"I'm not taking the chance. One guy's already dead."

"We should go to the cops."

"Are you crazy?" he almost shouted. "Who's going to believe us? All they have to do is switch horses again. You think they can't? And who could pin that groom's death on them? What are you, nuts? Here we have a chance to cash in big and you're turning Boy Scout on me. Come on, Shifty."

"What about Sam? You planning to tell him?"

"I don't know."

"We might need him," I said. "We'll have to scatter our action. Sam could help and he won't bet too much himself, maybe a couple of hundred."

"Now you're making sense," Jay said. "Now you're talking like a horseplayer. You had me worried there for a moment, Shifty. It isn't often you have a rush of morality to the head."

"But that is preposterous," Marina had said, when I reported to her later that evening on Jay's theory. "You cannot be serious?"

Point by point I had proceeded to list all the reasons Jay had given me. "He lives by his figures," I explained. "He trusts them. What do you make of it?"

In her agitation, she sat up on the edge of the bed and stared down at me. "Do you believe him?" she asked.

"I'm not sure what to believe now," I answered. "Jay can be very convincing with his numbers."

"But it is ridiculous." She had begun to pace around the room like an animal in a cage. "Surely he can't be serious?"

"He's very serious. And he's going to make a serious bet."

"And what do you think, Luigi?" She had stopped pacing long enough to fix me with a very intense stare, as if the fate of civilization in our time depended on my answer.

"I told you, I don't know what to believe," I said, "and that's true. I do think you ought to worry about your money."

"Why?"

"Because it's asking an awful lot of any horse to make the jump in class Buckingham is asking of Gran Velero," I explained. "Now, for the moment, let's assume Jay is right, that, for reasons of his own, Buckingham is pulling a switch here, it's still asking a lot. Both these horses of yours are newly-turned four-year-olds and they're being thrown in against the best older horses out here."

"What do you mean? Please explain."

"I am explaining," I continued. "All American horses' ages are figured from a common birthdate, January 1. South American horses date their ages from August 1. Different hemispheres, you see? Which makes both Balthazar and Gran Velero younger than their official ages; they just turned four."

"Oh, that makes no difference," she said, shrugging impatiently and resuming her pacing.

"Just thought I'd mention it," I objected, propping myself up against the pillows and watching her. "Still, I do think you'd better cut your downside risk. Don't bet the full fifty thousand, Marina. Your horse will be a big price. You don't need to risk everything. We can worry about whether your trainer's pulling a switch or not later."

She swung savagely around and came rushing to my side of the bed, taking both my hands in hers and moving in very close to me. "Luigi, I can't do that," she said.

"Why not?"

"I can't, I can't," she said. "I *have* to go through with this, I simply *have* to. I must trust Bert, I must have this money, or I lose everything. I cannot accept that he is cheating me or hope that the horse will pay a large price."

"The winner's share of the purse will be over eighty thousand dollars," I pointed out. "You're halfway there."

"No," she insisted, shaking her head, "no. There are so

many expenses, so many debts. And the jockey gets a part and Bert gets a part. It is not enough. No, I must go through with this. You will go, won't you?"

"Of course. I said I would."

"I must believe in Bert, I *must*," she said. "I believe in Bert and I believe in you. He would not do this to me and he would not run my horse in a race he could not win."

"Well, you're in luck in one way."

"What is that?"

"There's no monster in the handicap division this year," I said. "There are no Secretariats or Affirmeds or Spectacular Bids around. If your animal is as good as Bert obviously thinks he is, you ought to win, whether its name is Balthazar or Gran Velero."

"Oh, that is absurd," she exclaimed. "Jay is mad to think such a thing. We are talking about Gran Velero."

"Jay's a human computer," I said. "You put the information in, the numbers come up with an answer. This is the one Jay comes up with."

"I am not going to think about it anymore," she said. "I am going to believe that it is all right and that it is Gran Velero who will win." She fell against me and laced her fingers behind my neck. "And now, Luigi, will you help me?"

"How many times do I have to say yes?"

We had made love then, with an intensity I had never noticed before, an almost savage concentration on technique that had left me physically drained but curiously indifferent. She had left our Kozy Kabin earlier than usual, hurrying away from our time together as if it had become too dangerous for her, too full of intangibles, too vulnerable to doubt.

I had remained behind for an hour or more, lying on my back and thinking hard without arriving at any solutions to anything. The manila envelope full of money lay on the bureau beside the television set. I almost forgot to take it with me when I left, but then I had been thinking only of her, as usual, of late and not the horses.

The knock on my door shattered the silence of the room. I must have dozed off, but not more than another hour or so could have passed. "This is Gold," a male voice said. "I have your tickets."

"Slide them under the door," I answered, getting up and stepping to one side, against the wall.

"What's the matter with you?" the voice asked. "You got our payment?"

"I don't want to see you," I said. "Give me some identity and I'll pay you."

Whoever was out there hurriedly scribbled a note and slid it, a folded piece of pocket-sized Kleenex, under the door. On it, written in felt-tip, was the single word "Marina." I went quickly across the room, picked up the manila envelope, knelt to one side of the door and quickly rammed it out into the hallway. I heard my visitor tear it open, then leave without another word to me.

I waited until I was certain he had gone, then, on a hunch, went to the window and peered out through the slats. In the side lot the parked cars still baked in the merciless desert sun. A man came around the corner of the building and threaded his way unhurriedly between the rows of automobiles. He was short, stocky, in his mid-forties, with a round face, a mustache and a thick head of curly black hair going gray at the temples. He was dressed in expensive-looking gray slacks, a sports shirt and a dark blue blazer with gold buttons. Despite the heat, he looked as cool as a snake in the shade of a rock. I watched him climb into a cream-colored Lincoln Continental and drive away; the car seemed to float through the heat like a basking white shark in a clear, shallow sea. I had never seen the man before.

I got dressed, picked up my overnight bag and went out into the lobby to call Vince. "What kind of a shithole are you in?" he asked. "Don't you even have a phone in your room? I've been trying to call you."

"It's very cheap, Vince. And since I'm not staying here . . ."

"Are you all through with your business?"

"That's one way to put it. Vince, do you know what Angelo Rinaldi looks like?"

"Of course. He's short, kind of chunky, always very well-dressed. He's in his forties. Oh, and he has a mustache. Why?"

"I think I just saw him."

"What are you up to, Shifty? You're not involved in some sort of a caper with Rinaldi, are you?"

"No. A friend of mine is."

"Shifty, you're beginning to worry me. Are you ready to get out of there?"

"Yes."

"Good, I'll pick you up in twenty minutes."

I sat out in the lobby of the motel until Vince came by. I thought about calling Marina, but decided not to. I thought about calling Dawn, but decided I didn't want to. Every time I shut my eyes and tried to sort out what might be going on, I ended up remembering only that I loved Marina and that I had committed myself to believing in her and trusting her. I almost literally ached to hold her in my arms again, as if I had been separated from her for weeks instead of a matter of hours. By the time Vince's battered-looking blue Toyota sedan pulled up in front of the motel entrance, I had almost convinced myself nothing was wrong. Obviously, Rinaldi was just the sort of man you would have to deal with to pull off a betting coup of the size envisioned here. He would know how to run the money into the tote machines and the bookies without affecting the odds unduly and that was why Marina had become involved with him now.

That was essentially what I told myself, as I sat there, my brains scrambled by heat and love, and waited. The average horseplayer's gift for self-deception is boundless; we are all true believers at heart.

FOURTEEN

Misdirection

THE HOUSE was empty. Although I knew Marina wouldn't be there, I hadn't wanted to accept that reality quite yet, so I had driven straight from the airport to find the place not only empty but abandoned, with a sign out front saying the house was for rent and giving the name of an agency to contact. I went into downtown Del Mar and called to inquire about it. "Oh, yes, those people left," the woman who answered the phone informed me. "It's available week to week through September fifteenth, after which it's month-to-month until the start of the racing season next year."

"I gather Miss De Nevers has moved out," I said. "Do you know where I can reach her?"

"Who?"

"Mrs. Caretoni."

"Is that the lady who's been staying there?"

"Yes, the wife of the owner."

"I think there must be some mistake," the woman said. "The house is owned by my client, Mr. Jeffrey Selvin. It was rented for the season to some people from New York by the name of Harrison. I had assumed that was Mrs. Harrison staying there. Are you interested in renting the place?"

"No. I was trying to find the lady in question."

"I'm sorry, I can't help you."

"It doesn't matter. Thanks anyway."

I hung up and drove up the coast to Carlsbad. The Kozy

Kabin parking lot was empty, but I let myself into our room anyway. Our little nest looked cold and dingy, as if no one had ever stayed in it. On the bed lay a white envelope addressed to "Luigi." Feeling a little sick and with a mounting sense of dread, I sat down and tore it open. "Darling Luigi," it read, in Marina's bold, clear handwriting. "There has been a crisis with Dino again and I have had to go to New York for a few days. I will come back late Sunday night or on Monday, in time for the race. Please do not try to find me, as I am not at all certain where I will be and I cannot call you at home. Everything will be all right, you will see. Thank you for helping me. Gran Velero will win, I think, but you must tell no one and you must also try to persuade Jay from betting on him at all, although I know that will be difficult. I love you." The letter was unsigned.

I read it through a second time, after which I tore it up and flushed it down the toilet. I left the cabin and walked down to the beach. It was empty except for a group of teenagers sunning themselves on a blanket around a portable cassette player blaring acid rock into the cool, clear morning air. I kicked off my shoes and carried them to the water's edge, then began to splash up the wet sand away from the noise. Finally, alone again, I sat down facing the incoming swells and tried to sort out how I felt about things. I knew I had a lot of thinking to do and I was trying hard to remain objective, although everything in me cried out to her, urging belief. To concentrate even harder, I shut my eyes and bowed my head, the sun warm now on my neck and shoulders, the soft rush of the surf underlying the chaotic roaring in my head with its steady, indifferent beat. . . .

I had never seen Vince in better form. We had driven together to his stint that night in the Emerald Room, and I watched him work one group after another, almost without stopping. At every table he received what in the world of the big illusions would have amounted to a standing ovation. One of his best tricks, restoring a crumpled cigarette simply by sliding his finger along it, dazzled everyone including me, even though I had seen him use it as an opener dozens of times. His touch was so delicate, so understated but so masterful, that it always moved me. What he had wanted me to see most was a new version he had worked out of the Sympathetic Coins effect, a move in which he could pass coins through a table simply by tapping on it, or from hand to hand through the air. No one since the legendary Slydini of New York had mastered this move more gracefully and delicately than Vince, and I had marveled at its subtleties with as much delight as the diners for whom he performed. To my mind, he had always been the great master of the technique of misdirection, and as a stylist no one could now compete with him.

During his first break, we occupied a rear table and talked. "Vince, that was beautiful," I told him. "I'm glad I stayed."

"Wait," he said. "I want you to see my Paper Balls Trick. I think I've got it better than ever before."

"I'm not sure I want to see it," I said. "You're beginning to depress me."

"Why? You're every bit as good as I am. With cards no one can touch you. You could do it all, Shifty, if you'd give up the ponies."

"Come on, Vince, you're beginning to sound like my shrink."

"I don't want to be anybody's shrink. I just hate to see you wasting your time."

"There's magic in racing, too, Vince," I said, "only you can't see it."

He sighed. "I never will understand, I guess."

"Come on, talk magic to me, Vince," I urged him. "That's what I stayed over for, not a lecture on my profligate ways."

We had talked for about half an hour when Vince decided to get back to work. "See that group over there?" he said, indicating two middle-aged couples in a corner booth. "I'll open with coins and then I'll get into the Paper Balls. Keep an eye on me."

He started to get up just as Dino Caretoni came through the door. He was accompanied by a short, dark woman in a gown cut very low to reveal a spectacularly voluptuous figure. Her face was beautiful, but heavily made up, and her eyes were as blank as those of a mechanical doll. She trailed the producer across the room to where Renato, smilingly obsequious, bowed them into a booth and snapped his fingers at a waiter, who rushed accommodatingly over. Caretoni gave them an order, which they hurried off to fill, then leaned idly across the table and patted the woman's cheek. She stared blankly back at him and he gave up, apparently disgusted. He sat back in his seat, half turned away from her, as if he could now hardly bear her presence.

I took Vince's arm. "Wait," I said, my mind racing. "That's Caretoni, isn't it?"

Vince looked. "Yes. I told you, he comes in here often when he's in town."

"Do me a favor, will you?"

"If I can."

"Let me work their table."

"They'll tell you to leave. They always do. They just come in here to eat, then go off and gamble again."

"I'll take my chances, okay?"

"If you insist. Meanwhile, catch my Paper Balls.'

"I'm watching," I said. "Go to it."

But I wasn't, entirely. Vince began working his miraculous effect, in which he crumpled up one piece of paper after another, making each one disappear before one person's eyes at the table while tossing each ball back over the person's head for the benefit of the others in the group. While he was doing that wonderfully funny stunt I had seen him pull off before with unfailing verve, I kept my eye on Caretoni and the woman. They had not spoken a word to each other since they had first come in and it was clear that they were waiting for something to happen. I had a feeling it would be the arrival of Rinaldi, so, without having planned anything specific, I waited until Vince had seated himself and embarked into some of his coin routines, then I walked over to their booth.

"Good evening," I said, "can I interest you in a little magic?"

"No, that is not necessary," Caretoni said. "Thank you very much."

"Just one or two effects I think you will find amusing," I said, reaching over behind the woman's ear and producing a tiny sponge-rubber rabbit out of the air. "Where there is one rabbit, there must be two." I opened my hand to produce the pair in question. "And where there are two rabbits," I continued, "soon there will be dozens." I showered the table with bunches of the small rubber animals.

"Perhaps you did not understand me—" the producer began.

"Oh, Dino, don't be such a drag," the woman said. "He's more fun than talking to you, especially after what you did to us."

"It was bad luck," the producer said. "We will be better tonight."

"That's what you always say." She looked up and smiled at me. "Show us another trick," she said. "Show us how to win at cards."

She was indeed very beautiful, I thought, but her eyes were those of a child, a spoiled, dangerously self-indulgent child. "Cards," I said. "I love cards." I whipped out one of my decks, shuffled the cards, then spread them out to form a graceful, self-contained fan. "Now watch carefully." I rolled the entire deck over facedown, then faceup again, then over once more, then faceup, except that now all of the cards were blank.

"That's beautiful," the woman said, clapping her hands in delight. "It's like a dance."

I repeated the maneuver to restore the original deck, then riffled it and offered it to her. "Pick any card you want."

"Gloria, this is really very tedious," Caretoni objected. "Must you?"

"It's fun," she said to him. "Every time you lose, Dino, you're such a downer." She pulled a card out of the deck.

"Don't let me see it," I said. "You can show it to him."

"He doesn't care," she said. "If he can't bet on it, it bores him."

I made her restore her card to the deck, then I took her hand and said, "Let's see, that was spades, wasn't it?" I cut the card and exposed her card. "The seven, right?"

She clapped her hands in delight. "I love it. Do some more."

"You were talking about money," I said. "I can show you how to make money." I reached into my pocket and produced an empty money clip. I passed a hand over it and found a miniature dollar bill. "It doesn't look like much, does it?" I said. "That's what inflation does to your money. But magic . . ." I crumpled up the bill and unfolded it several times, gradually increasing its size until it had become ten times as large as an ordinary dollar bill. "You see?" I said, flaunting it before them. "I can make your money grow. That's more than any casino in this town can do."

"You said it, buster," Gloria agreed. "Hey, Dino, maybe we should take him along tonight. We can't do worse than you did all by yourself."

"I do not find that amusing," the producer said. "Please go away."

"No wonder Marina didn't want to come along tonight," Gloria snapped. "Being with you is like death warmed over. Can't you just have a good time?"

"Has Marina disappeared?" I asked. "Shall I produce her for you?"

"This is not entertaining," the producer said. "Please . . ."

"I can't produce her here," I began.

"Oh, yes, you could," Gloria interrupted. "Only she can't stand to be around him when he's like this. I wouldn't be here either tonight, except I'm hungry. When are we going to eat, Dino?"

"But I can produce her next Monday," I continued, the smile frozen on my face. "I can predict where and when."

Caretoni eyed me curiously and Gloria laughed. "Go ahead, magic man," she said. "You tell us."

I shut my eyes and improvised a quick trance. I waved my hand mysteriously over their heads, as if conjuring knowledge out of their brain waves. Cards snapped out of my fingers and I pretended to read each one before making it vanish again. "I see a tall, red-haired, very beautiful woman," I said. "I see grass and horses walking in a circle around the grass. And I see little men in different-colored costumes and white pants and boots. And I see all these little men on the backs of these horses. I hear a great roaring sound, like a big wave of people shouting, and I hear a bell ringing and I see all these horses running now." I paused and pretended to grope through the air again, as if I had lost contact.

"Go on," Gloria said. "Is that it?"

"No, not quite," I answered, snapping another card open between my fingers. "I'm not certain, but I see a large sum of money. It is all piled up into a kind of mountain of money now."

"How much?" Gloria asked. "How much money?"

I opened my eyes and smiled brightly at them. "I'm not sure," I said. "But how about two hundred thousand dollars?"

"My God, you're fantastic," the woman said. "Isn't he fantastic, Dino?"

The producer gazed stonily at me. "What is all this nonsense? Who are you?"

"I told you," I said. "I make magic."

"I think I know who you are," the producer said. "You are a *stupido*."

"Dino, that's so rude," the woman objected. She reached out a hand and patted my forearm, as if tranquilizing a small furry animal. "Don't mind him," she continued. "He's on a real bad losing streak. He always gets like this."

"I shall make myself disappear," I said with a little bow.

"Thank you for your time. I always appreciate a good audience."

I went back to my table at the rear of the room and waited for Vince to take another break. Before their food arrived, the producer and Gloria got into some sort of argument, which ended with him obviously trying to make peace. He reached over and patted her cheek affectionately, then took one of her hands in his and kissed it. She wasn't having any of it and became even more petulant than she had been, a development that clearly frustrated him. He ended his part in the scene by concentrating on their dinner and an expensive-looking bottle of wine, both of which arrived opportunely just when it looked as if she might get up and walk out on him.

"Did you catch it?" Vince asked, rejoining me a few minutes later.

"Terrific, Vince. Listen," I said, "I'm going to call a taxi and get out of here tonight."

"How come? You won't find a flight to San Diego this late."

"Maybe not, but there'll be one for L.A. I'm going to pick up my things and go to the airport."

"Well, suit yourself. How'd it go over there?"

"All right."

"Are you involved with them in some way? You look a little funny."

"Indirectly, let's say. The Signor Caretoni does not care for magic much."

"I told you. The lady with him is no bargain either. She's usually bombed. Sometimes they come in here with Rinaldi and sometimes a whole bunch of people. Doesn't this guy make movies anymore?"

"Not lately. He's in money troubles."

"The way he gambles, I hear, it wouldn't surprise me. You're not going to see Dawn?"

"I'll call her from the airport. She's probably working, though. How's Ronnie doing?"

"Fine, I guess. Shifty—"

"Yeah?"

"What are you mixed up in here?"

"Nothing I can't handle, Vince."

"You sure?"

"I'm sure."

"We're just a couple of public clowns, remember that," he said. "The people you're messing with are trouble, I hope you know that."

"Better than you imagine," I said. "Anyway, thanks for everything, Vince." I stood up to go. "Oh, and by the way, next Monday you can bet on a horse in the feature at Del Mar called Gran Velero. He's going to win."

Vince laughed. "Come on, Shifty, you know I don't gamble."

"It's no gamble," I said. "He's going to win and he's going to pay a big price."

"Thanks, but no thanks," Vince said. "I live and work in Las Vegas. If I ever start gambling, I'm through here. I couldn't survive. Go back to work, Shifty."

"Very soon now," I said. "Don't worry about me, Vince. I'm not yet totally hooked."

As I waited outside for my taxi, a cream-colored Continental pulled up to the curb and Angelo Rinaldi got out. Without a word to the parking attendant or so much as a glance in my direction, he walked past me into the lobby of the hotel. He moved, I thought, like a man in complete, confident control of his surroundings, a ruler inside the comfortable confines of his palace grounds. It impressed me.

Jay was sitting over his figures and sifting through his charts, still enmeshed in his daily creative toil, when I walked into our apartment. "Hey," he said, "you're back early. How was Vegas?"

"Unchanged," I said, dropping my overnight bag on the floor. "I came in late last night to L.A., but I couldn't get in here till now."

"There's some fresh coffee on the stove."

"I've had some. Listen, I'm going out to Oakview Downs."

"What the hell for?"

"I want to see that horse."

"You go out now, I'll bet they won't let you near him."

"Want to come?"

"No way," he said. "I've come up with two good numbers today, maybe even three. I'm planning to make myself and my investors some loot. You better get down, too, Shifty."

"Have you told Sam yet?"

"No. All in good time." He leaned back in his chair and clasped his hands behind his head. He looked as self-confident and pleased with himself as a stock market specula-tor with inside information on a merger. "I trust Sam and we're going to need him to help us run the money into the machines, but he's a negative force, Shifty, and I don't want to have to deal with him till the last minute. Anybody, even Sam, could flip out over this dead crab."

"Okay," I said, "now tell me how to get out to Oakview."

"I still don't see why you want to go there."

"Just a hunch I have, that's all. He was in Barn Two, you said?"

"Yeah." He drew me a map and again urged me not to waste my time. "Don't you want to hear what I've come up with today?"

"You can tell me later."

"Shifty, I don't understand you."

"You know me and my hunches, Jay. I've got a negative feeling about this one," I explained. "If I go to the track without checking it out, I'll lose. Sorry."

"I'll never make a horseplayer out of you," he said. "You'll always be a gambler."

The morning fog still banked along the coastline when I started out for Oakview, but within a few minutes, two or three miles inland from the freeway, I was in sunshine. Long before I reached the training facility, however, I could tel' that something was burning. What I had originally mi..taken for a fragment of a cloud bank that had somenow drifte inland toward the hills turned out to be smoke; it floated motionlessly, gray and menacing, over the scrubby hillsides. I heard sirens and, two miles out, I was forced to pull over onto the shoulder of the road to allow a fire engine to roar past me. I knew, without even having spotted the location of the blaze, exactly what must have happened.

When I rounded the last bend and could see Oakview in the distance, the sight was beautiful and dramatic. The hillside corrals and sloping meadows were full of horses, herded together but restless, uneasy in the haze. A thick column of dark brown, oily-looking smoke rose from behind the ranch buildings to feed the overhanging cloud I had seen from a distance, throwing the white structures on their hilltop into dramatic relief. People were rushing back and forth toward the barn area and I could hear shouts. A fire engine had parked beside the main building and was directing a steady stream of water against the sides and over the shingled roofs of the whole ranch complex. I parked halfway up the road and ran toward the fire.

By the time I arrived, the blaze had been brought under control. A couple of dozen men and women were busy stamping out sparks and embers in the area around the nearest row of barns, where a squad of fireman was pouring water at one end of the building from which the smoke still soared skyward. Others chopped and pried at the remains of the structure and the air was filled with the sound of splintering wood and the barked orders of the professionals at work. The smell of burned flesh suddenly filled my nostrils and caused me to turn away, my stomach heaving. From a distance I stood and watched, until, after another twenty minutes or so, it became clear that the danger was mostly past.

A large, fat woman was standing at the edge of the scene, tears running down her face, one hand clasped over her mouth. I approached her. "Excuse me," I said. "I came out here to meet a friend of mine. What happened?"

She shook her head miserably. "God only knows," she said. "Harry came running up the hill to put in the alarm and then we spent the rest of the time getting the horses out. We got most of 'em out. Everybody pitched in, thank God! We could have lost everything."

"You say you got most of the horses out?"

"Yeah, all but the ones in Barn Two, at the end where the fire started. It went up so fast we just had no chance. Harry said it must have been a short in the wiring. That's how these damn things usually start. But we had it all redone just last year."

"A spark's all you need, I guess, things being as dry as they are this year," I mumbled. "Barn Two, isn't that Buckingham's string?"

She nodded. "Oh, God, yes. Poor Bud. He came in early this morning to see how that big horse of theirs was gettin' on and now that sucker's gone. The fire was in that corner, over by the tack room, they say."

I left her and walked toward the barn, now reduced at one end to a pile of smoldering rubble. The sickly-sweet smell of flesh still permeated the air and I thrust a handkerchief to my mouth and nose. Bud Grover, his face and hands blackened, his jeans and shirt soiled, was standing bareheaded and alone, staring at the smoking pile of debris. A single charred horse's leg protruded from under the ashes. Grover did not move; he seemed hypnotized by the sight.

The man I later found out was Harry Brown, the owner of Oakview, now came up to Grover and put a hand on his shoulder. "Goddamn, Bud," he said, "I'm sure as hell sorry. We couldn't get 'em all out. We tried."

"I know you did, Harry," Grover said.

"I thought we had this place about as fireproof as you can get."

"Don't fret, Harry. I know it ain't your fault," Grover told him. "These things happen, they just happen. I guess I better go call Bert."

"Yeah, you better do that, Bud. Damn, I sure am sorry."

Bud Grover turned and walked up the hill toward the ranch house. He walked slowly and deliberately, like a very tired man with the weight of a tremendous sin on his shoulders. My eyes returned to the spectacle of that charred leg protruding obscenely from under the smoking debris. Behind me, the woman had begun to sob aloud. I think that if I had had a gun at that moment, I might have shot Bud Grover in the back. Instead I turned away and buckled over, emptying my stomach into the dust.

FIFTEEN

The Undertaker

"I'LL TELL YOU exactly how this race shapes up," Jay said. "I know exactly how it's going to go."

"It must be wonderful to be like you," Sam volunteered. "Too bad you ain't religious. With all that faith, you could maybe walk on water."

Jay laughed indulgently. "Good old Sam," he said, "I knew we could count on you for some dark clouds."

We were sipping weak coffee from plastic cups and standing by the rail, at the gap beyond the finish line. Behind us the empty grandstand yawned like a huge open mouth over the dark-brown earth of the newly combed racing surface and the tufted, bright green of the infield turf course. The fog had already burned away, while directly across from us, a strong late-summer sun beat down over the stable area, where the last of the morning's work was being completed and the horses tucked away in their stalls and open pens. Traffic along the freeway east of the track was still light and the outlying public parking lots were empty. By the time the gates opened at eleven, the traffic would have begun to back up on all the access roads and by post time the premises would be jammed, but that was still several hours away.

"Sam's right," I said to Jay, "you seem a little too confident. Something *could* go wrong."

"I can't worry about it," Jay said. "That's not my style. When I see a race I know I can beat, I have to step out. My money isn't scared like yours, Sam."

"I'll talk to you in twenty years," Sam said, "when I'm still here."

"Yeah, I know, you're a survivor. That's the difference, maybe," Jay said. "My goal is to beat their brains out." He waved his hand toward the empty stands behind us. "I have to assume it's them I'm in competition with, not the dark fates."

"Yeah, I know," Sam answered, "you told me already, like maybe a thousand times. I still think you ought to back off a little. Everybody needs a reserve."

"No way, Sam. I'm going for the K.O."

We had just spent the last hour running fifteen hundred dollars in dribs and drabs through the early-bird betting windows and were taking a break before going back to pump another five hundred into the machines. The sum represented one-third of the six thousand dollars Jay himself was betting on Gran Velero, everything he had in the world except for the coins in his water jug. For myself, I had decided to go along for the ride; I had eleven hundred dollars of my own still to bet, the last of my summer racing capital. If Gran Velero lost, we were out of action.

As for Sam, he had agreed to help us bet, but he had not declared himself as to his own involvement. Gran Velero was listed at thirty to one in the morning line, the longest shot on the board. Sam had not lasted as long as he had around race tracks by staking the contents of his shoebox on long shots coming out of maiden wins to go up against stakes horses for the first time. "I know you tell me it's this Balthazar, not the other pig," he said to Jay, "but we don't actually know that, do we? I mean, there is this tiny element of doubt, ain't there? A guy could go broke listening to other people in this game."

"So how does it shape up?" I asked Jay now. "I'd like to hear this."

Jay glanced at his program before launching into his recital. He was always at his best in these performances, like a great concert artist rising to the challenge of a packed house.

I always found them oddly comforting. Jay brought order out of chaos, imposed a structure and a logic on the great mystery. He would have made a terrific priest.

"Well, the six scratches are going to make it easier for us," he said, "because we can't assume Gran Velero will get out of the gate all that fast. I expect he'll break a little slow, but from his outside post in this ten-horse field, it won't make a hell of a lot of difference. He's got a good long run to the turn and Richards will get him over closer to the rail so he won't have to go too wide. I wouldn't want him to be last in this field and he shouldn't be. He should be in mid-pack, maybe six or seven lengths off the pace.

"I figure Twilight Zone will go," Sam said. "He drew inside and he's got plenty of speed."

"There should be a real duel up front," Jay continued. "Both The Smoke and Jack Point have sprint speed. I figure they kill each other off, with Twilight Zone laying no worse than third. McArdle will have him positioned perfectly I look for him to move at the three-eighths pole and he should be on or near the lead at the head of the stretch"

"With the short stretch here, he figures to win, right?" Sam suggested.

"He'll be tough, Sam," Jay agreed, "but you forget one thing."

"What's that?"

"That move of Gran Velero's. If Richards has him close enough to the half, the pace is right and he makes that big run of his, he wins," Jay said. "I don't care how wide he goes into the stretch."

"What about Machismo?" I asked. "What about Cheapseat Charlie? They'll also be coming."

"I'm not worried about them," Jay said. "Machismo will make his run, all right, and Luis will get the best out of him, but he'll come up short. He usually does and he's better on grass, anyway. As for Charlie, he's honest and real game, but I think he's seen better days. No, the horse we have to beat is Twilight Zone and he'll be the favorite. But I figure he'll have to go just a little too fast too early and that'll make him vulnerable. He'll be short-legged by the sixteenth pole and when our horse hooks him, I guarantee you he'll spit it out."

"You make it sound so easy," Sam said. "You know what I'd do, if I was you?"

"Tell me, Sam, but keep it positive."

"I'd back him up. Shit, he'll be a big price. What do you want, for Christ's sake?"

"All or nothing, Sam."

Sam did not answer, but he managed to look unhappier than usual. "You aren't going to bet him at all, are you, Sam?" I asked. "You don't believe us."

"*If* I bet the race," Sam said, "that's who I'm betting. Maybe across the board."

"You're terrific," Jay said. "I love you, Sam."

"All I know about this racket is, it's hard to steal money," Sam said. He looked at his watch. "Come on, we only got fifteen minutes. You want to bet some more now?"

"Let's go," Jay said, starting for the windows.

"Here, Sam, put two hundred on the nose for me," I said. "You don't need me for this action. I'll see you back at the house."

"Where you going?" Jay asked.

"I want to walk around a bit," I explained. "I'm going to the backside."

"What for?"

"I don't know. I just feel like walking, that's all. Maybe I'm nervous."

"Okay, but remember, we got to get back here early," Jay reminded me. "We got to watch the action and we got to start betting again early. We can't dump it in all at once."

"We have plenty of time," I assured him. "It takes me twenty minutes from the stable gate."

"So have fun," Jay said, turning to Sam. "Come on, sunshine. It's action time."

I set out on foot through the frontside barn area and around the clubhouse turn, the musky smell of horses in my nostrils. Nobody challenged my right to be there and I managed to look purposeful, like a stablehand on some small official mission. At that hour few people were about and no one paid any attention to me. At the stable gate, I looked up Buckingham's barn numbers, then stopped at the racing office to pick up the overnights and the bump sheets, more out of habit than anything else. I'm not sure now exactly what I had in mind, but I knew I wanted to see for myself whether anything out of the ordinary might be going on. I was restless, anxious; the fate of more than just my money was riding on this race. I was angry and I was bleeding inside, like a man with a hidden but possibly mortal wound.

Buckingham's string of about thirty horses, the largest on the grounds, was stabled opposite the guinea stand, near the five-eighths pole. I walked up a narrow road between the rows of barns, then cut back toward the track along another trainer's neat-looking shed row shielded by an elegant blue-and-white-striped awning. When I emerged from under it, I found myself facing a corner of the first of Buckingham's three barns. No one seemed to be around, but a very nasty-looking Doberman on a long chain lay stretched out in the sun. He raised his head to look at me, but I moved on and then turned down another shed row under another awning, a less fancy green one this time, until I finally stepped out onto the road running beside the track between the stables and the guinea stand, now basking emptily in the sun. Marina's white Mercedes, its top down, was parked at the end of the nearest barn, in the shade of a second-story balcony on which a thin, wiry young Mexican was spreading his drying laundry.

"*La señora es aquí?*" I asked.

The Mexican looked blankly down at me, shrugged and went back inside his room over the stables. I hesitated a moment, then I turned and climbed up into the rickety wooden stands, where early every morning the trainers and the backside help came to watch their horses work or gallop. I sat down on the top row directly above Marina's car and waited.

About ten minutes later, she appeared from under the

shed row, with Buckingham and Grover in tow. She was wearing a white dress, belted at the waist, that looked dazzling against her bronzed skin, and a wide-brimmed white straw hat that hid the upper part of her face. The trainer nodded goodbye to her and stood by the corner of the building as his foreman walked her to her car. I leaned over and called out to her. "Is he going to win?"

Startled, she looked up, her eyes still in shadow. "Luigi? What are you doing here?"

"I guess I came to see you. Got a minute?"

"I have to go, Luigi. We can meet later."

"I think we ought to talk now."

"But I can't . . . Where?"

"Right here," I said. "Just the two of us."

Grover said something to her and started back to the barn, but she took him by the arm and spoke quickly to him. He glanced angrily up at me, then disappeared from view. The trainer remained in place, arms folded, his hawk's face expressionless. Marina spoke to him, too, and without a word he now followed his foreman inside. She looked up at me again. "Are you all right? Is anything wrong?" she called out.

"I'm fine. And everything's wrong," I said.

"Oh, Luigi . . ."

She came up the steps and confronted me, her eyes still shadowed by the hat. "Did you get my note?" she asked.

"Yes, I found it very moving."

"I had to go to New York in a rush," she said. "I couldn't think of any other way to get word to you."

"I stopped by your house."

"I moved out of there," she said. "Dino rented it."

"The house doesn't belong to Dino," I said. "It belongs to a man named Selvin."

"Nothing Dino has is in his name," she said. "I told you that. The tax people are after him for everything."

"So how was New York?"

"Exhausting, as usual. Darling, I want so much to thank you—"

"I was sorry about your horse."

"My horse . . ."

"Balthazar. That was a terrible thing."

"It was," she said quickly. "It was ghastly. Bud said there was nothing they could do. The building burned in five minutes, like a torch. It was terrible." She turned her head away and gazed out over the track to the empty grandstand. "Please, let us not talk about that. We must think only about today. Gran Velero must win for me. I know he will."

"Yes, we're going to bet on him, too."

"We? You and Jay?"

"Yeah. Jay thinks he can't lose, but you know his theory. Of course, it would be hard to prove now, after the fire."

"Do you believe Jay? You know that is ridiculous. It is bad enough that Balthazar is gone. You can see what my situation is." She leaned toward me and put a cool hand against my cheek. "Oh, Luigi . . ."

"So how was Vegas?" I asked.

"Vegas? What about it?"

"Well, Dino and Gloria sort of missed you at dinner," I said, "but then later, after Angelo showed up, I imagine you all went gambling. Or at least some of you did."

She withdrew her hand and gazed at me in silence for a long minute. When she finally spoke, her voice had gone flat and dead. It matched the mood of the moment, all right. "You believe Jay, don't you? And you think I am part of it."

"I know you are, Marina," I said. "I know why you went to Vegas now."

"Why? Tell me."

"Because, after you learned from me that Jay had figured out what was going on, you knew what Buckingham and Grover would do," I explained, trying to keep my voice from shaking. "You knew they would eliminate half the evidence. The easiest way to do that was by fire, making identification of at least one of the horses impossible. With one horse destroyed, the game is a lot less risky. But you had to establish an alibi, be somewhere where you'd be known and be seen.

You went to be with your husband. Dino is still your husband, isn't he?"

"You know he is," she said, in her dead voice. "We are not yet divorced."

"Perhaps you never will be," I suggested. "Perhaps you'll have a true reconcilliation. You could see a good marriage counselor and Dino could join Gamblers Anonymous and go back to stealing from his production budgets."

"I do not find this amusing," she said, standing up. "I will go now."

"Sit down, Marina," I said. "I'm not through."

"But I am."

"I could tell this story to the California Horse Racing Board or to the stewards. I could even go to the police," I said. "I could suggest they match Gran Velero's markings with the ones on file."

"They would find nothing," she said, "nothing at all."

"Oh, I should have known," I said. "You've covered all the angles, have you? With the real poor old Gran Velero reduced to ashes, all the boys had to do was alter the records. Easy enough, I guess. Of course, there is the matter of that white blaze."

She sat down again and leaned urgently toward me. "Luigi, you can't believe I did all this—"

"I didn't say you did it," I countered. "I only say you knew about it, all of it."

"But you don't think I would do such a thing, you can't," she insisted. "And Bert, he—he is only the trainer. . . ."

"Only?" I smiled at her, but it could not have been reassuring to see. "I think you were upset about the first killing," I said. "I think you were angry about it, too. You saw no reason to kill Eduardo. You were not consulted about it. When you told Bud Grover or Buckingham that the groom had recognized Gran Velero at Oakview and knew something was going on, they went ahead and took care of Eduardo and that did shake you up."

"Luigi, listen—"

"No, I don't want to listen. You listen," I told her. "You had nothing directly to do with the death of Eduardo, I know that. You didn't see the need for it and you were right. He was a little man, a nobody, and he only spoke Spanish. He probably didn't even have the right work papers. He could have been paid off and shipped out, maybe back to Chile even. I can't blame you for being upset. I even sort of like you for it. It *was* an excessive show of force."

"You are mad," she said. "You are completely mad."

I didn't argue with her; I simply plunged ahead now, heedless of the possible consequences. "Harrison you knew about, however," I continued. "That one you saw was inevitable." She said nothing now, so I leaned back against the rail of the bench we were on and pieced my version of the story together for her. "He was supposed to bet the money he'd been given on Gran Velero, but he didn't. He invested it in a high-stakes poker game and he blew it. Your friend Angelo took care of Mr. Harrison."

"He is not my friend," she said. "I despise him."

"Yes, you probably do. And you're probably afraid of him, too. I know I would be."

"Guy was an idiot. He did not deserve what happened to him, but he was beyond help."

"I believe that, too. Do you want to keep on leveling with me now, Marina?"

"I have always told you the truth."

"Oh, Marina, hearing you say that makes me sad," I said. "I thought we had a chance there for a second, but obviously we don't."

"I told you Dino was a terrible gambler," she said. "What else could we do? He borrowed all this money from Rinaldi and he had to repay it. He still owes him a great deal, nearly a quarter of a million dollars. What were we to do? I had to help him. I would lose everything, too."

"Well, I realize your situation is desperate, Marina. After all, you've been in on two murders. Or should we say one and a half? Did you know it's a crime in many states to be an accessory to a killing and not to report it to the police? They actually put people in prison for that, Marina, even very beautiful foreign princesses."

"You are being cruel and unfair."

"Really? I worry about you, Marina. You're more cold-hearted than I believed possible."

"I really cannot listen to this. I must go now." She stood up again.

"I swear to Christ I'll go straight from here to the stewards and the police unless you hear me out," I said. "You might all still get away with this, but I'll do my damndest to get that horse scratched today. I'll also go to the press, Marina."

"You will not do that," she snapped.

"I don't want to, but I will. Unless we have this out now."

Without a word, she sat down again, her face once more in shadow. I sensed death in the air, not the physical fact of death, but simply a great emptiness all around us, a desert in which nothing would ever grow and flower again. "I didn't understand about Buckingham," I said. "I'm not sure I understand it all and maybe I never will. But I got a hold on it when I met his wife. I figure Rinaldi is into her, too, probably in more ways than one. Am I right?" She did not answer, so I proceeded. "Let's take a guess. I guess that she hooked into Dino's scene and borrowed from Rinaldi, too. Then maybe she tried to pay him off with her body and that worked, up to a point. The point at which her husband found out. Angelo, being the kind of gentleman he is, must have made it clear to old Bert exactly what the score was. One payoff and the trainer was out. So you all cooked up this little scheme together. Bert's off the hook and he's unloaded Gloria, who has got to be one of the major burdens of our time, especially for a much older man like Bert, who must regret bitterly the day he ever set eyes on her. He was married before, I know, but to a decent woman his own age, who died after putting up with him for over thirty years. He must have been easy pickings for a toothsome chippy like Gloria, who's got an ass every bit as nice as yours and knows how to peddle it to her advantage. Where did they meet?"

"I have no idea," Marina said. "There is no need to be coarse."

"I'm sorry," I said. "I didn't mean to sound bitter or anything. Now where did I come in? Would you like to tell me?"

"You would not believe me, if I told you."

"Not if it's about love, Marina," I said. "No, that I would no longer believe."

"Then you must believe what you like."

"I believe, then, that it was your original intention to use Jay," I said. "But then, after a while, you got a little tired of him, especially after you realized you were too far down on his list of priorities. Sam warned you. He said you could only hold Jay if you'd let him put a saddle on your back and run the three-quarters in one-o-nine flat. So when Jay began asking all these uncomfortable questions, especially about Balthazar, you decided he wasn't worth the risk and you dropped him. I was much easier pickings. You could actually make me fall in love with you."

"Is that all you really think it was, Luigi? You can't believe that."

I turned away from her again so I wouldn't weaken and kept right on talking, filling the emptiness with words, everyone of them a nail in my own coffin. "I wasn't that important to you," I continued, "but I could be useful. You needed a courier and I was the perfect messenger boy. You didn't want to take the cash to Vegas yourself, undoubtedly because you *are* being watched and not only by the IRS people. You're afraid of Rinaldi, aren't you? You don't know what he might try, including having someone hijack the money from you before you could deliver it."

She said nothing, but her hands shook slightly. It comforted me to know that she was suffering, too, if only a little bit and for quite different reasons. When I didn't immediately pick up the thread again, she looked up at me. I could see her eyes clearly at last. They looked large, very beautiful, but wary, like those of a big cat confronting an armed man in a cage. "Have you finished?" she asked. "Can I go now?"

"You should have gone to New York, Marina," I said.

"Then maybe you could have convinced me you were at least trying to bail out. I loved you, so I probably would have bought it. But when you ran back to Dino, it told me all I really needed to know about what I meant to you."

She stood up again and this time I did not try to stop her. "Goodbye, Luigi," she said. "You do not have the whole story. And I do care for you, I do. But this is useless now."

"You don't care enough, Marina. And I can't trust you enough now."

She started to walk away from me. "I hope the horse wins, Marina," I said. "I hope he wins for all our sakes. Don't you want to know whether I'll blow the whistle on you or not?"

She paused in her flight just long enough to glance back at me. "I know already you will not do that," she said. "You are a gambler, like the others. And afterward, who would believe you anyway? You have no evidence."

"No. You'd destroy this horse, too, I know that."

She reached the top of the stairs. *"Au revoir, chéri."*

"But if he loses, Marina, then what?" I asked. "How will that sit with your friend Angie the Pick? He's not betting on him, is he? He's just waiting to be paid off, isn't he? Guys like Rinaldi don't shoot craps, Princess, they're running the game."

She neither answered me nor looked back. Without another word, she walked to her car, got in and drove away toward the stable gate. A cloud of fine dust marked her departure, then floated airily away across the empty infield. I waited until I stopped shaking, then I followed her out. I don't know how long it took me to get home. I was like a crippled plater on his last legs and carrying enough weight to stop Man O'War.

Gran Velero had never looked better. His coat gleamed and he was clearly on the muscle, so full of himself that I began to feel nearly as confident as Jay about the outcome of the race. I had watched him in the walking ring, where Marina, Buckingham and Bud Grover had gathered around Lonny Richards, who seemed almost disdainfully confident in his pink-and-blue silks, and the horse simply radiated power and desire. Once Marina had glanced in my direction, but she had looked right through me. Then I had lost sight of her temporarily behind the crush of people in the paddock, as the horses and their grooms circled the ring. "Look at that," the man standing next to me said. "That claimer of Buckingham's is the best-lookin' thing in the race. Just shows you can't tell nothin' from looks. That Cheapseat Charlie, he's a wreck, four bandages and all, but he's won more money than any of these and he's gonna win this one, too. He just outclasses this bunch."

"I like Tim's horse," the woman next to him said. "He's cute."

"You don't know shit," the expert told her. "Charlie's gonna blow him down in the stretch."

The first blink of the odds had established Gran Velero at nine to two, a tremendous drop that had not passed unnoticed by the hard knockers and had sent Whodoyalike scurrying to our box. "What's going on?" he asked Jay. "That horse has no chance, does he?"

"None," Jay said. "The owners are betting him, but they're betting fools. I know them. Don't worry, the price'll go up."

"I sure hope so," Sam had growled, after Whodoyalike's departure. "I hope this ain't Vegas layoff money."

"He won't be thirty to one, Sam," Jay said. "I'll settle for a third of that."

"You ain't gonna get it," Sam said gloomily. "The word must be out."

Whodoyalike had been succeeded by Fido, Alex, Action Jackson and several other members of Jay's regular entourage and he had lied to all of them. We had bet our money early, getting it all down by the seventh. Now all we had to do was wait and hope the Vegas money wouldn't show up, or at least not too much of it. "First time I ever heard you lie, Jay," I said, between visits from suppliants.

"I can't share this one," Jay said. "This one makes my whole year. And you can wait a lifetime for this kind of bet."

"You better be right," Sam said. "You even hooked me into this one."

"How much did you bet, Sam?" I asked.

"Too much."

"Oh, come on, Sam . . ."

"Five hundred, okay? And it's been a lean summer, too." He shook himself like a wet mongrel and managed to look every bit as miserable. "I gotta be crazy," he muttered. "That fuckin' Richards, he could fall off this horse."

"Not with the money up, Sam," I said. "This is his big chance, the first good mount he's had in three years. He isn't going to blow it and he certainly isn't going to stiff him."

"I don't trust the sonofabitch," Sam said.

By the time the horses cantered past on their way to the starting gate, the odds on Gran Velero had risen to twelve to one. Twilight Zone had been installed a solid favorite, at eight to five, with Machismo the second choice at five to two and Cheapseat Charlie, the battered-looking old gray gelding, at four to one. The two genuine speed horses, The Smoke and Jack Point, were also drawing support, since Del Mar, like all California tracks, tends to favor animals that run forwardly, on or near the pace. Of the others, only Gran Velero was being taken seriously and we all thought we knew where most of that support was coming from. I focused my glasses on him as he loped, head bowed, around the clubhouse turn, Richards crouched over him next to an escorting pony and rider. He looked magnificent, unbeatable. "He sure looks like a winner, doesn't he?" I murmured.

Jay was focused on him, too. "He's the boss," he said. "These are good horses he's up against, but he's a champion. He's the boss, you can always tell. He's going to eat them alive."

By the time the horses reached the starting gate, Gran Velero's odds had dropped again, this time to seven to one. The action on him had begun to attract the lemmings, the bettors who watch the board and put their money only on what everyone else is betting, so it seemed likely that our horse would go off at a final price of no more than five to one. In fact, as the animals were lined up in the gate, poised to spring out when the starter released them, the final blink of the board dropped Gran Velero to nine to two, making him the third choice in the race, behind Twilight Zone and Machismo. "Somebody in Vegas caught on," Sam observed grimly. "That ain't just the lemmings up there."

Jay didn't answer. He sat like a stone, his binoculars trained on the stalls where the ten best horses on the grounds were tensed for competition. Sweat beaded his forehead and I could see his hands tremble slightly; after all, his whole reason for being was on the line here, to say nothing of his money. He had stepped out at last, like a poker champion betting his whole stash on one terrific hand. I had to admire him, because I knew exactly what it meant to him. As for me, I felt nothing. My last eleven hundred dollars was on the horse, but I had bet all of it without a qualm. Win or lose, it meant nothing to me; I had already lost much more than money.

The wait in the gate seemed interminable. First one horse, then another would turn his head up or lunge forward against the barrier; the starter, a solitary figure on his little tower facing the field, delayed, anxious not to spring the horses out into the clear until he could be sure each animal was ready. For a purse of this size, he wanted no one to be left; he wanted the perfect start, ten horses all out of there at once, in an even line, free and clear of each other, the ideal, trouble-free getaway. Motionless, inscrutable, he waited, while his assistant starters labored to align their skittish charges perfectly. "Get 'em out of there," Sam muttered behind me. "He's gonna leave 'em in there until one of 'em blows his top, the jerk."

The gate suddenly sprang open and the crowd seemed to surge forward, as if it, too, had been released from restraint to vent its excitement in a great tension-easing roar. Jay jumped to his feet beside me. "Oh, my God!" he exclaimed.

Gran Velero had bounced out of the gate like a cat pouncing on a mouse, nearly unseating Richards. The jockey snatched him up, jerking his head sideways. The horse bolted for the outer rail, with Richards hanging on now and fighting to get him under control. By the time he was able to straighten him out, Gran Velero was last, at least twenty lengths behind the leaders. As the field swept past us, Richards aimed him toward the inside to save ground on the turn, but he was now nearly thirty lengths behind and trailing the next-to-last horse by ten. "Oh, Christ," Jay said. "That fucking starter!"

"It ain't the starter," Sam snarled. "They don't call this guy Richards the Undertaker for nothing. He just buried us."

The two speed horses had gone to the front, exactly as Jay had predicted they would, with Twilight Zone in third, tucked in along the rail about five lengths back. Machismo was in mid-pack, boxed between horses, with Cheapseat Charlie and Gran Velero bringing up the rear. "Beautiful," Sam said. "Why didn't they just shoot him? It would have been kinder."

Jay said nothing. He sat down again, his glasses trained on Gran Velero, who had already begun to make up some ground, moving easily and powerfully around the turn. His task seemed hopeless, all right, but anything can happen in a horse race and perhaps today the Dummy God would take pity on us.

The Smoke and Jack Point did their thing perfectly. They ran the half in forty-four and four-fifths seconds and the first six furlongs in one-o-nine flat, a suicide pace that was certain to kill them off and did. At the half-mile pole, Twilight Zone quickly moved up between them and easily took the lead, even though he, too, had had to run faster than he normally wanted to by this stage of the race. Behind him, Machismo was charging into contention, with the rest of the pack strung out several lengths back. Gran Velero had moved up alongside Charlie and the two were now running as a team, about fifteen lengths behind Twilight Zone. Pete Oliver, the New York jock on Charlie, was not about to let

Gran Velero go by him and he was asking his mount to run some, which kept our horse outside of him as they neared the turn.

With three-eighths of a mile to go, Richards stung Gran Velero once with his whip and the big horse suddenly took off. None of us had ever seen a move like it and it brought us to our feet, screaming with excitement. Running on the outside, five wide around Del Mar's sharp, poorly banked turn for home, Gran Velero picked up one horse after another in a spectacular charge exactly like the one we had first seen him make weeks earlier, but this time it was even more astonishing because it was against class horses. By the head of the stretch, he had passed Machismo and caught Twilight Zone, then proceeded to open up about a length and a half with less than an eighth of a mile to the wire. It was the most incredible run I had ever seen a thoroughbred make, at least since Forego, the great gelding of a few years back, who used to make the same sort of explosive move to win many of his races. I found myself jumping up and down and pounding Jay on the back. "Sit down," Sam barked at me. "Can't you see he's done?"

Sam was right. Gran Velero had been asked to do the impossible and had almost achieved it, but not quite. He had lost ten or twelve lengths at the start and had had to be used early to get back into the race. Then he had made his great move going wide, at the cost of several more lengths. Even a great horse can't perform the impossible and now, as I saw him lower his head and shorten stride, I knew it was simply a question of whether he could just hang on long enough to win. Twilight Zone was also through, but Pelé had Machismo rolling along still and Oliver had kept Cheapseat Charlie on the inside, saving ground and moving steadily through as holes opened up for him. At the head of the stretch, he was able to cut the corner and come through on the inside to hook Machismo. The two of them now set off in pursuit of our exhausted champion.

I forgot the money I had bet on Gran Velero and I think

Jay did, too, at least temporarily. With Richards slashing and pumping, the boss dug in and somehow found the strength to make one last effort. He floundered gamely for the finish line, losing ground at every step as both Machismo and Charlie closed on him. The three of them hit the wire together, with nearly thirty thousand people screaming with excitement. I was on my feet again, shouting with the rest of them, because, win or lose, I had never seen a gutsier effort or a more exciting race.

The photo sign went up on the tote board and I looked at Jay. He was sitting straight up in his chair, his face bathed in sweat and drained of color. "He lost," he said. "They caught him on the last jump."

"Are you sure? I thought he hung on."

"No way," Sam said. "He lost. You got a gun? I'm gonna shoot that jock."

"Get the starter, too, while you're at it," Jay said, in a low, harsh voice, as if someone had clamped an ice cube against his larynx. "They stuck him in the gate too long."

"He was so ready to run," I said. "My God, what a move he made!"

"Death," Sam said, "death is too good for these guys. That animal ran his goddamn brains out and they got him beat. That's racing for you. Why do I do this to myself? Tell me that, huh?"

I couldn't answer him. I trained my glasses on the people swarming around the winner's circle as the horses came galloping back, but I saw no sign of Marina. Grover and Buckingham were out on the track, waiting for their horse to return, but they were alone. Gran Velero, lathered from the tremendous effort he had made, was moving slowly down the track along the outer rail, head still bowed, his jockey sitting glumly on his back. He was the last one to return, reaching his trainer just as the board posted the order of finish and the crowd roared. Cheapseat Charlie had won, with Machismo second and Gran Velero third. The photo finish camera would later show a margin of a nose and a head between the three of them.

I looked at Jay. He hadn't moved, his face stonily blank. "Nice call, Jay," I said. "We did everything right. We did everything right but win."

He didn't answer. "That's it for today, lads," Sam said. "I'm going home. There's too many ways to lose in this racket." He heaved himself wearily to his feet. "I should have done something else with my life. I know I'll feel better tomorrow, but right now I could chuck it all in." I watched him leave the box, moving slowly and heavily through the crowd like a barge drifting downstream. He was old and tired, I thought, and perhaps I was seeing a preview of myself in twenty years.

"Jay, are you okay?" I asked.

He put his head down on his hands against the railing of our box. "Just leave me, Shifty," he said. "I'll be all right eventually, but now I want to be alone. I don't want to discuss it, okay?"

I watched the photographers snap pictures of Cheapseat Charlie, his exultant jockey and his ecstatic entourage in the winner's circle. Then I went inside to watch a rerun of the race on the monitor. It was almost as impressive the second time and for a wild, improbable moment there, at the head of the stretch, I couldn't imagine our horse not winning. Had there been a God or any justice at all in the world, I thought, he would have won. But halfway toward the finish, as Machismo and Cheapseat Charlie began closing on him, a familiar angry voice blared behind me. "Watch this," Bet-a-Million said, "watch this dumb move the jock makes on Machismo. He goes to the outside instead of in, the dumb bastard! The horse should win by a mile! Look at that! You ever seen a dumber rider? I got ten times the best horse and my rider gets him beat, by a cripple that can't even run no more! The race is so bad the claimer almost wins it! It just makes ya sick, that's all!"

I couldn't take it anymore. I turned around and confronted him. "You are one dumb asshole," I said. "Why doesn't somebody put you out of your misery? They shoot sick animals, don't they?"

Bet-a-Million stared at me as if I had physically assaulted him and I immediately felt ashamed of myself. In horse racing, after all, as in life, all truths tends to be relative; reality is whatever you happen to think you saw. "The best horse don't always win the race," Sam once said, "but every man's best horse is the one he bet on."

SIXTEEN

Getaways

TEN DAYS AFTER the race, Dino Caretoni fell to his death from his twelfth-story office window on the corner of Fifty-third and Fifth Avenue, in New York. No one saw him jump, because the tragedy occurred sometime between three and four A.M., but foul play was not suspected. It was reported that he had been despondent over the forthcoming bankruptcy of his movie production company, as well as allegedly heavy gambling losses in Nevada, Atlantic City and elsewhere. The widow, who looked very beautiful in black, said very little to the press about her husband's death but admitted that she had been separated from him for some time. Nevertheless, she handled all the funeral arrangements impeccably, including the lavish service conducted in St. Patrick's Cathedral, at which hundreds of the biggest names in show business appeared, after which the producer's body was shipped back to his native Salerno for burial in the family tomb. The widow remained dry-eyed during all of this ordeal, but her dignified deportment was favorably commented on by most observers, one of whom, an anchor woman for a TV network, even compared her public style to that of Jackie Kennedy at the time of JFK's assassination. "Clearly a classy broad," was the way Action Jackson put it to me between races on a Saturday afternoon at Pomona.

It was the first time I had gone to the track since what I now called the Labor Day Massacre, but I left before the feature. I was depressed and disinterested, unable to make myself feel the old surge of excitement that had always made the track a special event for me, a communing with the secret forces of nature. I drove home, I remember, along the San Bernardino Freeway, my eyes streaming from smog, as if fleeing from a rendezvous with death. I had always thought of this trip, through some of the most polluted sections of the San Gabriel Valley, as a pilgrimage through a fart, but this time it was to have an especially dreary significance for me. I arrived home to find a message from Jay, telling me that Sam had collapsed that morning over his *Racing Form* and had been taken to the emergency room at Cedars Sinai, in Beverly Hills.

We found him in the Intensive Care Unit. He was propped up, flat on his back, plugged into a machine and with tubes stuck into his veins and protruding from his nose. Jay told the nurses we were his sons and they let us in to see him for exactly three minutes. Sam was having trouble breathing, but he recognized us and it was clear he had something important he wanted to say to us. I leaned over with my ear to his mouth. "That fuckin' Richards," he gasped. "Why couldn't it have been him?"

He had another seizure near dawn, lapsed into a coma and died without regaining consciousness. His heart had just given out, they told us, but Jay had his own explanation. "Sam lost one too many photos," he said. The next day, Jay reported that the shoebox under Sam's bed had contained nothing but a two-thousand-dollar insurance policy, enough to get him buried. He also left Jay and me a hundred-dollar bill with a note pinned to it instructing us to make one last losing bet for him, so there would be nothing at all left for his "shitty relatives."

The latter, consisting of a younger brother who owned a pizza parlor, his sour-looking wife and kids, and two fat, angry-looking sisters and their hairy, disapproving husbands, all showed up at the funeral. They were full of bitterness and contempt for the obviously not-so-dear departed.

Jay and I were the only ones of his racetrack cronies to attend the service, a dismal affair conducted on the cheap in a small Roman Catholic chapel off Sunset Boulevard, in downtown L.A. After the ceremony, conducted mainly in Spanish by a Chicano priest, as we were waiting to set out for the cemetery, Sam's relatives gathered in a tight, hostile knot around the hearse. They stared dourly at us, as if we had bells around our necks. "Hey," Jay said to them, "we didn't kill him. He picked his own horses." But they refused to talk to us and actually succeeded in making us feel guilty for Sam's own failures. When the cortege left for the cemetery, we chose not to go along. "Poor Sam," Jay said, "no wonder he ran away to the track. At least he didn't have to hang around with lifetime losers."

Jay looked badly shaken, however, and I asked him if he wanted to have a beer somewhere. "I could use one, couldn't you?"

"No thanks," he said. "I've got some things to do."

"Where have you been?" I asked. "I didn't see you out there the other day."

"I've been cooling it for a few days," he explained. "I haven't got it all together yet. I need freshening. I'm like an old sore-legged candidate for the vet's list running on bute and a prayer. I may go away for a few weeks." He looked uneasily away from me, as if not anxious to reveal the sort of turmoil obviously boiling up inside him. "I'll see you, Shifty. Keep breaking fast out of the gate." And he walked away toward his car like a man on a tightrope, one foot in front of the other and a pit yawning beneath him.

It was then I should have begun to worry about him, but I didn't call him for a while. I was too busy rebuilding my own life. I had gone back to work part-time in the magic store on Hollywood Boulevard and three nights a week I was in the close-up room at the Magic Castle. Several weeks went by when I didn't even think about horses and had no desire to go to the track. I was making my own magic and it was enough. Then, one night, when I was between shows and having a beer in the downstairs bar, I heard a familiar nasal bleat. "Hey, Shifty, how are you? How you been, honey?" I found myself confronted by Bunny Lehrman, big-bosomed and bucktoothed, perched precariously on spiky heels and dazzling in a purple-sequined dress.

"You are a fanfare, Bunny," I said. "Better, you are a Sousa march."

An immense, forbidding hulk loomed up beside her. "You remember Kretch, don't you?" Bunny asked. "We're still together, you know, only now I work for Kretch full-time. We got a game—"

"Shut up," Kretch said. "You got a mouth like a siren."

Bunny wilted, a petunia suddenly blasted by an Artic wind. "I'm sorry, Kretch, but you said—"

"I didn't say nothin'," Kretch told her. "Go and hustle your ass for a few minutes, babe."

Crestfallen, Bunny wandered aimlessly away into the smoke-filled night. Kretch heaved himself onto a stool and glowered at me. I tensed to spring out of there. "So how's it goin'?" he asked.

"Pretty well," I said. "I'm working here three nights a week. Next month I've got a three-day cruise to Vallarta, then I'm going to substitute for my pal Vince Michaels in the Emerald Room in Vegas for a few weeks, when he takes some time off. How's the game going?"

"I got three of them now," Kretch confided. "One in Malibu and two in L.A. I could be doin' better."

"Sure, you could have four games."

"Listen, this is all goat turds in here," Kretch said, waving a massive arm at the premises. "What do you get paid here?"

"Not much," I admitted. "I get a few tips. But I like the work. Close-up doesn't pay much, Kretch, but it's what I do and I'm good at it."

"Forget it," he said. "I can pay you a grand a week. You deal only for me."

"No, thanks."

"Next month I got a big game in Tahoe, with some real

high rollers," he continued. "I'll pay you five grand for the gig."

"Kretch, I can't afford it."

"What do you mean, you can't afford it? You ain't gonna make that kind of bread here in ten years, magician."

"Look, Kretch, see these?" I held up ten fingers in front of his eyes. "These are the only capital I've got."

"So?"

"So if something goes wrong here, if an ace falls out of my sleeve or something, I just laugh and crack a joke and go on," I explained. "If I fuck up with you or maybe we don't get along, who guarantees I'm not going to have my knuckles broken? I'm not saying I don't trust you, Kretch, but it's also the company you keep. I don't carry insurance."

"Just deal the Tahoe games," he said. "One week, maybe two. We clean 'em out and you're free and clear, with five grand in your pocket.

"I really appreciate the offer, Kretch," I said. "I really do. But no thanks." I stood up and smiled. "Forgive me, but I have to go kill the people now."

"You're a moron," Kretch said. "I'm sorry I wasted my time on you."

"I can understand that," I said. "I'll see you."

I went back to work, feeling as if an enormous white whale had been lifted permanently off my shoulders. That night I got a big round of applause for my Ring on a Stick and I worked for two hours without stopping and without repeating a single move. Vince would have been proud of me.

I didn't see Jay for several weeks, mainly because I had stopped going to the track. Sam's death had dampened my spirits and I had no real desire to go. During part of this time, too, Dawn and Ronnie paid me a visit. She had brought the boy in for a check up and he was doing very well. They stayed with me for three days, during which Dawn and I spent a lot of time holding hands and talking to each other. She asked me to stay with her during my forthcoming engagement in the Emerald Room and I agreed to. She kissed me on the mouth when she left to pick up Ronnie at the doctor's office on the last day and I asked her if Ronnie would object to my presence. "He suggested it," she said. "He's not such a bad kid, is he?"

A few days later, Jay called me at home. "Shifty," he said, "I need a hundred dollars."

"What's going on?"

"I got a good number in the fifth today at Santa Anita," he said. "Trouble is, I'm Tap City."

"Jay, what's been happening?"

"I'll meet you for breakfast in an hour at Big Boy's on La Brea," he said. "We can drive to the track together."

"I wasn't planning to go."

"Make plans," he said. "I'm telling you, this is a dead crab."

"There are no dead crabs," I said. "I thought you knew that."

"Be on time," he said. "I've got quite a story to tell you, Shifty." And he hung up before I could argue with him.

It *was* quite a story and Jay told it very well. "See, what happened was, right after Sam's funeral, I went into this terrific slump," he began, as I sipped my coffee across from him and watched him. "No matter what I did, I couldn't win for losing."

He couldn't sleep either and became convinced he was dying. He didn't call me, because he knew I was out of the picture for a while, but he began telephoning a lot of his other track cronies, especially Fido and Action Jackson, at all hours of the night to say goodbye. Every day, however, bone-weary, unshaven and unprepared, he continued to go to the track, where he lost steadily. Even Whodoyalike stopped coming around for his selections, and one morning Jay went to his closet and found the water jug almost empty; he had gambled away the last of his hamburger money. That day, broke and desperate, he stayed home, shaking and staring at his walls. "I was convinced Sam's ghost was haunting me," he said, "getting even with me for what I'd done to us at Del Mar."

At the end of that afternoon, Jay had picked up his telephone and asked for the local number of Gamblers Anonymous. "They have this twelve-step recovery program," Jay explained, "which includes attendance at group therapy sessions during which the members admit their compulsion, tell their personal stories and promise to carry the message to other compulsive gamblers."

"Sounds like a good thing," I observed. "Did it help?"

"Wait, wait," Jay urged me. He explained that he still couldn't quite bring himself to admit that he, too, needed help, so he had resorted to his favorite ploy. He told the man on the phone, who had introduced himself as Ned, that he was a journalist on assignment from a magazine to write a story about gambling. Ned had suggested Jay attend a meeting that night in Monterey Park, after which, if Jay so desired, they could talk privately.

No sooner had the meeting begun that night, shortly after eight-thirty, than Jay had begun to ask himself what he was doing there. "A couple of dozen of us were sitting around on these metal folding chairs around a big table," he said. "It looked like a set-up for a big poker game." Most of the gamblers present were men, ranging in age from mid-twenties to elderly, but there was a sprinkling of women, too. No one looked well. "They had kind of pasty faces and a lot of lines around their eyes and the women looked like plague victims," Jay continued.

He thought the effect might be due to the lights, overhead neon strips that were merciless to the skin, dropped shadows under eyes, accentuated wrinkles, daubed cheeks a pale, jaundiced yellow. Jay also remembered the room as being very cold, even though it was a warm night. The premises had been made available by a Methodist church and had a sterile, institutional look. Most of the men smoked and gray swirls hung in the air, contributing to the general seediness.

"I'm Ned," a fat man said, sitting down at the place reserved for him at the head of the table. He was about forty, sported a mustache and a goatee, and he exuded more confidence than Jay felt. He smiled at the group. "I'm Ned," he repeated, "and I want to welcome you all here. I'm glad to see such a big turnout." He went on to inform everybody that there was a reporter present and to ask if anybody objected to that fact. He explained that no notes or recordings would be made of the meeting and that no one would be identified by name in the story the reporter might write. He asked for a vote by show of hands on the reporter's presence. He got a unanimous endorsement, which pleased Ned, because he obviously wanted all the publicity he could get for his rescue mission. "I felt a little guilty about what I was doing," Jay admitted, "but I decided it was too late to tell them the truth."

Ned now explained the ground rules for the therapy sessions, then gazed around the table. "Let's begin with you, Bob," he said. "This is Bob's first birthday. He's a year old today." Everybody applauded.

Bob smiled wanly. He was a thin, blond young man with a scraggly mustache and the pale, darting eyes of a rabbit. His wife held on to his left arm with both hands, as if he might bolt for the lettuce patch. "I'm Bob," he said, "and I'm a compulsive gambler."

"Hi, Bob!" everyone exclaimed in unison.

Jay jumped in his seat at that one. "The chorus bit got to me," he confessed. "What were these people so afraid of? It was as if they were treading water and holding hands so as not to drown."

Bob went on to say that he had begun gambling at sixteen, mostly on horses and later in Nevada casinos, but never realized he was hooked until his wife had forced him to confront the truth.

His confession and those that followed interested Jay, though it soon became clear the session would last much longer than anticipated. At the start of the evening, Ned had asked everyone to limit his remarks to five or ten minutes, but most of the speakers had ignored his request. Several of the older men around the table, in fact, had rambled on until Ned himself had been compelled to intervene. Jay wondered if they had been trying to impress "the reporter" present. If so, they had partly succeeded. The litany of failure resounded off the walls, clanged like bells of doom in Jay's ears.

Some leitmotifs began to dominate. Nearly all of the men had first heard about Gamblers Anonymous from their wives, who had also been the first to call a G.A. member to set up meetings for them. "The one woman gambler there," Jay explained, "a poker addict, had called for herself, after her husband had threatened to throw her out and seek legal custody of their two kids." Many of the gamblers in the room had become violent in order to go on gambling; all admitted they would not have hesitated to use violence, even against their own families, in order not to be deprived of a chance to get a bet down. They had all tried to hide their gambling from their families and lied about the extent of it when cornered. Most of the men admitted they had gambled also to achieve some sense of masculinity; one man even compared its effect on him to having an orgasm. They had all stolen, from their wives and children as well as strangers, in order to bet. Most had been arrested; some had done time. The melodies, in minor and major keys, did not cheer Jay up, but he felt estranged from these people, as if their problems were not his.

Some stories even made him want to laugh. For instance, Walker, a middle-aged man with a face sculptured in tapioca, had blown four marriages. On his fifth wedding night, in Las Vegas, his bride had asked for an aspirin. Walker went downstairs at about nine o'clock to find her one and disappeared for two days. Egbert, a heavy-set old man under a gaudy Mexican sombrero and with a cigar impaled between his false teeth, declared that since he had stopped gambling, he could now invest in wildcat oil wells and penny mining stocks. William, a twitchy ex-accountant, recalled a time he had driven to Las Vegas from Riverside in September, with his wife and two young kids in an old station wagon. He left them, gasping like stranded guppies, outside the Flamingo

Hotel in order to go in and book a room, but got waylaid at the craps table, where in twenty minutes he blew the family's vacation money. They drove back to Riverside that night and the following day his wife had asked for a divorce.

"As I sat there and these doomsday tales went on," Jay told me, "I suddenly began to feel better. Basically, I guess, I realized I had nothing in common with these people. They were all gambling to get away from their real lives. They were substituting gambling for everything else. But gambling *is* my life. I don't care about anything else. Gambling on horses is not a substitute for what I do, it's what I do best." He beamed at me. "You understand what I'm talking about, Shifty?"

"I think so," I said. "So now what? Obviously, you're going back to the track."

"Of course. Listen, I spent the last three days working the *Form,* until I could come up with something I really like," he said. "You remember that old plater Hullabaloo you cashed a ticket on at Del Mar?"

"I'll never forget him."

"He's been freshened and he's in again today against a field he can beat on three legs. Did you bring the bread?"

I took out my wallet, pulled out two fifties and gave them to him. "I hope you're right," I said. "But what if he loses? He could break down."

Jay laughed. "Forget it, Shifty," he said, "there's always fresh."

Hullabaloo won easily and paid nearly ten dollars for every two-dollar ticket. It was the start of the biggest winning streak of Jay's career. Every time he opened the *Form* that fall, some horse jumped out at him. We didn't lose a bet for three weeks and I was able to quit my job at the store, although I stayed on at the Magic Castle until it was time to leave for Las Vegas.

'You're going to miss a lot of good action," Jay warned me on my last day at Hollywood Park, in early December.

"Somewhere, every day of the year, there are horses running and people betting on them," I said. "You'll be here when I get back, Fox. That's the only dead crab I know."

Balthazar, the fake Gran Velero, never ran again. He broke down on the track early one morning, a month after the Del Mar Handicap, and had to be vanned off the premises. He had a broken sesamoid and a bowed tendon. They retired him to stud duty at a small ranch near Santa Barbara. He had no real racing credentials, apart from the one great effort in a graded handicap, so his stud fee was put at only a thousand dollars a pop, but I promised myself I'd watch for his first progeny and bet on them when they got to the track, several years down the line. One of them, at least, I figured would inherit that great move of his and some of his heart, enough to make him a winner.

I toyed with the idea of telling my story to the racing officials, but I had no firm evidence and I was afraid they'd destroy Balthazar, too, if I put the authorities or the press on the scent. I knew by then that Buckingham, Grover and the rest of them would stop at very little to protect themselves and I really couldn't bear the idea of picking up the paper one morning to read about another fire or some mysterious illness striking down our champion. I settled for silence and, though I'm not proud of it, I tell myself I had no choice, really. I comfort myself with the idea that the horse is safe, well cared for and happy at his duties as a professional stallion. Someday, Jay tells me, we'll get out on him and maybe he's right.

As for Marina, I never spoke to her again, but I did catch a brief but rewarding glimpse of her one day. I was working a convention of jewelry salesmen at the Beverly-Wilshire Hotel and I showed up there one morning in mid-January to find Marina standing in the lobby surrounded by Vuitton luggage and holding a small terrier in her arms. As I walked in the door, she looked straight at me, but without a glimmer of recognition. Her eyes were cold and her face as beautiful and lifeless as a statue's. I smiled at her, but she turned her head away. Angelo Rinaldi came around the corner from the elevator landing. He was dressed in dark-gray slacks and a checked cashmere jacket and moved, as usual, with an arrogance born of contempt for the whole human race. His appearance caused a flurry of activity in the lobby, with bellhops whisking suitcases out toward the sidewalk and obsequious clerks bidding goodbye from the front desk. Marina did not move, however, until Rinaldi took her elbow and steered her out the door himself. She had become another of the man's possessions, nothing more than an expensive piece of meat to be consumed at his leisure.

I looked at my watch and saw I was five minutes late, so I hurried upstairs to my hustlers of stones and metal trinkets. Time, as always, for magic.